A Model Murder

The Dead Ex Files – Book 2

Claire Kane & Stan Crowe

ISBN-13: 978-1-938327-23-0

PROLOGUE

A woman ran blindly through the Seattle parking lot, dodging cars and shooting frightened glances over her shoulder. During a glance back, her shoe snagged on a break in the sidewalk, sending her sprawling. She hit hard, rasping her hands on the concrete, but scrabbled to her feet again and ran on.

Rounding a corner, she ran directly into a man with biceps the size of small logs. "Gotcha!" he said, seizing her arms.

The woman shrieked. Blond hair flaring, she struggled in the man's grasp, managing to connect a kick with his shin. He growled and struggled to subdue her, but she managed to knee him in his groin. He doubled over, and she sprinted away.

"That's it," he growled, staggering slightly as he dashed after her. "I don't care if you call me the baby daddy or not. You're dead."

*

Lacey Ling woke with a scream, cold sweat beading across her face and neck. She paused to listen to Nainai, only to find the woman barely halted her snoring. Grateful she hadn't woken her grandmother, she placed a hand on her chest and fought to bring her heartrate and breathing back under control. It had all been so real—so vivid. As though she'd actually been there, watching that poor woman being murdered.

The worst part of it was that she recognized the victim.

Jessica Simcox.

Feeling violated, Lacey got out of bed and, still shaking, made her way to the shower. "What *was* that, Victor?" she murmured, uncertain whether her ex-boyfriend might actually hear her. "Why have I had such weird dreams since you left? And why are they turning violent?" She turned the shower on to as hot as she dared, then undressed as it warmed up. When it was ready, she stepped into the steaming stream, wondering whether the water heater would hold out long enough for her to really think.

Jessica had been Victor's girlfriend some time before Lacey had come to know him. Though Lacey had only ever met the other woman once, and under embarrassing circumstances, she'd heard enough from Victor to be glad he hadn't stayed with her. Jessica had even falsely claimed that Victor was the father of her unborn child. Beautiful, well-dressed, and predatory, she was the kind of girl guys' moms warned them about.

Yet, Lacey could hardly believe Jessica deserved to die—especially since she was pregnant.

Lacey wet her hair, exulting in the warmth that coursed over her. Feeling the urge, she poured a large dollop of body wash in her palm and went to work scrubbing off the icky feeling remaining from the dream. She'd practically been able to *smell* the fear, the stench of the murderer's breath, and the reek of the back street dumpster Jessica had passed.

"It was just a dream, right, Victor?"

And yet, Victor was gone. Not just dead, but *gone*. She'd felt clearly that he'd finally passed into Heaven, wherever that was, and knew it was time to get on with her life. Living with his ghost had been strange enough that she wasn't sad to not have to deal with his random appearances or the fact that he could read her every thought and feeling.

So why did she still miss him so much? She'd dumped him for good reasons.

She scrubbed vigorously at her scalp, as if she could scratch out the memories. She had more important things to think about now.

The hot water ran out in just under five minutes, leaving Lacey a sodden, freezing mess. She hastily finished rinsing off, then practically leapt out of the shower, wrapping an extra towel around her against the cold made worse by the fact that it was only a couple of weeks before Christmas. She deflated at the sudden reminder that she hadn't gotten anything for Nainai yet. Rather than dwell on it, however, she dressed as quickly as she could, then ran for her room, pausing only to crank the thermostat to as high as it would go before diving under her thick bedspread.

Maybe she'd still be able to salvage some sleep.

ONE

"Tell me, Miss Ling," a friendly-looking woman in a blazer festooned with embroidered candy canes and mistletoe said, "what is your interest in this position? I really should have asked that at the beginning of the interview; I hope you'll forgive me."

Lacey had seen this question coming a mile away; it was a standard question for any job she'd ever had since college. Behind her, a floor-to-ceiling window looked out over the elevated freeway running along the Seattle Pier, and directly onto the best clam chowder shop in town. Though it was barely past four o'clock, the sun hovered just above the horizon, a testament to the approaching winter solstice. The sounds of rush hour were muted by the window and by the Christmas music playing softly from somewhere down the hall. The office Lacey found herself in felt surprisingly cozy and matched its occupant. The whole setting put her at ease, and her toes curled in delight. She knew she'd aced this interview, and could practically see the job offer in the other woman's eyes. One more perfect answer, and it was in the bag.

She straightened slightly and looked the woman in the eye. "I've been researching Bowler and Bowen for some time now. They've got some excellent reviews, and—" suddenly, something caught in her throat, gagging her. She tried to clear it, but even as she did, her mind seemed to go mushy.

"Excuse me," she rasped, coughing into her shoulder.

"Take your time," her interviewer said sympathetically.

Lacey straightened again. "As I was saying," she started, yet her thoughts refused to come. The polished answer seemed to blur, but her mouth carried on working anyway. "Yeah, so B and B totally made me think of 'Bed and Breakfast,' and it sounded like a totally sweet place to work."

Her mind reeled at the words coming out of her mouth. What was she saying? And why did the room suddenly look so dark? She struggled to correct herself, but was stunned to hear her voice continue, "So it's like, totally a place that could be great for late nights—the whole 'bed' part of B and B—and then breakfast. So you go to sleep, working super hard in your office, and then wake up and your secretary feeds you breakfast. Who *wouldn't* want a job like that?"

The interviewer's jaw was virtually scraping the floor. Lacey felt herself freeze, and wished she could crawl into a hole. Something *insane* had just happened, and already she could hear herself being politely thanked and invited to leave. Instead, the PR woman composed herself and hastily jotted some notes.

"Thank you, Miss Ling," she said, standing and extending a hand to shake. "I must say that's one of the most unique answers to that question I've ever heard. Your honesty was… stunningly refreshing."

Lacey managed not to groan and hide her face, but instead smiled professionally and stood as well, shaking hands. The interviewer gestured at the door. She didn't have to ask twice. The happy woman did Lacey the favor of stepping into the hall with her. "It was a pleasure to meet the great Lacey Ling. I must say, seeing your resume come across my desk was actually quite the little thrill. We don't often get *celebrities* applying for our firm."

Lacey cocked her head and smiled. "Thank you, but I'm not all that much of a celebrity. I only did the morning news."

"But you did it so *well*," the lady said. "I'm surprised you left them. Surely some *other* station must be *dying* to bring you on board."

Lacey hesitated, hardly missing the implications of the compliment. She kept her smile even, her eyes shining. *If only you knew, lady,* she thought.

"If nothing else," her hostess continued, "I'm sure *someone* is looking for an investigative reporter to dig into the recent disappearances."

Lacey frowned. "Disappearances?"

The PR woman's eyebrows shot up. "On campus? U of W? You really haven't heard? Oh, well, maybe you wouldn't have. I only know because my best girlfriend's daughter attends, and she's heard the rumors. Some sorority girls, or models or something. It may be nothing, but it doesn't hurt to be safe."

Lacey's brow wrinkled in thought. She *worked* on campus but hadn't heard anything yet. Maybe it was time to start nosing around. Lacey smiled one last time. "Thank you again for the interview."

"Thank *you*. It was a pleasure. We'll contact you if we decide to select you. You did have some superb answers. Have a wonderful day and a very merry Christmas."

Lacey took the hint and made to leave. She hadn't gotten three steps away before the interviewer called to her again. She turned, and the woman had produced a small notepad and a pen from somewhere.

"Miss Ling, one last thing," the woman said, before blushing. "May I... may I have your autograph? And the secret for how you keep your hair *so* lovely? You're just so beautiful all over. I could only wish for a face like yours, but I *must* know how you keep your hair."

Lacey sighed inside, but graciously penned her signature in the notepad and gave the woman some basic hair tips anyone could pull off the internet.

And with that, Lacey Ling walked away from an unexpected and inexplicable failure of massive proportions. She wandered toward her car, still somewhat in a haze, but her concern over her bungled interview was already giving way to the idea of shady business brewing in the city. First her horrible dream about Jessica. And now some disappearances. And from the same campus Lacey now worked at? Speaking of which, her shift was set to start all too soon. Glancing at her watch, she hurried her steps; Mrs. Jones, her boss, considered tardiness for work was a cardinal sin.

*

"A double mocha latte for you," Lacey said, carefully sliding the mug and saucer onto a table between a couple of guys who looked to be new freshmen at best; nothing particularly unusual for the morning crowd, whose murmurs mingled with the buzz from the TV. Lacey refused to even glance at the screen, since someone had set the channel to KZTB.

It still hurt to think that, despite the TV station's pretty-sounding promises to bring her back after the incident with her previous boss, nothing resembling a job offer had materialized. Her savings had gotten slender quickly, and out of desperation, she'd picked up some part-time work at a coffee shop near the campus of the University of Washington.

Only telephone sales would have grated at her more than her new job.

"And a peppermint espresso with extra whipped cream and a candy cane for you," she said, placing a second saucer on the table and ignoring the way the guys at the table openly stared at her. She'd learned quickly to wear baggy turtlenecks to work. "Can I get you gentlemen anything else?"

One of them snickered, and the other one blushed and swallowed hard before pasting on a cocky expression Lacey was sure he'd practiced in the mirror. "Yeah." He whipped out his phone, and before she could think, she heard the click of a camera shutter. "How about your number? Or just your digits." His friend stifled a guffaw in his fist.

Lacey maintained her professional composure. *This job is only temporary,* the former news reporter reminded herself. "Yes, I have some numbers for you. One moment." She stepped nimbly over to the register and rang up their tab, printed the ticket, and walked it back to their table. "There you go," she said, placing the ticket on the table. "No charge for the extra whipped cream."

"I meant your *phone* number, you dumb chick."

"That," she said with a smile, "is reserved for *men.* Get back with me when you figure out how to treat a lady, and maybe we'll talk."

The guy's face flushed, and his friend muttered, "Burrrn." She knew she'd just killed any chance of a tip, but in this case, she was fine with that.

"And this breaking news just in," said a voice from the TV. Lacey recognized the voice. She knew the anchorwoman personally; she'd once competed for that same position.

"Seattle PD reports what appears to be a homicide near Seneca and Western, this morning.

They say the body was found in a dumpster, with multiple stab wounds."

Lacey whipped around, nearly bumping into a patron who was making her way past. She apologized quickly, then strode over to the TV, her attention now riveted on the screen. A crime scene played out before her eyes—flashing lights, police tape and all. The anchorwoman continued to speak.

"No suspects have yet been taken into custody, but investigators say the victim is Jessica Simcox, a twenty-five-year-old female. She had reportedly been returning home from a photo shoot for a local modeling agency when the incident occurred." An image appeared on the screen, freezing Lacey's blood. The Botox-enhanced lips, the flawless makeup, the bleached hair with stylish highlights. It was unmistakably Jessica.

Lacey stumbled backward, colliding with a table. Something clattered to the floor and broke.

"Hey! What's your problem?"

Lacey spun, mortified, and noticed a girl in a nice outfit sporting a glower and a large, dark stain on her blouse. A shattered mug of coffee lay at her feet.

"So sorry," Lacey hastily said vacantly. "Let me get something to clean that." With that, she all but ran for the back room. When she returned, the girl she'd spilled coffee on was just stalking out the door. Mrs. Jones shot Lacey a glare from behind the till. Lacey gave an apologetic nod, and hurried to clean the mess. She stooped, dabbing at the spill and doing her best to ignore the TV.

"This is creeping me out," she overheard a girl at the next table say. "First Brittany, then Shayla. Now this other girl on the news?"

Lacey paused and peeked over the table just in time to see a redheaded girl nod. "I'm locking my windows at night. My roommate is starting to freak out a little, too." She knew the girl and her companion by sight, if not by name, and she'd served them often enough to know the redhead liked a caramel mochaccino with extra whipped cream and caramel sauce, while her petite, brunette friend took her coffee with a little cream and sugar, and a bagel.

The brunette bit her lip and stared into her coffee. "D-do you think they'll figure it out?"

The redhead nodded. "I'm sure they will. Stuff like this just doesn't happen without someone doing something about it."

Lacey couldn't help but be curious. Formal news was one thing, but scuttlebutt had its own value; she'd gotten plenty of leads from "word on the street." Quickly wrapping up her cleaning, she stood and stepped over to the two friends, adopting her most relatable, innocent air.

The girls noticed Lacey immediately and looked up at her expectantly; the brunette peered at Lacey with a hint of a shy smile on her lips. Still shaken, Lacey glanced over her shoulder. Her boss had retreated to the back room, probably for daily inventory; Lacey knew she had at least twenty minutes. "Uh, hi, girls." Lacey smiled. "How are your drinks this morning?"

The girls responded encouragingly, and Lacey took the cue to continue. "Apologies if I was eavesdropping, but I couldn't help but overhear you talking about… things."

The girls shot glances at each other, then looked back up.

Remembering her conversation at the PR firm, Lacey said, "Sounds like I've missed some news lately." Her heart beat hard, as she tried to talk low. "Have there been *other* murders?"

The brunette recoiled slightly and looked at the floor, but the redhead shrugged meekly, and said, "We hope not. I mean, a couple of girls from our sorority have gone missing."

"Missing?" Lacey repeated, eyes widening as she crouched next to the table. "For how long? Who are they? D-do you know them?"

Again, the redhead spoke. "We know *of* them. They come here. They've been missing for, like, a week." She glanced at the brunette. "Emily, didn't Brittany say something about maybe going home early for Christmas?"

The other girl, Emily, nodded. "I think her parents were taking her to Cabo or something."

"Oh," sighed the redhead. "She is *so* lucky."

Lacey sensed the subject getting away from her. "You said they're both your sorority sisters," Lacey repeated. She gestured at the TV, where the news had moved onto a weather report. "Was the girl on TV in your sorority as well?"

The brunette shook her head. "No."

Lacey pursed her lips. "You seemed to think that murder could be related to your girlfriends' disappearances; why's that?"

The redhead grimaced. "We don't *know* if they are. It's just all really freaky, with the timing and all. And, like, the girl on TV—she's drop-dead gorgeous. So are Brittany and Shayla. Our sorority sisters. Maybe there's some kind of psycho perv out there." She shuddered. "I don't know. I don't want to talk about it anymore. I think we've had too many late nights," she said, locking eyes with her tablemate. "Don't you?"

The brunette nodded vigorously as she sipped at her drink. "Yeah. I should be thinking about finals."

"Or about *Bret*," the redhead retorted. Her friend's face flushed, and she swatted at the redhead.

"Okay," Lacey said, sensing she wasn't likely to get anything else out of them. "I just, well, I'm in a bad neighborhood. It got me thinking. Thanks for your time."

"Sure," the redhead said. "Nice meeting you."

The brunette grinned suddenly, an impish glint in her eye. "You know, *you're* actually just as pretty as that girl on TV. Maybe you're next." She made a spooky noise, then the two girls laughed. Lacey forced herself to laugh along with them, hiding the fact that her insides were quivering. She thanked the girls again, then headed for the back room to put away her cleaning supplies. All she'd gotten was the hunch of a pair of college girls, but she knew well enough that even a hunch should never be totally dismissed. She pursed her lips and pulled out her phone. She may not have a job at KZTB any longer, but she still had connections.

A few seconds later, a text message to an old friend marked her official entry into the investigation of the murder of Jessica Simcox.

TWO

Lacey stepped out of her black Lincoln MKZ into the cracked parking lot of her new apartment complex. Thankfully, she already owned her expensive ride. And the high-priced security system with GPS tracking. She glanced back at it; the elegantly sleek lines and shine of pure luxury didn't quite fit in with the random beaters nearby, one even spray-painted. Another had its front bumper off and hood up, nobody nearby working on it. Gazing a little farther down the row of cars, she caught sight of an Escalade, though it would do well without the ridiculous rims and window tats.

Pulling her purse up higher on her shoulder, she headed toward her bottom-floor apartment. A swirl of smoke caught her attention, leading to a man in a tank top. "'Sup?" he said with a mischievous glint in his eyes. Lacey gave a curt hello and hurried on her way, hearing her neighbors shrieking at each other all the way through the stucco walls. Something about not locking a door. Before locking, and chaining, her own front door, the sound of an ambulance whined in the distance.

"Nainai," she called toward the backroom. "I'm home." She didn't expect an answer—her grandmother was usually asleep when she got home—but it made her feel better all the same. She slipped off her shoes and turned her thoughts carefully back to the morning news. She hadn't been able to get it off her mind since first hearing about it, and she had difficulty believing the other disappearances were merely coincidental. A healthy dose of paranoia and over-analysis, she found, had helped propel her as a good investigative reporter. Yet before she could do much investigating, she still had to deal with the home front.

Surveying her tiny new living room, she sighed at just how much work moving was, even after hiring someone to do the hauling. Knowing that moping was useless, she reluctantly grabbed a box cutter and went to work on the nearest box.

She had barely gotten the thing open, and was fishing out some plates, when her phone buzzed once; a text. Lacey nearly dropped her load, but managed to safely stash the plates on the counter while she scrabbled to unlock her phone. Cathy Higgins, her old editor from KZTB, had texted her back. *This place sucks without you*, the message read. *I wish they'd come to their senses and hire you back.*

Lacey tapped out a reply. *I'll be fine. Have you happened to hear anything more about that Simcox murder?*

She waited a moment before another buzz. *Not yet*, Cathy said. *Why?*

Lacey bit the corner of her lip, hesitating. *Who was the witness?* she finally typed.

Right away, the reply came. *You know that's confidential.*

It was. Cathy would never be caught texting confidential information. She could lose her job. So Lacey pressed Cathy's contact picture on the phone's screen, and it started ringing.

The answer was quick, Cathy's voice an excited whisper. "Hey, Lacey."

"So spill," Lacey said, raising her brows expectantly.

"Okay, so sources say it was a homeless man. Goes by the name Teddy."

"A homeless man?" There were plenty of homeless people on Seattle's streets. "Teddy?"

There was an audible sigh. "That's all I've got."

"Thanks. That's good. I appreciate it. Looks like I'll be busy calling the name 'Teddy' at random transients."

"Wait—*what*?" Cathy said with disapproval. "You're not really going to look for that man, are you?"

"Yes, I am," she said as naturally as if she were speaking of shopping.

"But why?"

"B-because," she stammered, thinking of the dream. "I-I have to know more. The victim was Victor's ex."

A pause. "You mean, like you." Lacey heard a pregnant silence on the other end of the line. Eventually, Cathy exhaled slowly. "Is there something you're not telling me? What am I missing?" Lacey could imagine the suspicious squint behind her friend's cat-eye glasses.

"N-no, it's nothing. Just chalk it up to the investigative journalist in me. Hey, listen, I've gotta go." She didn't, but there was no way she was up for being interrogated by a fiery redhead on a roll.

"*But—*"

"Gotta go."

"*Wai—*"

Lacey pressed the "End" button with her French-tipped thumb. She went and sat on the living room floor in thought. "Oh, Victor," she said, brushing wisps of long dark hair behind her ears. "I could really use a listening ear right now."

An old woman's voice answered, "What was that?"

Lacey started and lithely leapt to her feet, hastily smoothing her blouse and hoping her eyes didn't show how she felt. She'd been so focused on her conversation that she hadn't heard her grandmother getting up. But as she looked at Nainai, who was wheeling herself into the room, she knew there was no fooling the older woman.

"Nothing, Nainai. Just talking to myself."

"More like talking to that studly guardian angel," the woman said, eyes twinkling.

"He's not my guardian angel, Nainai. You know I don't believe in those." She knew her lie wasn't fooling anyone. She'd not only *seen* the spirit of Victor St. John, her one-time boyfriend, but had interacted with him for weeks, as, together, they worked to figure out who exactly had killed him and why. She shuddered at the memory of how that had ended.

Nainai piped up. "Remember, Confucius say, 'Better a dead boyfriend who still loves you than a living boyfriend who is a jerk.'"

Lacey sighed and changed the subject. Her grandmother was known to say made-up Confucius sayings on a whim to get a point across. "I'm almost done unpacking." It was partially true. At least she'd had the help of a moving crew to move her out of her luxury condo. She shuddered to think at how much of her dwindling savings had been shunted toward their assistance. Were it not for her need to care for Nainai, she'd have just done it herself.

"Then sit, Lacey. Sit on the couch and talk to your grandmother for a while. You've been so stressed lately, and it makes an old woman sad to see it."

Lacey grimaced but complied, resisting the urge to bury her face in her hands; it wouldn't do to let Nainai see just how desperate she'd become. "Yes, Grandmother?"

Nainai frowned. "You haven't called me that since the night Victor died. And you took *forever* to tell me that he had. Shame on you for making me think you still had a good prospect you weren't panning out."

Lacey closed her eyes so Nainai wouldn't see her roll them.

"I saw that, baby girl."

"Of course you did."

"Confucius say, 'Until senile dementia sets in, Nainai gets smarter with age. Notices more.'" The woman rolled up alongside the couch and gently placed a hand on Lacey's knee. "Lacey? Look at me."

The former TV reporter bit her lower lip, but, after a protracted moment, did as Nainai asked. She saw wisdom and a comforting love in her grandmother's gaze. She wanted to dissolve into tears and throw herself into Nainai's arms as she'd done when she was a child. Only she wasn't a child anymore; she was a big girl, and she could handle this just fine.

"You're young, yet, Lacey," Nainai said quietly. "You have so much time left to live and love and make mistakes."

"You think it was a mistake for me to quit KZTB?"

Nainai shook her head and held open her arms. "Come, child."

Lacey hesitated again, but, once more, obeyed her grandmother and embraced her.

"When you first told me you had quit your job," Nainai said, "I thought the loss of my Feng Shui had cursed us. Only now I see that you left behind employment for a wicked man who wanted to abuse you. You were right to leave."

"So why doesn't it feel right? Why won't they take me back?"

Nainai squeezed her granddaughter. "Such questions are beyond even Confucius sometimes. But perhaps the universe has something larger for you than just being on television. Besides, maybe they will come to their senses and offer you your job again. In the meantime, at least you have some work."

Lacey pulled away from her grandmother, grimacing openly. "Yeah. As a barista on the U of W campus. Two, part-time shifts a day."

Nainai raised her eyebrows. "And what's wrong with that? It pays you, it gives reasonable hours, and it lets you meet plenty of young men closer to your age."

Lacey pulled away, making a disgusted noise. "No, it means I'm a professional woman making minimum wage at a job where I get ogled by frat boys and yelled at by little girls who don't have half my education but think they're smarter than me just because I wear an apron with a logo at work." She thought, briefly and bitterly, about her failed attempts to sell a ring worth $22,000. She'd been unable to get an offer over $2,000. Even if she took the offer, it wouldn't be much of a financial cushion.

"Gratitude is a hard attribute to cultivate, granddaughter."

Lacey stood. "Please don't go philosophical on me, Nainai. I worked hard to get where I am. I had my future in the palm of my hand." She looked around her apartment again, then out at the priceless view of the Puget Sound. "And I went and gave it all away like an idiot. And now we've got to move into a hovel just to make ends meet."

"But you are still alive," Nainai said. Then, in a firmer tone, added, "It is time you stop complaining and *do* something about your life. Your life is a blessing. *Use* it like one."

Lacey's fists clenched, and she checked the time on her phone.

"I'm going to make some tea while you vent to your man," Nainai said. "Let me know when you decide to take charge of your life again."

Lacey heard the rustle of rubber tires on matted carpet, but didn't watch as her grandmother rolled herself to the kitchen. She fought the urge to help, knowing she'd be rebuffed yet again; in the three months since Lacey had left KZTB, Nainai had insisted on taking care of herself as much as she possibly could, and proved that Lacey's stubbornness was, indeed, an inherited trait.

Glancing back at her phone's texts, Lacey said out loud, "I *am* taking charge of my life. Life just isn't cooperating." She took a deep breath. "What would you do, Victor?"

Nainai's words echoed in her mind. *Perhaps the universe has something larger for you than just being on television.*

She decided a brisk walk was in order, where the news said Jessica's body was found. At the cross streets of Seneca and Western.

THREE

Heaven was a place fit for a king. Of course, it had a King, so that made sense. Victor chewed on a grape, in thought. His first Elvis sighting had happened just hours after arriving here, or rather "crossing over," as they called it. Now the sideburned singer played the ukulele in the shade of a palm tree, not far away, in the Grand Courtyard. Women still fawned over him. Why he insisted on wearing jumpsuits, up here, was beyond Victor. At least the white color and blingage fit in with most other angels who preferred light, airy colors. Victor, on the other hand, opted for a simple blue shirt and jeans. He liked the frayed knees, jokingly referring to them as his holy pants; other angels didn't seem to get his sense of humor. Maybe they'd been dead too long.

"Eyes up, pretty boy," a familiar voice said, interrupting his thoughts. There, suddenly sitting on his patio-style table, was Rao, his former pet cat and now spirit guide. "I've got news."

"I don't care about your Quidditch tournament."

"Croquet. Croquet! Anyway, that's not what I was going to say…"

"Well, then, what?" Victor crossed his arms, leaning into the table.

The black and gold tabby raised a brow. "You do know angels aren't supposed to be depressed, right?"

Victor raised his dark eyebrows in return, as if to ask, "Is that all?"

"Look around you! This is Heaven, for goodness' sake! Stop with the moping already. It's getting sickening."

Victor sat back with a huff. "Do you blame me? It's been months now since I've spoken to Lacey. I haven't even been allowed a glimpse at her in The Pool." That reference had nothing to do with catching a peek at his ex in a bikini. The Pool was a beautiful patch of crystal-clear water where angels got live visions of their loved ones down on earth. It was considered a privilege, and not to be taken advantage of. Most angels had to earn it.

The tabby rose to all fours, staring emphatically with her sparkly green eyes. "Listen to me, my news has to do with Lacey."

"Do I get to see her in The Pool?"

"Not if you paid Peter in a pound of shillings," she said.

That earned an eye roll. "Then what? Tell me!"

"She's in danger, Vic."

*

It was dark out, the sun slipping away in a deep purple horizon behind downtown's myriad of skyscrapers. Lacey stepped along the damp streets, having parked in her old spot in the KZTB garage. At least she still had that perk, until her pass expired. She soon left behind the KZTB tower, its lit-up letters glowing red behind her. Western and Seneca were quite a walk, but the transient nature of homeless people meant she might find this "Teddy" anywhere. She may as well start somewhere.

She searched while she walked, and while most of the next hour was fruitless, if pleasant. Lacey struggled not to be distracted by the decorations scattered throughout downtown ahead of Christmas. The local storefronts, and even some apartment complexes, were beautiful. Wreaths adorning doors, Christmas trees glittering just within. The window displays were especially attractive, with their fake snow. Despite the distractions and the growing cold, she pushed on, talking to what seemed like dozens of shiftless vagrants. A startling number of them were women, and none answered to the name "Teddy." As she shivered, she wondered whether she'd be giving herself away too much by simply visiting the various shelters nearby. She worried that she might have to, and began contemplating how she'd do that without drawing attention to herself. The obvious answer was her old standby—undercover work.

She was still sorting out the particulars when she finally reached Seneca and Western.

As she passed a nail salon, a tinkling bell caught her attention. Lacey glanced over to see a man who almost looked homeless himself, a threadbare black beanie on his head, standing next to a hanging money bucket. "Merry Christmas," he called at her. "Ho, ho, ho, and all that."

She stopped and pulled out her wallet. Unzipping it, she quickly confirmed all she had was a Subway Sandwiches punch card and one shiny Macy's card. "I'm sorry," she said, her eyebrows pressing together. "I-I wish I could."

"It's for the kids, lady," he insisted, his raised eyebrows melding into his beanie.

"I'm sorry." Lacey kept walking.

"Rich brat," he muttered.

Lacey scowled, speeding her pace. *What was that about?* she wondered, making a mental note to call the store manager with a stern complaint. Shoving her wallet back in her purse, she peeked in at the gun nestled beside it.

Looking back up, Lacey started at the realization that, in her distraction, she'd nearly *stepped* on a homeless man who was nestled between a pair of hedges ringing a parking lot. She stumbled around him, in his thick bundle of tattered blankets, catching her breath and pulling her red coat closer around her. She wanted to move on, to get out of this place. She had nothing particular against the poor, but she'd been around long enough to know that rich, attractive girls should best avoid certain areas of town at night—and certain people. Still, she was Lacey Ling, investigative reporter extraordinaire.

She'd always been able to handle herself just fine. And so she crouched beside the man, whose scraggly, gray hair poked out from beneath a trapper cap, and nudged him. The only reply was a small mumble and heavy snoring.

Settling on her haunches, she nearly whispered, "Sir?" Hesitantly, she reached out to tap him. "Teddy?" she finally said. "Are you Teddy?"

The man groggily changed positions, his pink eyelids still shut, a string of drool trailing from his chapped lips. He looked like all too many of the other destitute people she'd encountered tonight. Cringing, she tapped him once more on his shoulder. "Teddy? Sir?"

With a snort, his lids blinked open, the whites of his eyes badly sun-damaged. "Huhrr?"

Lacey sympathetically smiled, tucking some of her long hair behind an ear. "Hi. I'm so sorry for waking you."

He blinked some more. "You talkin' to me?" He made another gurgling "Huhrr" sound from the depths of his throat.

"Yes, sir. Is your name Teddy?"

"*Teddy?*" he repeated loudly while cupping an ear. "I haven't had a teddy since... since I was five!" He lifted a nearby crumpled cup. "Spare change?"

Embarrassed, Lacey glanced around. A couple of window-shoppers didn't seem to care or notice. But the black-beanied bell ringer who'd insulted her had stopped to peer at her like a watch dog. Never had a five o'clock shadow looked so menacing. She returned her attention to the vagrant. "I'm sorry for

28

bothering you." She stood, pulling her purse close against her body.

Crossing the parking lot, Lacey sucked in a deep breath and exhaled slowly. She spotted another homeless man sitting against a concrete pylon that supported Seneca as it merged onto the Alaska Way viaduct. Even from several yards away, he had a different feel than any of the other transients she'd met tonight. Something... dark. Her heart beating hard, she wondered if she should dare approach him. One foot in front of the other, as if possessed by someone stronger, she went forward.

A rat skittered across the shadowy pavement, squealing in the cold. Still, Lacey pressed forward, her high-heeled boots clicking loudly no matter how cautiously she stepped. The man didn't seem to notice, focused on something in his lap.

Lacey's shadow was suddenly paralleled by another, from behind. She made to spin but wasn't fast enough; a large hand seized her left arm.

FOUR

Her breath caught the instant she saw her captor. There stood the bell ringer, black beanie askew, his face menacing beneath. His former, vacant look had been replaced by a chilling clarity.

"Let go of me," she ordered. Although her voice was strong, she was shaking within.

He pressed his face close to hers, and she recoiled from the stench of cheap coffee and cigarettes. "First, you pass up my donation bucket," he said, teeth stained and voice dripping with disdain, "then you harass a sleeping man. Who *are* you?"

It didn't help to know she was probably within fifty yards of the spot where Jessica had been murdered. His grip crushed her bicep, refusing to release her.

She started, "I'm just—" Her right hand stealthily continued reaching into her purse. "I'm looking for someone."

Squeezing even harder, making Lacey wince, he said, "Do you know what happened in here? Do you want it to happen to you?"

Her right hand now having a firm grip around her pistol's handle, she asked, "Why? Are you the murderer?"

The man growled, then chuckled at Lacey's reaction. She wondered whether she'd managed to keep the fear out of her eyes.

Without warning, a calm, familiar voice chimed in her mind, making her gasp in surprise. *Pull out your gun.*

"Victor?" she muttered.

"Who's Victor?" the man asked. "Don't you mean Teddy? Isn't *that* who you're looking for? Yeah, I heard you."

"Yes," she finally said, her heart hammering. Had she just hallucinated? Had she just willed a memory of Victor's voice?

The man jerked Lacey in his grip before letting go. "Here I am."

"Wh-what?" Lacey's eyes narrowed, blood returning to her arm.

"I'm Teddy, so what do you want?"

Was this part of his game before the attack? "No, you're not Teddy."

"Of course I am."

Lacey ripped the gun from her purse, pointing directly at his face. "Back up."

A sudden yelp and the sounds of panicked retreat behind her—probably the vagrant she'd been intent on moments ago—caught Lacey's ear, but she kept her eyes focused on the man in front of her. If she had to guess, it was probably the vagrant she'd been intent on moments ago; probably not a fan of guns. "Back *up*, I said."

Raising his hands slightly, he looked surprisingly amused. Still, he complied with her demand. "I am Teddy."

Shaking her head, Lacey said, "Teddy's homeless."

"Right," he drawled sarcastically. "I really live in the Escala Condos. This is just my night job." He rolled his eyes. "Of course I'm homeless."

"No, you're not. You're a liar and a creep. And I'll put a bullet in your head if you don't start telling the truth." She savored the sense of power that surged through her at having the upper hand. "Who are you?"

The man carefully pulled off his overcoat, dropping it carelessly into a puddle. He then started unbuttoning his shirt, not shivering even a bit.

"What are you doing?" Lacey demanded. This man was more sick in the head than she supposed. "Why are you undressing?"

He stopped unbuttoning at the top of his paunch, and exposed his hairy chest. Through the forest, she could barely make out the tattoo in bold black letters: Teddy.

Lacey's eyes widened. Cocking her head, she conceded, "Okay, so you're Teddy."

"Like I said, rich brat." He smiled a winning smile. "You going to put away the gun now?"

"No. You going to stop being a creeper? Didn't think so."

"What do you want from me then?" he asked.

"You know what I want."

"Details about the other rich brat's murder." He spread his arms. "Am I hot?"

Lacey nearly barfed in her mouth, until she realized *hot* meant *right*. "Yes."

"You sure you want to meddle in this, rich brat?" There was a dark gleam in his eyes.

"Yes," she replied, keeping her elbows locked, the gun motionless. "And stop calling me that."

"What?" His brows went up. "Rich brat?"

"Yes. I'm not a rich brat."

"Now *you're* the liar," he said. "Tsk, tsk. Wait a sec. Ain't you that Asian reporter? Lacey Ping?"

"Ling," she corrected, lifting her chin a touch. "What's the fact that I'm Asian—? Never mind, no more tangents. I have some questions for you."

Teddy relaxed and started rebuttoning his shirt. When he finished, he retrieved his coat and fished a cigarette and a lighter from a pocket. He lit up and gestured at Lacey with the pack. She wrinkled her nose and stepped away.

"Suit yourself," he said. "Not like I got many to share anyway. But I see. You want an interview." He shook his head and snarled quietly. "You know, I *knew* I couldn't trust cops. Information gets leaked when they say it won't. Now it's *my* head on the chopping block, if you know what I'm sayin'. Well, you can't intimidate Teddy, even with that shiny thing in your dainty little hands." He took a long drag on his cigarette and blew it out into the chilly air. "I'm not available for comment." He turned around and stuffed his free hand in his pocket, clearly convinced that Lacey wouldn't pull the trigger. "Excuse me, but I have a job to go to."

Lacey stepped forward. "Wait, that's it?"

"Got a donation for my bucket?" he called over his shoulder. His tone said he didn't expect a yes.

Lacey huffed, glancing at the concrete, then back to him. "Seriously?"

FIVE

Standing on an unimaginably green stretch of grass, under brilliantly blue skies, would have been Victor's dream, once upon a time. Granted, watching a herd of cats play croquet would *only* have ever happened in a dream, but now, it was the stuff of reality. And it was driving him *insane*.

"You're killing me here, Rao," Victor said, his blue eyes bulging.

The black-and-gold striped tabby floated about a foot above the plush grass, aiming her croquet mallet at a wicket. "Could you give me some space?" she said, waving a furry arm at him. "You're the only spectator in the middle of the field. You know, they have benches for a reason."

It was true; hundreds of human angels watched in wait beyond a white perimeter. There were only cats on the green, one black one, in particular, now eyeing Victor with disdain.

Defiant, he stayed put. "Look, you're the one who told me Lacey was in danger. And now you're asking me to stand around while you play stupid games? I *want* to see her. I *have* to know what she's up against. Talk to me," he said, nudging her.

Rao swung, hitting the yellow ball. It zipped just past the wicket, a little too much to the right. The crowd moaned in disappointment. His former pet turned, glaring at Victor. "See what you made me do?"

Victor could have pulled his hair out if he weren't made of spirit matter. "This is wasting time. There are more important things than *this*."

Giving Victor a sidelong glance, Rao challenged, "You're questioning Heaven's wisdom, here. Now, listen…" She hovered up to face him straight on. "You aren't scheduled to 'go down' until after this round of the tourney. I have it on good authority, the *best* authority, that Lacey will be fine until then."

"You mean to say," Victor's dark brows went up, "I get to actually go down… to see her… on Earth?"

"More than that, bub." Rao winked. "You get to be her guardian angel."

*

Who knew a Subway sandwich would be more convincing than a gun at getting information? Slouching against the corrugated steel wall of the pierside storefront, Teddy dove into his foot-long ham and pastrami, pieces of lettuce spilling out of the corners of his mouth, littering the sidewalk. Lacey wished she'd had the time to take him to a regular Subway, where they could have gotten in out of the cold. "We gotta hurry," he said. "Like I was saying, I have a job, you know."

"Right." Lacey cleared her throat, having foregone eating for the sake of talking. "Look, I know you're afraid of information being leaked. You wanted to remain an anonymous witness. I respect that. All this is off the record."

The hunger in his eyes was replaced with skepticism. "Sure."

"I mean it," she said, slapping the steel wall in emphasis. "I'm not even a reporter anymore. KZTB is in the past."

"Then why do you care?" he asked through another large bite, a hunk of meat falling from his lips.

She paused, her mouth hanging slightly open. "Because. I simply have a personal interest in the case."

He cocked a brow, and a hint of respect shone in his eyes. "A vigilante thing going on here? Gonna be like the female Asian Batman or something?"

Lacey blinked, her hand still wrapped around the gun tucked in her large purse. She shook her head. "No. I mean, I don't want revenge. I don't plan on—"

"Killing him," he finished, smacking his chops.

That was actually an interesting question. What was she doing exactly? Lacey pressed her full lips together in thought. "No."

Teddy pointed with a knowing smile. "Ya know, you sure don't sound sure of yourself."

"*I'm* supposed to be the one interviewing *you*." She flipped some hair behind a shoulder, trying to get serious again.

"Where are you working at now?" he ignored her words. "You know, even though you're a rich brat, if you're looking for work, you wouldn't be half bad as a model."

"I'm not… looking to be a model." This was getting tiring.

"Why not? You know there's some agencies close by."

Lacey shook her head emphatically. "Listen. First question, tell me everything you saw."

"That's a big question. Not even a question, technically. I might need a soda to go with this sandwich."

"Argh. I don't have any more money. I get paid Friday. Please. Just tell me what you *saw*."

"It's just—for an investigative reporter, you'd think—"

Lacey slapped the wall again, earning a frown from the employee working behind the window. "*Enough*. I got you your stupid sandwich. Now *talk*." She lowered her voice, in case any of the few passersby had heard her little outburst. "A deal is a deal."

His countenance softened, and he set down the other half of his meal. "Okay. So I was finished with my shift for the Salvation Army, and I was heading to my usual spot for the night. A couple other guys share it with me. It's where we sleep. Anyways, as I was walkin' back to my 'home,' I heard a skirmish. This blond chick was—who was dressed very rich, by the way—"

Lacey felt like rolling her eyes, but since he was on a roll, talking, she refrained.

"Anyway, I saw this scrawny guy threatening her with a knife."

"Scrawny? A knife?" Lacey repeated. That's not what her dream, or her vision, or whatever it was, showed.

"That's what I said. Do you want to hear the rest, or no?"

Lacey shifted her stance. "Go on."

"Okay, so anyway, I nearly called out to the guy, to tell him to get off my turf and leave the brat alone. But I was too late. She was stabbed."

Lacey took a deep breath. "Just a moment," she said, pulling her phone out of her woolen coat pocket. She quickly pulled up the Internet and Googled. Nothing new on Jessica's case. Just the usual spiel from the cops, looking for information and hoping to weed out false testimonies.

Teddy stood quickly and crowded Lacey, peering at her phone. "Whatcha doin'?" He made to snatch it, but Lacey jerked it away. He narrowed his eyes at her. "You're not texting someone what I'm saying, are you?"

"No." Lacey apologized, putting away her phone. "I was just checking something. What do you mean by scrawny?"

Teddy's dark eyes continued to study her suspiciously. "What you mean, '*What do you mean*'? I mean he was… scrawny. I'm more buff than him." He flexed slightly and kissed his bicep before laughing sarcastically.

Lacey looked at Teddy's arms, easy to see through his thermal button-up. They were strong. She flashbacked to that moment in her dream, where her focus was zeroed in on the murderer's biceps. They were eerily similar to Teddy's. Bulky, thick like small logs.

"What? What're you thinking?" he said gruffly, breaking into her thoughts.

Lacey shook her head while closing her eyes a moment. "I'm sorry. I'm feeling a little out of it. Must be my hunger," she lied.

Teddy slid the sandwich closer to him, possessively.

"I have to go," she lied again, standing. "I'm feeling sick."

From beneath the ridge of his beanie, Teddy eyed her. "Sure you are," he said. "Hey, you know what I'd do if I were you?"

Lacey paused out of curiosity. "What?"

"Stop meddling." He took a bite, and with a full mouth, said, "Or else."

A chill went down Lacey's spine, and she hurried away, though trying to act cool. Once out of Teddy's line of sight, she jogged toward KZTB's parking garage, feeling like she had a hundred miles to go instead of two. Suddenly, all the city's Christmas decor wasn't comforting. The streetlamp bows now appeared blood-red. An inflatable sidewalk Santa even had a menacing look in his jolly smile. She couldn't get to her car soon enough.

Once in the garage, and with keys ready, she rushed toward her car in the dark distance. She hated how easily she could scare. It didn't help that nearly every horror movie had a moment just like this one. Closing in on her ride, she beeped it open, the sound echoing eerily through the garage as though it had come from everywhere at once.

Just as she pulled on her driver-side door handle, someone again grabbed her arm.

SIX

Lacey jerked with a yelp and spun out of the grasp, her hand shooting into her bag for her gun.

"Whoa, Lacey," a woman said.

There, before her, was Cathy, bundled up against the cold, toting a bag stuffed to the brim with binders and folders. Her eyes bulged behind her cat-eye glasses, and Lacey wondered how big a fool she'd made of herself.

"Sorry for scaring you!" Cathy said. "I saw you here, and was so surprised I couldn't speak."

Lacey clutched at her chest, taking deep breaths. She looked up at her former editor in rebuke. "You nearly gave me a heart attack."

Cathy awkwardly fixed a bit of her short red hair, a look of concern in her eyes. "I'm really sorry. My car's right here," she said, pointing at the yellow Volkswagen in the next stall. "I wanted to catch you before you left."

"Well, you *caught* me." Lacey straightened her back, running her slender fingers through long tresses.

"I wanted to tell you that I put in a good word for you with the new station manager."

"Well, thank you," Lacey said, still waiting for her pulse to slow.

"Is that why you were here? Were you trying to talk to her?"

"No, I don't even know who the new manager is." Lacey felt instantly apologetic at her curtness. "I mean, thank you. I'm just using this place to park. I was downtown. Shopping."

A nearby Exit sign suddenly buzzed and flickered before going out.

The women looked back at each other, obviously both spooked. Cathy giggled nervously. "Going to have to call Maintenance in the morning."

Cathy's eyes flicked back and forth between Lacey's hands. "Shopping?" the woman asked.

"Yeah, just got a *little* something." Lacey pointed at her big purse as explanation. A pang of sadness welled inside, knowing she *still* hadn't gotten Nainai a gift; worse, she wasn't sure that she'd be *able* to afford anything worth giving. She pushed the thought aside.

"Ah. Okay," Cathy said with a knowing glint in her green eyes. She gave Lacey a quick hug around the bulky bag of binders. "Well, it was good seeing you again. Take care of yourself, okay? Don't do anything you'd regret."

"I won't," Lacey said, hiding her wounded pride under a smile. Cathy, of all people, should know Lacey better than that; Lacey was a strong woman, and could handle herself. She opened her car door and said goodbye with another smile before sliding inside.

*

Lacey was happy to be home, with her door double-locked, but still groaned at the sight of her new cramped confines—it looked far smaller than the model she'd toured—but at least she'd been able to find a two-bedroom apartment; there was no practical way Nainai's special bed would have fit in the same room as Lacey's, even if they hadn't had dressers and a desk.

At a grating peal of laughter from upstairs, Lacey buried her head under her pillow. Nainai snored on as she did every night, and Lacey wished she could sleep so well. She had work in the morning, and resented the fact that taking the day off to move would take a chunk out of her paycheck. Even Cathy's assurances, in the parking garage, did nothing to help with that in the short term. She needed a good job *three months* ago, so why were her prospects so dim? She was well-qualified for several professional-level jobs.

Frustrated and desperate for sleep, she grabbed her phone and cued up some relaxation music. Setting the phone next to her head, she did her best to focus on the soothing sounds. But sleep eluded her. Every time she closed her eyes, visions of

Jessica running, screaming, or being tossed into a dumpster assaulted her.

"It wasn't my fault," she said into her pillow. "It was just a dream. Even if I *had* called the cops, they'd have never believed me. What could I have told them?" And yet, she couldn't help but think she could have done something to prevent it.

She *knew* why she had to solve this. Teddy was wrong—it wasn't about seeking vigilante justice; it was about reclaiming her peace of mind.

SEVEN

Lacey pressed the power button to her Mac laptop with a buffed fingernail, watching in anticipation as the screen flared to life. Her hair back in a low ponytail, strands of fly-away hairs shrouded her tired face. The morning shift had been hectic, to say the least, and it wasn't even over. The fact that Lacey didn't get good sleep last night wasn't helping. She had so much on her mind.

Quickly opening an Internet browser, she typed in the search field: "breaking news Jessica Simcox." A few results popped up.

"Hey," a crabby female-voice intruded. It was Mrs. Jones, her boss. The woman, whose brown hair bulged like a Chia pet's against her hairnet, glared down at Lacey. "You know the rules. Take your apron off during break."

Immediately, Lacey fingered the knot at her back, pulling it loose. "Yes, sorry about that." She folded it neatly, setting it atop her tiny table for two.

"Seven more minutes. Quit milking our wi-fi. That's for customers. And wash your face before you return to work. You have something… right there." Mrs. Jones slid a finger over a saggy jowl in emphasis, then stalked off to the front counter.

Lacey touched her cheek, leaving a white residue on her finger. Dried whipped cream. Lovely. It must have been from the last order, where the frat boy wanted so much whipped cream it was beginning to resemble a melting snowman. "Wonderful…" She rubbed face hard with a scratchy napkin.

Quickly scrolling through her results proved there wasn't any actual new news. She huffed, before her eyes fixed on a different result. An online portfolio for Jessica's modeling. She clicked the link, and was met with a variety of composite pictures of the young woman posing. Lacey clicked on a bikini picture, Jessica's blond hair feathering in a light wind, seaside. Even she had to admit, the girl was gorgeous. Eyes hungry for more information, Lacey quickly found a "Booking" link. She clicked it. A page with contact info to Trend Modeling Agency popped up, with the words beneath saying, "This model is currently unavailable."

"*I'll* say…" Lacey muttered- under her breath. Looking back up at the agency's address, she realized it was near B & B. The feelings of utter failure at her recently bombed interview crept up the back of her neck.

Never before had she so roundly *murdered* a job interview. The most disturbing part was the feeling that she hadn't actually been in control of herself when answering the last question. She *never* would have given such a bimbo answer like that, and yet, she *had*.

Reflecting on the strange sensation of darkness she had felt during those final moments of the interview, she frowned and glanced through her booth's window toward the sky. "Victor? Is there something you forgot to tell me before you left? I'm not possessed or anything, am I?" Of course, there was no response, but she took some comfort in the fact that his essence had survived death. It was nice to think he was still watching over her. She giggled at an unexpected thought that Victor, now dead, may be the Patron Saint of Lucky Charms and Godzilla toys. Then, an unexpected sense of emptiness settled upon her, and she felt the faint beginning of tears.

"Dang it, Victor, I wasn't supposed to miss you. Don't go making me fall apart like this. I've got too much to do right now, and if you're not going to help, then stop embarrassing me." Lacey wiped a small tear that had broken loose. Self-conscious, she set her jaw, willing her eyes dry.

That crabby voice broke into her thoughts again, this time from a distance. "Seven minutes are up, girlie! Back to work."

*

Lacey's shift hadn't ended soon enough; in fact, when Lacey's replacement failed to show early, Mrs. Jones had insisted on Lacey staying to provide coverage until the guy arrived, at which point the older woman had fired the guy, meaning there was a gap in the schedule for an additional hour. Lacey cursed the fact that she needed overtime pay so badly, but she stayed anyway.

Yes. It was well past time that Lacey get a new job. And she had just the idea.

As soon as she clocked out and stashed her apron, she'd made her way to the address she'd found for Jessica's agency, though she doubted they'd be open this late. Parking had been only a mild a nightmare, but she'd been fortunate enough to find something pierside, right across from B and B's—as if today hadn't brought enough painful reminders of her failure. Worse, she wasn't all that far from where she'd met Teddy. She wondered whether he might be somewhere nearby.

Watching me, maybe? She shook her head clear of the thought.

Evening was already upon the city, and the air was bitterly cold and unusually foul smelling. Lacey attributed it to the rush of cars passing overhead, but knew that it was as much psychological as anything. She walked quickly away from her car, but almost immediately sensed a presence behind her. Without stopping to look, she picked up her pace as she hurried toward Alaska Way. The traffic light changed just before she could cross, forcing her to stop. The dark presence that had assaulted her during her interview was still there, and she tensed, praying the light would change soon. As she lingered, a cold recognition descended on her. Whatever had caused her to botch her final interview question felt *exactly* like what she'd felt looking at the homeless man; or, perhaps more accurately, what she'd felt the instant before Teddy had grabbed her. A chill coursed down her spine.

Glancing behind her, she saw nothing unusual, and when the light changed, she hurried across the street, eyes scanning the area, and into the building that was supposed to house Jessica's one-time employer. Again, nothing unusual.

The lobby was blessedly bright and warm, and decorated for the Christmas season, as expected. Lacey's heels clacked against stylish tile flooring as she made her way toward a chic reception desk occupied by a gorgeous brunette in a smart pantsuit. Lacey had, of course, done her makeup again during the drive, and had even handled most of the flyaways. She may be temporarily poor, but she couldn't afford to look it, especially not now.

"Seriously, Victor," she murmured to the air, "if you can pull some of those heavenly strings I'm sure you've got..."

Her stomach rumbled, and she wished she'd stopped at the chowder house on the pier. It was too late for that. She had already made up her mind. She stopped at the desk and smiled politely at the receptionist, who returned the smile.

"May I help you?" the brunette asked. She seemed tired, and was clearly not thrilled to be there.

Lacey recognized her own employment frustration reflected in the woman's face. She had to give the lady credit for still putting on a professional façade.

"Trend Modeling Agency," Lacey said simply.

The woman nodded, and without missing a beat, said, "Suite two-oh-two." Lacey already knew this, of course, but thanked the other woman graciously, and made her way to the elevators.

Darkness closed around her mind again, bringing with it serious doubts. "Why am I here?" she asked herself. What had she been thinking, deciding to go into modeling? She could get information about Jessica as an outsider. And the other missing girls weren't even confirmed as models; even if they were, what were the odds they'd come from the exact same agency as Jessica? Further, she had no desire to sell herself for money. Who cared how she looked? Then again, she couldn't *stand* to work for Mrs. Jones another minute. But *modeling*? She'd almost rather go into telemarketing.

An elevator opened in front of her, the small whoosh of air playing with her hair. A pair of stunningly handsome men in designer business suits exited, a shorter ginger and a tall, lean man with a chiseled face and dark hair in perfect waves. Lacey turned quickly away, pretending to be preoccupied with her phone to avoid making eye contact.

"I'll see you tomorrow morning," the shorter one said.

The dark-haired man smiled and waved. "Yes, tomorrow. And I know you'll bring me news about the replacements. Turnover is one thing, but what happened to Jessica…"

Lacey perked up. *Jessica?*

Lacey saw the man shudder. "Murder. That's just beyond the pale. I'm going to miss her." He shook his head sadly.

The redheaded man frowned. "Me too. Don't worry. We'll get someone."

"Thanks, Jenners," the taller man replied. "I'm going to grab a late bite. You have a good evening."

"Likewise."

And with that, the taller man was off.

Gamble on a walk-in job interview, Lacey asked herself, *or follow a probable lead for resolving Jessica's murder? I guess this one's a no-brainer.*

Lacey only hoped she could afford dinner at wherever the guy was going.

EIGHT

"Table for one?" the hostess asked her as Lacey hurried through the doors of the vintage hotel and into the ground floor restaurant, arms still wrapped tightly around herself for warmth. She nodded, and was escorted to a table near the back of the restaurant. She tried to look casual as she scanned the room, hoping to find the dark-haired man; she'd forced herself to wait five minutes before following him through the door.

The place was nice—she'd actually been here several times before. On summer days, back when she'd been rich, she'd eat out on the patio. Tonight, however, was better done indoors. The main dining area, with its warm, wooden accents, ample booths, and elegant decor, was surprisingly empty, even for a Tuesday night.

Thankfully, when her hostess finally seated her, Lacey blushed as her eyes found the man from the agency, and she realized that she could see him easily from where she sat. So easily, in fact, she found her eyes briefly roving his face again while she tried not to get lost in those stunning eyes.

He had a phone pressed to his ear and wore an expression of mild agitation. "Look, Geo," he said into his phone, "a deadline is a deadline. We set them for reasons." He paused. "I know there's a personnel shortage. I haven't been happy about it myself." Pause. "Look, don't worry. We'll take care of it. We'll have the project wrapped up by the end of next week, and have the ad running just ahead of Christmas week. Just like we promised the client. The girls will look fabulous, I promise."

The rest of the conversation was clipped as he finalized whatever details he was discussing. When it ended, he sighed again—it was a strangely beautiful sound—and laid his phone gently on the table before rubbing his forehead. By chance, he glanced in Lacey's direction, startling her. When they locked eyes, a jolt of electricity coursed through her; she immediately hid her face behind her menu.

When the waitress arrived, Lacey languidly ordered a sweet potato gnocchi and some risotto, and agreed to the waitress' suggestion for a wine to complement her meal, and forced herself not to think about just how hard this would hit her bank account. She found she was more than a little reluctant to give up her menu, for all she could hide behind it, since the guy was still clearly in her line of sight. But she was a big girl and knew better than to let a handsome face get the better of her.

As the waitress walked away, Lacey felt an unexpected gust of chilly air. She looked up just in time to see the man walk out onto the patio, where he propped himself up against the low railing and looked up into the evening sky. Lacey doubted he'd see much of it, between the buildings of downtown Seattle and the night lights, but there was something serenely soothing about the mere gesture he was making to the universe.

Am I really doing this? she asked herself. But why not? Oh, right. Her grandmother. Nainai, whose health had been a rollercoaster for the last several months. Nainai, who had trouble feeding, clothing and bathing herself. Nainai, who would be all alone for hours on end, trapped in that... place... Lacey had been forced to stoop to renting for lack of better income. Nainai, for whom she had nothing to give for Christmas.

Nainai, for whom Lacey had given up a glorious afterlife.

Maybe she could go back to Bowler and Bowen and explain that she hadn't been herself during the interview; maybe find some way to salvage the last-second trainwreck she'd caused. She bit her lip. When had life become so complicated as to blunt the decisiveness she prided herself on?

Just give me a sign, here. What am I supposed to do? Teddy's compliment entered her mind: "You wouldn't be half bad as a model."

Dinner came, and dinner went, and while the food was excellent, as always, concerns over how much she was spending on the meal, and the blandness of her new life, spilled over into her enjoyment; she found herself unable to finish. She signaled the waitress and asked for a take-out box and a check. Waiting for the girl to return, she found herself unable to avoid glancing toward the table with the dark-haired man. He'd long since returned from his foray onto the patio and, from the looks of it, he was nearly done with his meal; unlike Lacey, he seemed to be enjoying—no, *savoring*—it. She was disappointed when he didn't look over at her, but she was awed by his easy manner and placid appearance, especially after what had seemed an agitating phone call.

"Your take-out box, miss," the waitress said. Lacey pulled out her credit card, but as she made to hand it to the waitress, the girl shook her head and smiled. "The gentleman at table six has already paid your ticket."

Lacey gasped, whipping up to look at him again, but his table was empty. Searching quickly, she saw his back as he made his way out the door and into the December evening. When she turned back to the waitress, she saw a knowing smile and a twinkle in the girl's eye. "Not that it's my place to say," the waitress added in a conspiratorial whisper, "but his ring finger was bare."

Lacey managed to neither blush nor gasp, but felt a strange combination of thrill at the news, and violation that a random stranger would be trying to hook her up with another random stranger. Instead, she smiled politely and left a generous tip; after all, she knew firsthand just how much a good tip meant.

Lacey hurried off to catch the man. She knew it'd look desperate, but how else would she get the chance to say "thank you" in as busy a city as Seattle? She couldn't pretend his magnetism had nothing to do with her need to offer the gesture, personally, and the last thing she wanted to do was put up a listing under Missed Connections in Craigslist.

So she pushed through the lobby door, jogging down the sidewalk in her heels. "Hey, sir! Wait!"

He was just rounding a corner of the building, and disappeared out of sight.

"Shoot!" she muttered, slowing her pace.

The man suddenly re-appeared with a curious expression. He smiled, making eye contact. "Me?" he said.

Of course you! Lacey thought. Smoothing her windblown hair from the chase, she smiled back. "Yes, hi."

They approached each other. This was the most pure animal attraction that she'd felt for a man in a long time, since the night she'd met Victor. Their eyes locked for a long moment, not uttering a word, until she finally did. "Thank you."

*

The Pool made Ultra 4K HD look like television from the 1930s. Looking into the normally invisibly clear liquid, Victor found that not only could he see Lacey, but he could change his viewpoint at will, and could see and hear everything as though he were there. Further, he found he was still fully connected to Lacey's thoughts and feelings, just as he had been on Earth.

Watching her walk away from "Tall, Dark, and Handsome," his heart both ached and rejoiced at the way her emotions fluttered after the encounter. Yet there was something pervasively *wrong* about the whole thing, and he couldn't put his finger on it.

"I thought you said I wouldn't get to see Lacey in The Pool," he said to Rao, not looking at her.

"No," she answered mildly, "I said you couldn't bribe an Archangel to give you a peep show."

"You have such a dirty mind for an angel," Victor retorted.

"Semantics," the cat said, waving it away. "You know what I meant. At any rate, can you see why Lacey is in trouble?"

Victor pursed his lips. "Of course. She's falling for a guy who's all looks and no substance."

Rao politely smacked him upside the head. "Enough with the jealousy. You know you're happy she's moving on, even if it's not with you."

Victor frowned. "Yes and no. I want her taken care of. If this guy will do it, great. It not…"

"So what's the *real* problem, Victor? Take some time to think about it."

Victor focused on The Pool, moving all around the scene and trying to pick out what was really bothering him. Lacey, however, proved to be too much of a distraction. Suddenly, the image rippled, then vanished, replaced by the face of a glaring tabby.

"I don't even think about my old toms as much as you think about your former girlfriend. Focus, Vic. Focus."

Victor gritted his teeth. "I couldn't tell, okay? And I haven't seen Lacey at all before now. Give me a break."

"Doesn't that bother you?" Rao asked archly.

Victor frowned. "What happened to your feminine powers of observation? Of *course* that bothers—"

"I mean," Rao interrupted, "doesn't it bother you that you *can't* figure out what's wrong?"

He paused, letting the idea percolate. At last, he looked up at the cat. "So you're saying that guy really *is* bad for her?"

Rao shook her head. "Not specifically. It's that *in the area around Lacey* there was a decidedly dark presence."

"You mean Leg—"

"Ah, ah, ah!" Rao shushed him quickly. All around, Victor felt thoughts of concern and surprise. "We don't speak that name in Heaven. This is a holy place. A clean place. The Dark Ones chose to leave; we're not inclined to invite them back."

Victor shuddered at the memories of Legion, the horde of demons he'd had to deal with during his time between death and Heaven. Rao was right—*no one* in their right mind would want anything to do with them.

"Get to the point, Cat. When do I get to go back? Or did you just bring me here to taunt me?"

Rao adopted a look of supreme innocence. "I'm an angel. Why would I taunt anyone?"

Victor rolled his eyes and gave her an unmistakable stare.

Rao smirked and carried on. "Angels are agents, Vic. Meaning, we're occasionally given assignments. Your girlfriend is about to walk into something unquantifiably dangerous without enough knowledge to be safe about it. Normally, one of her ancestors would be tapped to handle a situation like this, but the Big Man knows how much you still love her, and He's granting you a real favor.

"Angels in the Seattle area have reported that really dark things are afoot, dark enough that Heaven's intervention is required to keep things from really going off the rails. Because you once lived there, and because of your connection to Lacey, we're giving you a chance to prove your stuff by helping us figure out *what* is going on, and helping us avert anything truly harmful."

Victor's brow wrinkled. "Can't God just tell us the answer? I thought He knew everything."

Rao smiled. "He does. But *how* He knows doesn't necessarily work the way mortals think. You'll figure it out soon enough. Angelic messengers serve a variety of purposes. Right now, yours is to do a little nosing around."

It made little sense to Victor, but he could tell Rao wouldn't be swayed. Besides, a chance to visit Lacey was not to be passed up for any reason. "I'm in. When do I start?"

Rao smiled. "Right about... *now.*"

NINE

Primping in her bathroom's cracked mirror, Lacey couldn't help but feel a little giddy. She was going on a date. At least she thought she was... The man who'd paid for her dinner last night, Jack Beals, wanted to meet up for dinner today. He was a modeling scout, by profession. He had told her she had beautiful bone structure off the bat.

Lacey started to wonder.

"He didn't technically call it a date," she told herself. "Don't get your hopes up too high. He deals with beautiful women all day. Maybe this will be more like a job offer, instead." And she could really use one, right about now, even if it was in something she detested.

Dabbing her blush brush in a beige powder, she nodded, before fluffing it across her nose, muting a few freckles. Freckles Victor loved. She switched her thoughts back to her quasi-date. "Besides, he should be the one nervous to go out with *me*." She never did approve of girls acting desperate. Herself especially. Either way, this man could be a good distraction. A distraction from thinking about Victor so much.

On the way out, Nainai said, "I want to hear every detail." She hacked, stirring a heartier series of coughs.

Lacey went over to the portable heater beside her grandmother's bed and switched it on. "Stay warm, Nainai. Do you need a cough drop?"

"No." The old woman waved away the offer. "It's nothing."

Lacey paused, staring at her grandmother, her shoulder-length white hair thin and wispy against a fragile face of puffy lids and wrinkles.

"Don't look at me like that!" the woman insisted. "I have plenty of time left on Earth. Trust me. I'm not dying yet."

"Okay." Lacey hesitated. "I won't be long." Before leaving the room, Lacey straightened the lucky cat on the end table.

"Have some fun, dear!"

*

At dinner, Lacey's stomach embarrassingly growled loudly in front of Jack. Like a gentleman, he pretended not to hear. Instead, he turned his attention to the food being brought over by the waitress.

"Your steak, sir. And your fettuccini Alfredo, ma'am."

The plates were hot.

"Thank you for taking me out," Lacey said. "This is nice."

Jack's eyes smiled, the green in them sparkling. "The pleasure's mine. Trust me. Tell me about yourself. Besides the calm and collected reporter we all know and love..."

Lacey crossed her legs beneath the table. What part should she divulge first? The dead ex who'd haunted her, the grandmother seemingly on the brink of passing away, just getting a job as a barista girl, or being neighbors to the cast of Cops? Ugh, none of it sounded good. Better to fall back on the basics. "When I'm not reading, I like to indulge in a Netflix marathon."

"Oh, really? If you could watch a marathon tonight, which show would you choose?"

"NCIS, or maybe Criminal Minds..."

Jack nearly choked on his bite, and took a long drink of water. "No way. You're into crime dramas, too? I've seen every Criminal Minds episode there is."

"Really?" Lacey smiled.

"Yes!" He adjusted his tie and leaned forward. "What's your favorite color?"

"Blue."

"Your favorite music?"

"Hmmm. Classical."

"Breakfast? Wait, let me guess: veggie om—"

"Veggie omelet." Lacey nodded, surprised. How did he know *that* one?

"Mine, mine, and mine, too! Wow, we're so alike, Lacey," he said with a purposeful boyishness that was humorous and charming at the same time.

She simply laughed in return, giving him what he wanted.

Jack's eyes were suddenly penetrating. "Excuse me," he said. "I'm not normally this goofy. It's rare I feel quite so at ease with a woman, especially one I barely met." He smoothed his cloth napkin over his slacks.

Lacey found herself holding her breath as he leaned forward slightly. He was so handsome.

He smiled and chuckled lightly as he shook his head. "This is—"

"Insane," she finished with a dreamy sigh. "Like we're in that scene from Frozen."

He arched a brow with question.

"It was on Amazon Prime." Her tongue nearly stumbled over the explanation. "I watched it after NCIS's season was over. You know..."

"Yes," he said in contemplation. "It's okay. Even if your guilty pleasure is Disney, I'm still happy to be on this date with you."

Date. She should have never mentioned the silly movie. Victor liked silly movies. "Same here," she smiled, adding, "and just so you know, Disney happens to be a well-respected company, loved by all ages... and social statuses." What was she rambling about now?

"Of course," Jack said, eyes gleaming. "Hey, don't tell anybody, but I've seen Finding Nemo more times than any kid in diapers. True story." He took a long sip of wine and winked.

"So," Lacey said after taking a sip of her own wine, "you tell me a bit more about yourself."

Jack tilted his head in thought. "Hm. Okay..." He took a long pause, gazing in the distance, allowing Lacey to stare at his handsomely pursed lips.

"Hard question?" Lacey said after a moment longer.

Jack turned his eyes back to her. "A bit. I'm a hard worker, I guess you could say. Own a nice lil' home not far from here, where I just finished installing hickory wood floors."

As he cut his steak into neat pieces, he talked on about further upgrades. Lacey found herself mesmerized as he described the kitchen's backsplash, a "groutless pearl-shell tile"; the foyer's stonework "imported from Italy"; a pointillism painting "acquired from the local museum." And so on and so forth. None of it sounded boastful in the least, although he was clearly describing very expensive items. Everything was spoken of in a hushed reverence, as if the art of it all preceded its cost. Yeah, Lacey would definitely spare him info about her own crib.

When Jack finished his list, his eyes settled into hers again as he said, "I guess you can say I like beautiful things."

She caught the drift, which was nice and warm. Still, the woman in her couldn't help but say,

"Which is why you work in modeling," thinking of all the opportunities.

He quickly shook his head. "I hope you know, while yes, many women can be beautiful, the girls at Trend, they're simply sisters to me."

There was a faraway look in his eyes, suddenly, that begged the question, "I heard on the news that a model had been murdered recently. Jessica something. Was she one of yours?" Lacey uttered with a quiet respect. "Was she like a sister?"

"Uh, yes, yes." He cleared his throat, coming back to the present with a frown. "Jessica Simcox. She was..."

Lacey went against her instinct to pry. Instead, she nodded in sympathy before twirling some creamy noodles around her fork. When Jack finally took a bite of his steak, she mirrored him, slipping her warm forkful into her mouth.

Eating in silence wasn't awkward. Lacey dipped a salty breadstick into some Marinara and took a bite, savoring it. She thought of Jack's mention of needing a replacement model. "I'm sorry, but I have to admit I overheard you talking about finding a 'replacement'. I," and she glanced away, "I know I'm not Jessica Simcox, but maybe I could help you out. What... would you think my prospects would be for breaking into modeling?"

Jack's eyebrows perked up. He finished chewing and swallowed. "You're thinking of modeling?"

Lacey bit the corner of her mouth. "Possibly. I'm taking a break from newscasting. A small one."

"As I said yesterday, you have great bone structure." His eyes seemed to scrutinize her lines and angles all over again. "And it's always nice having a fresh face, someone unique, like you."

"I'd be very interested," she exaggerated.

Jack shrugged a shoulder. "I can have you do a test shoot with my photographer, Geo. I'm sure you'd do well, but are you sure this is something you want to get into?" He set his elbows on the table, clasping his hands and leaning forward. "The client demands can be pretty intense. And acting is a big part of it. You're basically pretending to be someone else the whole time. I know *I* feel that way as often as not." He chuckled lightly.

Lacey nearly retorted with her resume of undercover work, but bit her tongue, knowing better. This *was* undercover work. She was no stranger to acting. Still, Jack's reluctance was unmistakable, and Lacey nearly asked him to forget she mentioned it.

"Geo," she repeated. "Funny name for a photographer. But," and she straightened, "yes. It's something I want to get into."

A strange, sort of supernatural, chill swept over Lacey at that declaration. She shook it off and took another bite of her dish, feeling her determination rising. She was well on her way to finding a resolution to the murder of Jessica Simcox.

*

"I had a really good time tonight," Jack said, lingering by Lacey's car after their meal.

"Me too," she said with a smile.

Their faces inching closer and closer, Lacey was lost in Jack's eyes. She silently sighed into the coming kiss.

"You really like this guy?" The voice came out of nowhere, slicing through Lacey's euphoria and startling her back into a cold reality. Lacey's eyes flew open. There, almost like a mask over Jack's face, was a vision of Victor St. John.

TEN

"Ah!" Lacey stumbled back with a yelp. Three months of silence from Victor, and he had the nerve to show up *now*? His blue eyes were supremely incredulous, and his frown spoke volumes.

Jack blinked in surprise. "Wh-what? What's wrong?"

Victor, floating between them, said to Lacey, "We need to talk. We don't have time for *him*."

"Not right now," she said through clenched teeth.

Jack's brow furrowed in confusion. "I'm sorry. Too soon? I know it's our first date, but—"

Lacey's face went red hot in embarrassment. She stepped right through Victor and up to Jack. Placing a hand behind his head, she pulled him down, pressing her lips against his. He jerked slightly in surprise, but warmed quickly to the kiss.

"Mmmm," Lacey said.

"Mmmm," he replied.

Victor plastered a hand over his face, shaking his head. "This is the kind of *welcome back* I get?"

Lacey continued to kiss Jack. *This,* she retorted mentally, *was just the absolute* worst *time you could have appeared. Can't you see what I'm doing?*

Victor rolled his eyes and began pacing, refusing to watch. "Yeah, sucking face with this guy you hardly know."

Hands running through Jack's hair, and lips still entwined in his, she pled, *Can you give me just five minutes alone, please?*

Victor pursed his lips in anger. "Two minutes," he said.

Fine! Two minutes!

Victor teleported to a corner of the hotel restaurant's parking garage. He watched the cars zooming by, surprised at how he had to readjust his senses to life down here. Heaven was so much simpler and cleaner: no cars, no commercial buildings with tacky signage, and no darkness. He glared at a life insurance office, ignored any jokes he might have once made, and settled on peering up at the evening sky, admiring the vast expanse of Heaven as seen from Earth. The sky in heaven was never dark; it had the kind of perfect sunshine that even Cabo San Lucas would envy.

Although he had no physical heart, Victor couldn't help but feel a blow to his ego. The *love of his life* was making out with some dude not twenty feet away. Realizing he didn't have a watch or phone—because what's the use of such items when you're an angel?—he started counting down. "One-hundred and nineteen, one-hundred and eighteen..." At least Lacey appeared to have a type. The dude resembled Victor in coloring and height, but Victor was sure he could take the guy in a fight; not that he fought these days.

"Where was I? One-hundred and seventeen, one-hundred and sixteen, one-hundred and fifteen..." Even though Pretty Boy looked smoother than Rico Suave, he was certain to have some faults. Lacey'd thought Victor had been perfect when they'd first met, too. He wondered where he'd gone wrong, to cost him her good graces. "Uh, one-hundred and ten? One-hundred and nine..." *It's just, how can she move on* that *fast?* Then he reminded himself, she had moved on long before he had died. It was *he* who hadn't moved on. Since when was two minutes so long, anyway?

Victor tapped his foot and crossed his arms. Braving a glance over a shoulder, he saw Lacey was already done kissing Pretty Boy. He was opening her car door. As soon as it was shut, Victor teleported himself into the Lincoln's plush passenger seat. "Miss me?" he said.

Lacey yelped again, accidentally pressing her horn in surprise. The honk got the attention of Jack, who looked back at her through the window in expectation. "Accident," she simply said, internally cringing. Jack nodded and waved goodbye, walking off to his car somewhere amid all the other vehicles in the lot.

Fixing her hair before clamping her hands on her steering wheel, Lacey finally said, "Hello, Victor." She wasn't even looking his way.

"Hi, Lacey." Sensing Lacey's stoicism, Victor quickly reconsidered things. "I suppose I should apologize."

Lacey's fingers softened their grip, and she turned to him. Surprisingly, her beautiful almond-shaped eyes were red and watery.

"Woah," he uttered. "I didn't mean to—"

Slowly shaking her head, Lacey said, "Where have you been?"

Victor blinked, his mouth hanging open. "I, uh, was in Heaven. Didn't you know?"

Her brow furrowed. "Of course I knew. I felt that you had ascended, or whatever it's called, after your murderer was arrested. I just..." she paused, choking slightly. "Things have been really hard lately." Her voice squeaked, and a tear fell. She furiously rubbed it away. "I hate crying."

Victor leaned closer to her. "It's okay to cry, Lace. Remember, you saw me cry."

A memory of a shiny blue teardrop rolling down Victor's ethereal face came back. "I remember," she said softly. Setting her jaw, she willed her eyes dry, anyway. "Do you know Jessica's been murdered?"

That was definitely news. "Uh..." His jaw dropped again. "She was? Jessica Simcox?"

"Yes, your ex-ex-girlfriend."

He bit his lip, looking down. "She was pregnant."

Lacey didn't reply. It was horrible news to process. She just sat there, taking in a deep breath, trying to relax into her seat a bit.

"Wh-when did this happen?" Victor looked back up.

"A couple of days ago..."

"Are you okay? Has anything happened to you?" He recalled Rao's warnings of a new darkness over the city, a spiritual battle that Victor would somehow fight against... for the sake of Lacey. He suddenly felt way in over his head. Especially if Legion were involved.

"I'm fine," Lacey firmly said. "Other girls have disappeared, but... as for me, I'm not in danger."

Should I say it? Victor wondered. "You're in danger, Lacey."

A sudden pounding on the driver side window startled them.

It was a meter maid.

"What's a meter maid doing in a paid parking garage after dark?" Victor asked. "Garages don't even *have* meters."

Lacey ignored the remarks and rolled the window down a touch. The rough-looking old woman in an orange vest barked through the crack, "You're in a handicapped spot."

"I am?" Lacey said. Glancing forward, she spotted it, the blue stencil of a figure in a wheelchair, spray-painted on the wall.

The lady scowled. "Do you know the fine associated with unlawful parking?"

Lacey turned the key in the ignition, and the engine thrummed to life. "My mistake," she said. "I'll leave now. I promise I didn't know this wasn't a regular parking spot."

The woman's frown deepened, and she withdrew a small pad of paper from her vest. "Slow down there, missy," she said. "We had a complaint about this specific vehicle. That's what got me here in the first place. I'm afraid I'm going to have to cite you tonight."

Victor raised an eyebrow and focused on the woman's thoughts. "Ah. She's looking for a Christmas bonus for exceeding her quota."

Not helpful, Victor, Lacey thought at him.

"Well, maybe not, but," and he stroked her hair just to do it, "I've picked up a few tricks since being away. One sec. I'll be right back." And with that, he was gone, flying around the parking garage at the speed of thought. Within moments, he'd located what he was looking for: spare cash lying around.

Okay, Vic, he told himself, *You can do this.* He concentrated on the cash, letting himself relax and trying to let his mind feel the fabric of the twenty-dollar bill. When he managed that, he reached out to the air around him, feeling it quiver slightly in response to his request. He smiled and kept on reaching. This would work.

ELEVEN

Lacey grimaced more at the now-empty passenger seat than she did at the old woman bent on fining her for a mistake. She drummed her fingers on the wheel, wondering what kind of idiot thing Victor had abandoned her for this time. She turned when she heard a ripping sound, and groaned inside as the woman finished tearing the citation off the pad. She proffered it to Lacey.

"Five hundred dollars. And don't even try to contest it."

Lacey hesitated to reach for it, but the meter maid shoved it toward her, only to have a stiff gust snatch it out of her hand and send it swirling away into the garage. The meter maid dashed after it, in vain, hands flailing to retrieve it. Lacey watched in surprise.

A voice broke her trance. "Pretty neat trick, huh?"

Lacey yelped a third time, and spun on Victor, who looked smug. "Will you *stop doing that*?"

Victor had the good graces to look momentarily sheepish. "Probably best that we leave. It'll take her a minute to catch up to that. But she'll find a nice reward at the end."

Lacey peered at Victor. "What did you *do*?"

He shrugged and gestured toward the exit sign. "Gave her a little holiday cheer. I couldn't have asked *you* to give her money, since that'd be bribery, but Heaven has interesting little ways of meeting people's need without resorting to anything illegal. She'll get what she wants, and you'll get what you want. You made an honest mistake, and this time, you're not being punished for it. Unless you sit here long enough for her to come back."

Lacey put the car in reverse, and looked over her shoulder. "She'll remember my plate. She'll just run it and then mail the ticket."

Victor chuckled. "Oh, she doesn't *have* to remember it."

Lacey shot him a glance. "You can mess with people's memories?"

He shook his head. "Not something they've taught me yet. But you don't have to be supernatural to know how to distract people. She'll forget all on her own when she finds the spare change I rustled up for her."

Lacey wasn't sure whether to be impressed, but she wasn't about to pass up the chance to avoid half a month's worth of rent in fines. In moments, she was back out on Seattle's streets. On mental autopilot, she started for home.

"You have no idea how good it is to see you again, Lacey. And not just in The Pool."

Lacey felt strangely violated. "You've been watching me in my *bathing suit*? That doesn't seem like something a good, Christian angel would do."

Victor groaned. "Geez. Walked *right* into that one. No," he said. "I mean, Heaven has this amazingly clear pool of water that serves as a portal for viewing mortals. And before you ask, I have *not* seen you naked, nor in any embarrassing or awkward situations. We're only allowed to look for good purposes, and at certain times. In fact, I haven't been allowed to check on you until right before I got here. And now, here I am." He threw his arms wide.

"Here you are," Lacey replied quietly.

Victor frowned and leaned over. The mental connection they'd formed shortly after his death was as strong as ever, and there was no mistaking the waves of sadness, confusion, and betrayal coming from her. With the barest of probes, he caught up on her life during his time away. The sadness made him shudder.

"I'd forgotten just how depressing Earth life could be," he said softly, reaching out to stroke Lacey's face. Though he knew she wouldn't feel it physically, he knew their spiritual connection would convey the same kind of comfort as if he were there in the flesh.

"Why haven't you answered me, Victor? You said you loved me, and then you just *left* me here. Do you have any idea what I've been going through? And now I've just sold myself to a modeling agency because... because..."

"Because you figured it was the best way to solve two problems at once, no matter how much you hated the idea?"

She pouted. "Yes. And stop reading my mind. You should already know I just need to vent."

He nodded. "Go on. You've got a voice that would make the angels jealous. I could listen to it forever."

Lacey couldn't help but feel a little flattered at the compliment, even if she wasn't in the mood for it. Seeing Victor again was an emotional explosion, especially with his timing. No, she didn't *seriously* care for Jack, but there was something undeniably fun and exciting about him, and she could use a little of that in her life right now. Something to remind her that she was more than just some stupid little waitress in a dead-end life.

"I bet you look really good in your barista uniform," Victor joked. "I'll have to visit you at work."

Lacey glowered but had to fight a giggle. "Stop it, Victor." Determined not to wallow in self-pity, she brought her thoughts back around to Jessica. She sensed Victor's instant attention.

"Like I said, Jessica was murdered just a couple of days ago. Stabbed and thrown in a dumpster."

Victor ground his teeth. "And you're going to track down her killer."

She threw up a hand in exasperation. "Someone has to. Why not me? I did fine figuring things out with your murder."

He leveled an unmistakable stare at her. "Lacey—let the cops do their job. You flirted with death a little too much the last time we were together. I'm eager to get you over to this side with me, but not *that* eager. Remember all the reasons you want to stay here?"

Lacey did, of course, and sighed. "The cops are already on it, yes, but I *need* this, Victor."

He knew she did, but Rao's warning echoed in his mind. "What do you think you have that the police don't? They use trained detectives to investigate this kind of thing. Besides, Jessica Simcox? You barely even knew the woman. With me, I get it—we were an item. But her?"

Lacey blew out a breath. "She was a woman, Victor. Maybe not the kind a guy would want to take home to his parents, but still a human being, and someone I at least passingly knew.

"You're right—I'm not as well trained as some detectives, but I can *do* this."

He shook his head. "I never did understand your penchant for chasing danger. I'll make you a deal. You give me one good reason why you *need* to be part of this, and I'll quit badgering you about it. Otherwise, as your official Guardian Angel, I'm going to do what I need to to keep you safe."

Lacey bit her lip. "I'm going undercover. As a model. I'm *positive* the cops won't do that."

Victor opened his mouth to speak, but Lacey got there first.

"Before you say it, no I *don't* think they have any sexy female detectives to assign, even if they do think to look into this venue."

"I wasn't going to—"

A look from Lacey paused him.

"—put it *quite* that way," he finished after a beat. "I was going to ask, 'Why modeling?'"

Lacey turned a corner and headed for the Alaska Way viaduct. She merged into the light, evening traffic, and headed north toward home. "Because other girls have gone missing from the U of W campus. They may have also been models. I know it's not much, but something I heard at work led me to believe there may be a connection—one the police won't even consider."

Victor raised his eyebrows. "You really think they're that dumb?"

Lacey threw up her hands in frustration. "I *don't* Victor, but can't you just let me do this? Why are you always standing in my way?"

He turned in his seat to fully face her. "Because—"

"Because you love me," she cut in. And for a moment, she couldn't help remembering the closeness they'd shared during the time she'd helped him solve the riddle of his own murder. A big part of her wished she could have that with him. With *someone*. But now wasn't the time for sentiment.

Victor sat back in his seat. "You're going to do this no matter what I say, aren't you." It wasn't a question, and they both let the ensuing silence linger for a while.

Eventually, Lacey broke the reverie. "I've been having dreams, Victor." She exited Alaska and merged into surface street traffic, pausing at a red light.

"Oh?"

She hugged herself tightly. "They... haven't been good."

He examined her. "Could I... have a look? I mean, provided I don't make the memories conscious?"

Lacey bit her lip. "Mostly, it's just the one about Jessica that got me. I've ignored the rest. But ever since you've been gone, I've had lots of little things in dreams that have been coming true in real life. I just keep telling myself they're coincidences, and put them out of mind. But when I watched Jessica die..."

He took her meaning. "There's something else you're not telling me."

Lacey nodded, pursing her lips and trying to decide how to say it.

"It's okay," he said. "I already know what you're trying to ask."

She rolled her eyes. "Do you have any idea how annoying that is? Why do you think Stephenie Meyer made Bella's mind unreadable by her man?"

Victor chuckled. "Don't even get me started. But to answer your unspoken question, I don't know."

"You don't know what?" she said. The light changed, and she eased forward.

"I don't know whether our connection has contributed to your dreams. I mean, it *could*, and we *do* get a lot of sneak previews in Heaven, but I'll have to ask whether it would work that way—you being able to see into your future because you're tied to me."

Lacey nodded. "I know that sounds kind of silly."

"Not at all. So what are your plans now?"

"Well, Jack wants me to do a test shoot to see whether I'll be accepted into his agency."

"Jack? That's suck-face dude, right?"

She exhaled meaningfully. "If you must be so childish, yes. That's his name."

"Well, then, I'll make sure to let you get your beauty rest tonight."

She eyed him. "You mean you're coming home with me?"

He shrugged. "You're the one driving. Is that where we're headed?"

Lacey considered pulling over and asking him to leave, but realized it would do no good. Besides, she knew she could trust him to behave. "Just don't keep Nainai awake, okay?"

He nodded, and they completed the drive in silence.

As they pulled into her parking lot, Victor could sense the dark things around them. Nothing on the order of Legion, thankfully—though he was more prepared to deal with them now than he had been at first—but he could see beyond the obvious signs of broken down cars and shady characters. As ever, he was glad Lacey didn't know what she was missing.

They made their way to her new apartment—Victor knew better than to ask about it—and Lacey set her purse down in the living room.

"Nainai? I'm home."

"Oh, hey," Victor said. "Before you go to bed, would you mind leaving the TV on? You can turn it way down; my hearing is perfect. I just have several months of CSI to catch up on."

Lacey ignored the comment as she filled a glass of water in the small kitchen and grabbed some medicine bottles. She then hurried to Nainai's room, absently flicking the TV on just to satisfy Victor. The woman was still and white in the dark room. Moonlight sifted through the old blinds, eerily striping her face. Lacey walked over to her slowly, set down the pills on the nightstand, and felt her wrist for a pulse.

"I told you I'm not dead!" her grandmother spouted, springing up to a sitting position like a Jack-in-the-box.

Lacey clutched her chest with her free hand, nearly spilling the water. "You scared me!"

"You scared *me*!" Nainai protested, fluffing her hair. "I was having an amazing dream you've just interrupted. With Tom Hanks."

Lacey visibly cringed. "Tom Hanks? I mean, he isn't so bad… but *Tom Hanks*?"

"Yes." Nainai smirked. 'It turns out he knows quite a bit about *Hank*-y panky. Get it?"

Lacey tried to blank her mind. "Ew, I did *not* need to know that."

Nainai looked wistfully into the middle distance. "We were castaways on an island, trying to make our way out of there. Then we realized, why leave this beautiful, tropical island? Especially since we have each other, and I could make him babies?"

"This is getting weirder and weirder," Lacey said, putting up a hand. "You can stop now. I just wanted to let you know the date went well."

"Was there a kiss?"

A few. "Yes." Lacey smiled, humoring her. "But we better get to bed. Let's take your pills."

After her grandmother happily downed the medicine, Lacey kissed her forehead. "Goodnight."

"Goodnight, baby girl."

With Victor quietly watching reruns of crime dramas on the living room couch, Lacey settled into bed. She pulled the bedspread up to her neck and took a deep breath. Tomorrow was her test shoot with Geo; she *would* need her beauty rest. Lacey thanked God, finding she could actually fall asleep more peacefully, tonight, knowing Victor was nearby.

TWELVE

The one good thing about working at the college café was repeat customers, especially when Lacey had some further interrogations in mind. Maybe if she had more than a hunch about the missing girls it could satisfy Victor's cynicism over her solving the mystery. The brunette and redhead she'd seen a few days ago entered at the busiest time, noon, patiently taking their place at the end of a long line. Lacey worked harder and faster than ever before, ringing up customers and getting them their orders, not wanting the girls to have any reason for suddenly leaving.

A strawberry banana shake was in the works when the girls were finally next up in line. Mrs. Jones shot a curious glance at Lacey rushing to slam a banana into the nearby blender, followed by some cold, pink mix from the refrigerator. Shoving the puree button with a thumb, Lacey nodded to the sorority sisters with an eager smile.

Cold splatters across Lacey's face took her breath away. She looked down at the blender that was flinging more pink goop across her apron and even the counter. Lacey unplugged the spinning monster and exhaled in embarrassment. She wiped her face with her forearm and stood there dazed as the young man who had ordered it spurted a suppressed laugh.

"Oh my gosh…" the redheaded young woman was heard saying.

Mrs. Jones stomped over. Her hairnet was on the brink of popping off her puffy hair, her red face sure to erupt. "What's wrong with you?! Can't you do anything right?"

Lacey still didn't move from her stance. She simply licked her fruity lips, upset.

"Can you hear? Are you deaf?" Mrs. Jones continued.

The customer quietly cut in, "It's okay. It was an accident. I'll come back later."

Lacey's boss glared at him before returning to what she did best. "Now clean up this mess, apologize to our customers, and stop being such a show-off."

The guy scurried out of there, followed by the sorority sisters, all of them embarrassed over the fiasco.

Instead of cleaning up, Lacey calmly undid her apron's bow, dropped it to the ground, and headed to the back to grab her carry-all.

Mrs. Jones was on her heels, rattling on, but Lacey had suddenly grown the amazing ability to tune her out. There were more important things than Mrs. Jones' temper tantrums. Jessica was dead, and other girls were missing.

As Lacey hurried out the entrance, Mrs. Jones' calls were more like a distant rumble. Lacey picked up her pace, seeing the young women not far away, rounding the Student Union building. What the hay? She had already supremely embarrassed herself; what was a little more? "Wait!" she called after them. "Hey!" Flailing her arms, she took off running.

Nearly colliding with a skateboarder, Lacey quickly apologized, letting the long-haired guy pass.

The girls she'd been chasing finally turned around, spotting Lacey, then quickly eyed each other with arched brows. Jogging, Lacey caught up to them. "Hi." She smiled. "Sorry about what happened back there."

"No worries," the redhead said. "That woman you work for is a beast."

"Like Jabba the Hut-beast," the other agreed, shuddering her shoulders for added drama.

Lacey laughed, louder than expected. "Good news—she's not my boss anymore." She internally cringed, hoping she didn't just shoot herself in the foot.

"Congratulations," the brunette said with sincerity in her blue eyes.

"Anyway..." Lacey composed herself a bit more, wiping away a pink smear from her nose. "I need to know—any news about the missing sorority sisters? Who was it—Brittany and Shayla?"

"You didn't hear?" the redhead's expression fell. Lacey looked back and forth between them, sensing something awful.

The girls traded glances. The brunette sucked in a breath, and the redhead bit her lip and turned her eyes to the ground.

Lacey's heart sank. "No. What?"

"Brittany was found... last night," and she paused as her voice hitched. She sniffled suddenly, and Lacey could tell the girl was struggling to compose herself. Finally, she said, "She was found in a dumpster."

Just then, a movement caught Lacey's eye. She glanced up to see a couple of police officers striding fast in their direction "Oh, no. I have to know," she quickly added, "What sorority? And were these girls models? What agency? Who did it?"

But the young women had frozen up at the sight of the officers.

One cop, pointing to the two girls, said, "Rebecca Halliday and Emily West?"

"Yes," they responded, their expressions a mix of fear and knowledge.

The other officer came up to Lacey and lightly touched her arm. "Ms. Ling. Some privacy, please," he said. "We'll notify the media later with details."

She nodded sullenly and turned to leave. "Where's a dead ex-boyfriend when you need one?" Lacey muttered to herself, feeling frustrated and defeated.

Victor *poofed* beside her, his arms crossed, like an obedient genie. "Someone call for a hunky angel?" he said, arching a dark brow, his matching hair sifting handsomely in the wind. Must have been another of his new tricks; his spirit body wasn't affected by physical things, like wind.

Lacey didn't have time to smile. "The police. Right there. They're talking to those girls about the disappearances." The officers were standing on a dead patch of grass, serious expressions wrinkling their brows. "They must really think they have some good info, to hunt these girls down, here, at lunchtime."

"I'm right on it," Victor said, whooshing over instead of teleporting. Lacey leaned up against a tree and watched as Victor stopped next to the cops, crossed his hands behind his back, and began pacing like a courtroom attorney from a bad TV drama. She rolled her eyes and massaged her forehead. What *else* would she expect from him? She turned away as he worked.

...didn't know she was stabbed, came a sudden, female voice in her mind. Lacey jerked upright and looked around. The voice sounded familiar, but she couldn't immediately place it.

And you said you saw the victim, what was it, five nights ago? A male voice this time; authoritative, demanding. Then it hit her. Lacey peered hard at the sorority girls. The redhead was nodding vigorously. The instant her mouth began to move, the voice in Lacey's head resumed.

That's right. Last Thursday night. We actually ended up studying for the same final. She finished before I did. She said she was in a hurry to get somewhere, but I was too busy reviewing my notes to ask. And then she was gone.

Lacey's eyes widened. Victor *had* picked up some new tricks. And some incredibly useful ones at that. She called to him in her mind. *Victor? Can you, um, share your sight with me, too?*

From across the way, she felt his smile. *You may want to have a seat first,* he replied. *You don't have to close your eyes, but for you, it might be easier if you do.*

Lacey raised her eyebrows, impressed, then looked for a dry spot to sit. Finding no benches, she debated whether she wanted to retire to one of the nearby classroom buildings. The only problem with that was that she'd lose sight of the sorority girls if she did. Though she suspected Victor could keep tabs on them, and help her find them again, she wasn't sure how she'd explain her supernatural ability to stalk them. And so, she crouched on the grass and rested against her tree. Even before she closed her eyes, the vision came upon her, as though she were standing right back where she had been before the cops had arrived. The first cop—the one who had addressed the sorority girls—was jotting notes as he talked with them. The second cop was scanning the area as though he expected an attack. The vision flicked back and forth from one speaker to the next, and Lacey realized she could hear perfectly well, now, too.

"So," the first cop said, as he finished scribbling on his pad, "did Miss Lareaux give any indication as to when she expected to return?"

The redhead shook her head, frowning. "Like I said, I was too busy with my notes. I *hate* micro-bio. Worst class ever. It's no wonder Brittany quit early."

The officer gestured. "Did you have any other activities scheduled with her? Any time you would have expected to be with her again? An activity, another study group? A class?"

The brunette cut in, gnawing on her lip and looking nervous. "I'm sorry to interrupt, but I think I can answer that. We were *going* to have a big pre-finals party on Friday night. The guys from Zeta Psi were going to join, and it was going to be really big, and really fun, and have DJs and dancing and—"

"Relevant facts only, miss," the first cop interrupted.

The brunette wilted. "Oh. S-sorry. I just don't get to go to many parties. But Brittany does. She goes to all of them. She would have been there for sure."

The redhead scoffed. "Brittany was always a bit snooty."

The cop nodded and made some more notes. "And her place of employment? Was she heading into work that night, perhaps? Would they have any additional contact information?"

Both girls looked at each other and shrugged. The redhead cleared her throat and dabbed at her eyes before answering. "We just know that Brittany was a model. I think she worked for some place called 'Fad' or 'Trend,' or 'Trendy'. Something like that. She was starting to do a lot of shoots. I even saw her in a couple of local magazines."

"Is there anything else," the cop said, "either of you can tell us about the victim?"

Both girls traded looks again, then shook their heads as one. The cop frowned, clearly unconvinced, but nodded.

Victor? Lacey called to him. *They're hiding something. What can you get from them?*

There was a pause. *Lots of emotions. And something about cellular mitosis in fetal pigs.*

Lacey groaned. *Yeah. Really useful. Thanks.*

Hey, he retorted, *I'm doing my best. I'm still new at the mind-reading thing. Most people's thoughts are a superficial jumble of whatever. It's not like I can just plug in and download everything in their mind. I don't have that same connection as I do with you. But trust me, I'm working on it.*

"Wait," the brunette squeaked as the cop turned to leave. "I did just remember something."

The officer stopped and glanced over his shoulder. "Yes?"

The brunette fidgeted, then said, "Well, I *think* Brittany had a new boyfriend. Or, maybe he was a boyfriend. But he could have just been a good friend who was a guy, but—" She halted at a look from the officer. "Sorry. I tend to ramble. Anyway, some guy had been visiting her in her dorm the last few weeks before she disappeared. I'm not saying he killed her—please don't think that—but he just always creeped me out."

The first cop turned fully around, his notepad coming out again. The second cop even took another large step closer. "And can you describe this guy?"

The brunette swallowed. "I really *don't* think he killed her—"

The redhead sighed and interrupted. "Ripped guy. Didn't shave. Between that and that stupid beanie he wore, he looked like a panhandler. Our dorm mom threw him out a few times."

It was the cops' turn to exchange looks. "On what grounds did your dorm mother evict him?"

The redhead shrugged. "Because he was a creepy-looking guy hanging around a dorm full of hot girls? I don't know. He never really *did* anything, but I have *no* idea why Brittany kept spending time with him."

"And did you get the gentleman's name?"

Again, both girls shook their heads.

"Anything *else* about this man, or anything that may or may not have been unusual in Miss Lareaux's behavior in the days or weeks leading up to the murders?" Again, a negative. The cop thanked them, and, with his partner, left the scene, talking into the radio on his shoulder.

The girls hurried away, and the vision faded from Lacey's mind, leaving her stunned and disoriented as she suddenly found herself slumped beside the tree. She hadn't even realized she'd toppled during the incident. Victor appeared overhead, looking down at her sympathetically.

"I'm glad you took my advice to sit down first," he said. "I've never been a private broadcasting station before, and I wasn't quite sure what it'd do to you."

Lacey glared at him, head swimming, breath shallow. "Thanks for the timely disclaimer."

He shrugged one shoulder. "I knew it wouldn't *hurt* you, or I'd never have done it. But I've learned, in my time in Heaven, that mortals don't always have the fortitude to handle visions. Especially not detailed ones. That's why most visions come when people are already asleep and laying down. They're far less likely to get hurt that way."

Lacey shook her head to clear it, but was only partially successful. Using the tree for support, she slowly pulled herself to her feet. "Well, thank you for your concern," she said.

"It kills me that I can't help you up," he replied softly, reaching for her.

Lacey felt his sincerity, and it touched her. Victor may be a doofus, but he was a thoughtful, charming, and very handsome one.

"You really should have married me," he said.

Lacey blinked hard against the still-fading vision. "Maybe some other time," she said dismissively. "Think it's too late to follow the girls?"

Victor gave her a meaningful look. "Or just too creepy. Give them some time. I can tell you already know they visit your old coffee shop regularly. Oh— and I've read your thoughts on your old boss. I'm glad you're not working for her anymore, but she's actually a lot nicer than she lets on. You may be surprised by the pain she's been through."

Lacey sighed. "Focus, Victor." She shouldered her purse, cast one last look at the retreating college girls, then started, slightly shakily, for her own car.

She suddenly had some spare time, now that she was no longer waiting tables, and she may as well put it to good use ahead of the photoshoot. Though she could have hoped for more from the girls' discussion with the cops, she was glad for what she had heard.

"They were really holding out on me the other day," she muttered. "They said the missing sorority sisters weren't close friends, just acquaintances. Now they suddenly have all this info?"

Victor nodded in sympathetic agreement. "They were probably just nervous. Think about it—since when are sorority sisters relegated to mere acquaintanceship? I'm sure they know each other's shoe sizes, probably did pedicures on each other many times."

Lacey pointed at her chest emphatically. "*I* should know all these girly details, not you. But you're right. They're *sisters*. How could I have been so naive? And why in the world would they be nervous to talk to me?"

Victor gave her a look that practically screamed, "Really?" He shook his head. "Lacey, you're an investigative reporter. Ninety percent of the city knows that. Even college kids probably know you. Didn't you get looks or requests for autographs when you were working over at that little joint?" He jerked a thumb in the direction of the coffee shop. "They probably didn't want to tell you anything in fear of it splashing across KZTB's nightly news."

Lacey sighed. "You're right. Even people who don't own a TV know my face," she said, thinking of Teddy again, troubled at how closely the description of Shayla's "boyfriend" seemed to match. "Well, now that you know that the disappearances were indeed related to Jessica's murder, are you more on my side?"

"I'm always on your side," he said, stepping close to her. "I trust you. I'm just worried about you getting wrapped up in things again."

Lacey grimaced. "Okay, well, I'm going to say this one last time—I'm going to *continue* getting wrapped up in things. Starting with attending the test photo shoot Jack arranged for me.

"I knew danger well before you came into my life. That's not going to stop now. So if you're any kind of guardian angel, like you say you are, you'll do your part by giving me freedom up until the moment my very life is at stake."

He stopped and waited until she met his gaze. His blue eyes were all the more sparkly now that the cold sunshine shone through him. Lacey felt her chest tighten just a little, realizing that she was, indeed, looking at a literal angel. One who cared very, very deeply for her.

Then, without moving his lips, he answered, *That's what I'm afraid of.*

THIRTEEN

Later that evening, Lacey reminded Victor, "Freedom, remember?" She was standing outside Trend Modeling Agency in a large overcoat, her legs peeking out, tan and fit. "Nothing is going to happen during my shoot. I promise."

"I know," he replied only somewhat sullenly. "But I really think I should be there while—"

She whipped up a hand to stop him.

"I—"

"Tsk!"

He relented with a deep sigh, knowing she wouldn't miss the meaning. Her answering scowl told him she hadn't. "Just… be careful. The idea of you parading around in skimpy attire while men take pictures of you—"

"Stop, please," she said with an earnest quiet. "I'm having a hard enough time going through with this as it is. I really don't need reminders of *why* I don't like this idea."

Victor pursed his lips and nodded. "Okay. Love ya', babe. Knock 'em dead. *Especially* if they try anything funny."

Lacey rolled her eyes, but Victor sensed she was touched by his concern. "I'll call you when I'm done. Now, don't you have to be at church or something? It's already dark." Before he could answer, she disappeared into the building, leaving him alone beneath the Alaska Way viaduct.

He waited on the curb for a while, reminding himself of all the reasons he'd let her go in there alone. The list was very short. And yet, he'd promised her, and that was reason enough. And so he took to roaming the streets he was so familiar with, hoping he'd find something to help Lacey's investigation, or maybe something related to Rao's concern about the rising darkness in the area. He banished a flickering thought of Legion. He could sense them in the area, but they no longer terrified him as they once had, now that he knew a little more about warding them off.

Part of protecting himself involved turning his mind to more pleasant thoughts. He let himself get lost in nostalgia. Here was Christmas in Seattle, complete with decorations and people ringing bells for charity. He'd spent much of his life in here, with the odd break for vacations, his graduate program, and an internship in Japan. He really wished he'd survived that internship; he'd had a great job lined up. But the prospect of being a wage slave paled utterly in comparison to life in Heaven. Even now, back on earth, he was still without any obligation except to Lacey. No hunger, fatigue, illness, boredom—nothing of that muddled daily life could affect him anymore. But as he passed various vagrants and signs of aging buildings, he realized just how *depressing* life on Earth could be.

It's no wonder they take away your memory of Heaven when they send you here the first time, he thought. *Who'd want to stick around for seventy-five years if they remembered what they'd left?*

The so-called Emerald City was a far cry from the one in The Wizard of Oz, but Seattle was certainly no New York or LA. Even when he'd been alive, he'd always felt relatively safe walking in downtown, even at night. Sure, there were a couple of neighborhoods to avoid, but he supposed every big city had places like that, and its share of transients.

"Speaking of which," he said. He called to mind the discussion the sorority girls had had with the cops. He'd been able to pick a few snatches from their minds at the time. The brunette—Emily—had pictured the man very clearly for several seconds.

Tall, surprisingly muscular, unkempt. She was right—he really did look like a vagabond. His black beanie didn't help the image either.

"You're not supposed to be here."

Victor stopped and glanced to his right. One of the greatest perks about death was that his senses were extremely sharp. Immediately, he picked out the speaker, a man standing by a handing donation bucket, ringing a bell. Almost as if by divine design, it was the same man Emily had remembered.

Victor glanced around to see whether the man had been speaking to anyone else. The few pedestrians in the area seemed to be paying no attention to the guy, however.

"That's right, dead boy. Your kind ain't welcome here."

Victor materialized right next to the guy and examined him quickly. "You're him."

The guy shrugged and continued ringing his bell. "Him, who?"

Victor tried probing his mind, but the guy waved a hand with surprising violence, and Victor felt himself actively shoved out of the connection.

"Nuh-uh," he growled, shaking his head. "I don't play like that. You got questions, you *ask* me. I don't wanna answer, I don't answer."

Victor frowned, stunned. "Who the heck *are* you? And how do you even know I'm here?"

The man glanced quickly at him, sizing him up. "I'm just a guy doin' his job. And I know you're there because I can see you. How's that for a stupid question?"

Victor pressed on. "But *how* can you see me?"

"With my eyes. Got any more bright questions?"

Victor shook his head. "I'm a little bit *dead*, pal. And you don't look like Bruce Willis."

The guy actually cracked a smile at that. "You ain't gotta be a Hollywood star to see dead people. You just gotta know the right folks. Or, you know, find some other way to tap into things the eye can't normally see."

Victor was intrigued, but clearly getting nowhere. *Rao*, he called. *Is there something you forgot to tell me?*

There was a brief pause, then the cat's voice floated through his mind. *Yes. I failed to mention that I won my round of croquet and have advanced to the semi-finals. You can watch the replay when you're done.*

He rolled his eyes. *Maybe it's better I couldn't hear you when we were both still mortal.*

Agreed, came the reply. *I don't think you could have handled the truth about your morning breath when I tried telling you.*

"You talking to someone?" the bell ringer asked. "You are, ain'cha? I can see that far-away look in your eyes. Probably looking for answers old Teddy doesn't want to just give away."

Victor flicked a glance at the man. "So what's it take to get a guy like you to talk?"

The man nodded appreciatively. "There we go. Now you're catching on."

"Did you already forget the part about my being *dead*? That means I don't have anything."

Teddy shrugged again, and called out for donations to a passerby. A man dropped some change in the bucket, and Teddy smiled and wished him a Merry Christmas before replying to Victor. "I can see right through you. That means you're either incorporeal, or on a weight-loss program that would make you a billionaire overnight."

Victor looked down at himself, and then at Teddy. "'Incorporeal' seems like a pretty big word for you."

Teddy stopped ringing his bell and stared right at Victor. "Insults ain't becoming an angel. Now are you going to go back to where you belong, or do you got something for me? Being homeless can be a full-time job."

"Again," Victor said, gesturing at himself, "kinda dead here."

"Heaven's always got something for guys like me. Why do you think we keep doing business with you?"

Victor frowned. *Rao? A little help here?*

He felt a sigh. *It's just Teddy. Tell him you've got a couple of ten spots, but that you think he's just telling you tales about him being homeless, then walk away.*

Victor frowned. *And?*

And what? Just do it, and you'll find out. I'll explain more later. My set is up, and I just found the perfect mallet.

The former Seattle resident groaned and buried his face in a palm. "Thanks for nothing."

"'Scuse me?" Teddy said.

"Look," Victor said, feeling like a liar and hating it, "I don't think you really need the twenty bucks I have. You're just scamming me. I've got other things to do. You have a good night. Merry Christmas." With that, he turned and walked away.

"Twenty bucks?" Teddy called at his back. "What? Did Heaven suddenly get a budget?"

Victor continued to walk, hoping his trust in Rao hadn't been misplaced. Then again, she'd never misled him before. He was still disturbed by her elusiveness, but not surprised. More disturbing was the fact that some random guy—with unnervingly coincidental connections—could both see and hear him, to say nothing of blocking Victor's ability to read the guy's mind. Though he knew angels could hide their true identity from mortals when the situation called for it, he'd heard nothing about things going the other way. Maybe this was part of the dark situation Rao had mentioned before she'd sent him here?

He made his way up Seneca, his spiritual senses probing outward for pockets of darkness. His feelings brushed across a few pockets of dark spirits, and he even caught a strong whiff of Legion, but they seemed to sense him as well, and he could feel them grudgingly recoil. All the same, he didn't welcome any attacks.

He hadn't gone half a block before he heard Teddy's voice behind him. "Angel Boy!"

Victor stopped and glanced over his shoulder. A few pedestrians were eyeing Teddy warily, but they carried on as though he were crazy. One of them muttered, "Stupid homeless druggie."

Then something clicked for Victor, and he walked back to meet Teddy. "Drugs. You *are* on drugs, aren't you? It's how you can see me."

Teddy waved him off. "Twenty bucks is twenty bucks." He held out his hand expectantly. "And I *ain't* lyin' about my unfortunate condition. I don't take kindly to being called a liar."

Victor paused, knowing he didn't *actually* have any cash.

"Well?" Teddy demanded.

Victor opened his mouth to speak, but was interrupted by a stiff gust of wind that swept a pile of debris in front of it. Some of the debris smacked against Teddy, who—as though he expected it—clutched at it. Victor's jaw dropped as Teddy unclenched his fist to reveal a pair of ten-dollar bills.

"Took ya' long enough," he murmured. "You must be a new guy. This your first day on the job? Probably haven't even finished reading the manual, have you?" With that, he turned and walked back the way he came.

Victor simply stared.

A few yards later, Teddy halted. Without turning, he called, "Well? Ya' comin'?"

Seattle's newest guardian angel bit his lip, and took the offer.

FOURTEEN

Trend's receptionist greeted Lacey with a rude "You're here." She snapped her headset off, shoving it in its charger beside the desk phone. "I've gotta go."

Lacey opened her mouth to acknowledge the tired young woman, but was distracted by her hurriedly picking up a purse and Starbuck's coffee cup, and rushing to the elevator.

The offices behind the reception desk looked dark. There was a loud silence throughout. *Of course*, Lacey reassured herself, *this appointment was after hours*. She spun to ask, "Where's Geo?" but the doors swished closed on the woman's careless expression before she had the chance.

"Hello?" Lacey called, stepping forward, the clacks of her heels echoing lightly. "Geo?"

She couldn't help but feel a little disappointment over the fact that Jack wasn't there, ready to greet her. Especially after their date having gone so well. *This is business, Lacey*, she scolded herself.

Stepping around the large, sleek desk, she headed to the offices on the left. "Geo?" There was still no answer. A chill overcame her and she literally said "Brrr" at the sudden feeling, pulling her overcoat tighter. Hesitantly approaching the first door, Lacey considered opening it. She gently pushed down the lever door handle. Locked. She went to the next door. Locked. Why did she suddenly feel like she was in a scene from a horror movie? Maybe it *was* a bad idea to have sent Victor away.

As Lacey pressed down the next lever door handle, music suddenly played. She glanced up to see the speaker in the ceiling, like at department stores. A soft tune of *Careless Whisper* by George Michael played. Lacey pulled her phone out of her purse, thinking to call Jack, but realized they hadn't even exchanged numbers. Someone had turned the song on. For the briefest of moments, Lacey imagined Jack hiding somewhere with a dozen roses, waiting to dance. But the chill came back, and the song took on an undeniable eeriness.

"There you are!" a voice came from behind Lacey. She spun on her heels and caught her breath. There was a man in a Hawaiian shirt, his brown spiked hair bleached at the tips. His smile was huge. "Oh, you are lovely. Let's get to work, shall we? Come, this way."

"Geo?" Lacey uttered, following him down the hall.

"That's my name!" He walked like a woman on a catwalk, his hips lightly swaying, one foot perfectly in front of the other. "Come along."

Soon enough, Lacey was posing in front of a white screen, with what looked like a glowing umbrella propped and pointing at her, subduing any glares from the camera's flash. "You look a-*mazing*," Geo kept saying. "Beals is going to love these."

"Are we almost done?" she asked nearly a half hour later. Surely the hundreds of snapshots were enough to determine her skills. But Geo paused, shaking his head, with another big smile. "It's not that easy, honey." He walked over to a rack of clothes, scoured it, and found a black bikini. "Quick, put this on," he said, holding it out.

Lacey gritted her teeth at the swimwear. She glanced down at her attire. A white silk blouse over a black pencil skirt. Classy. She looked back up at him with a questioning look.

"It's standard procedure," Geo said. "You didn't think this is just about your face, did you?" When Lacey didn't respond, he burst out in laughter. "Oh, honey, are you sure you know what you're getting yourself into?"

Lacey lifted her chin, striding over. She snatched the bikini out of his hand with a smile. "It just takes some getting used to, being objectified," she blurted.

Geo lifted his eyebrows in condescension. "Oh, Lacey Ling, you didn't know all of Seattle was objectifying you when all they could see were those slender but curvy legs crossed beneath KZTB's desk?"

She glared at him. Legs were one thing. This was something else.

Geo put hands on hips. "Okay, maybe Beals didn't thoroughly explain the job description. I don't know if you're aware, but we are currently understaffed by *two* girls. Trend Modeling doesn't cater to the runway market. We like girls who have a little more up top, if you know what I mean. Now, we have spots to fill, and frankly, twenty girls who want in."

Clearing her throat, Lacey mustered a more professional composure. "I apologize. Of course you do. It's just a job." She paused, daring to ask, "Are you sure you have that many in line, though, with, you know, the recent murders?"

Geo narrowed his brown eyes, his usually over-the-top upbeat countenance fallen *dead* serious. "Listen, it's not like me to gossip"—Lacey doubted that—"but those girls got too hot for their britches."

"Yes?" Lacey said with tempered interest.

"Jessica and Shayla were the epitome of the word 'diva'. Even after Jessica got knocked up, and she was gaining this horrid back fat, she thought she should get special treatment. It was always, 'Geo, do *this*. Geo, do *that*. Call and cancel *here*. Get me a job *there*. I can't go to work today because of *this*.' She was *never* satisfied with her bookings. But when you start gaining weight around the midsection, modeling opportunities become limited, to say the least." He blew out a breath in frustration. "I mean, clients only want to use Photoshop so much before the shoot is a total bust."

"Mm-hmm." Lacey slowly nodded in false sympathy. "You got tired of it."

"Of course I did," he huffed. "Then here comes Brittany, traipsing into the agency one day, catching Beals' eye, thinking she was God's gift to us under the circumstances. She somehow knew of our plight over Jessica's pregnancy. She had the body, but so do half the sorority girls at the University of Washington."

Maybe the question was too obvious, so soon, but Lacey could tell the man was on a roll, confiding. She wouldn't stop him now. "Who do you think murdered Jessica and Brittany?"

Geo's countenance turned dark, his eyes gleaming with unnervingly sure knowledge. He stepped closer to Lacey, so their faces were close to kissing. She quietly gulped, keeping her gaze strong. Finally, he said, "There's evil all around this city. It can be right in front of you, and you wouldn't even know it."

"It can?" she said, wondering if she needed to call Victor, goosebumps dotting the back of her neck. Her gun was more than twenty feet away, in her purse, behind a dressing shade.

An amused smile crept on Geo's face, his usually happy glow returning. "Enough talk about gloom and doom. Put that thing on, and let's wrap up your shoot, pronto. I'm getting hungry, and there's a glazed honey ham with my name on it at home.

"If it's any reassurance," he quickly added, touching her shoulder, "Jack has very high hopes for you being in the agency. Unless you totally screwed up the test shoot—which you didn't—I can promise you, you have the job."

Lacey smiled. Her plan was working. She was employed with better pay, and she'd soon be in the very center of all the murderous drama.

*

Had he still had a body, Victor's breath would have caught when Teddy stopped at Occidental Park Station. He'd been here before, on occasion, but the historic trolley station had always been just a background to him, its pleasant square of trees providing shade in the summer and a bit of cover from the rains that so often soaked the area.

The area, decorated in its usual winter attire—trees with knit coverings on their trunks, and a few inches of snow—was normally alive with people playing on the outdoor foosball or ping-pong tables, chatting with friends, or grabbing a bite from a food vendor's truck. Now, it hosted a few passersby—clearly eager to be elsewhere—and a group of maybe a dozen vagrants who were probably just getting warm until a police patrol ousted them. Victor had seen homeless people plenty of times in his life, and was aware of the unfortunate conditions they lived in. But now, he saw them with new eyes, the kind mortals *didn't* have.

Victor could feel the way the December cold bit through their worn coats and gnawed at any exposed skin. They didn't even have the comfort of a 55-gallon drum to start a fire in. Worse, though, was the despair; an almost universal cloak of despair hung over the entire group, like an anchor around the feet of a drowning man. Though every individual had a different aura about them, and some even seemed actually cheery, he could practically taste a sense of hopelessness, with a side of endless worry on the parts of two different mothers who each ushered a child or two. Victor wondered why they hadn't made their way to one of Seattle's shelters, but before he could ask, a sick hissing sound scraped at his mind.

Oh, great, he thought, immediately alert. *Them.*

He hadn't had to deal with the Legion since he'd finally been taken into Heaven. As a full angel, he'd been shown how to combat them, the way Rao had banished them after the first time they'd attacked him, but he'd been warned that even angels could still fall—as evidenced by Legion—and that the forces of darkness were not to be trifled with.

Shortly, a cluster of the ragged, shadowy figures slid out from behind trees and wrapped themselves around some of the more visibly depressed transients, seeming eager to drain any life or hope out of them.

"Ain't pretty, is it?" Teddy said, gesturing.

Victor shook his head. "Can you see… them… too?"

Teddy glanced over at Victor. "You mean the bad spirits? The ones that look like starving zombies without faces?"

Victor shuddered at Teddy's casual tone. "I guess that answers my question."

Teddy shrugged. "I leave 'em alone, and they let me be. But maybe you'll take my point now."

Victor frowned. "And which point is that?"

Teddy gave Victor a dark smile. "Just wait a while and see. In fact, here comes a perfect example now." He gestured up the street, and Victor looked. Coming toward them was a well-dressed couple. As they neared the park, the man caught sight of the cluster of vagabonds. He pulled his wife closer and pointed across the street in the direction opposite the park, clearly in an effort to distract her. His free hand went into a pocket, and Victor could sense the man's desire to keep a tight grip on his wallet as he picked up the pace.

Several pairs of eyes watched the couple; even without his angelic senses, Victor could see the longing in their eyes. One older man in a worn army coat held up a cardboard sign with the usual silent plea for help. Victor felt a small ripple of repulsion tinged with guilt from the well-dressed man as he actively turned his attention fully to his wife. His wife happened to catch sight of the man with the sign, and hesitated. Victor felt her weighing whether or not to give him something, but when her husband tugged insistently on her arm, her thoughts immediately switched to justifying why she *shouldn't* give; Victor vaguely caught the woman's internal homily about "not supporting laziness, drunkenness, and drug abuse," as she let her husband pull her onward, away from the disappointed eyes.

Victor frowned. "You brought me here to show me people passing up chances to help the homeless?"

Teddy scoffed. "Spoken like a true rich kid. I bet you had it all, in life, didn'cha? Nice place to live, family support, probably went to some fancy college, had a great job, working car. The whole nine yards."

Victor made to protest, but stopped at once, realizing that Teddy had more or less accurately described his life.

Teddy smiled coldly. "See, some people just ain't that fortunate. Sometimes, when you fall on hard times, you don't get back up. Maybe your dad don't like you anymore, calls you a lazy bum and says he ain't gonna help you. Or maybe because you don't have a mailing address, ain't nobody wanna hire you on account of you being shiftless and undependable, as they see it.

"It's like a whirlpool, kid," he said, walking toward his fellow transients. "One some people never get out of."

Victor started to follow, but hesitated at the presence of Legion. "But what about homeless shelters? Government assistance? Job programs."

Teddy barked a sharp laugh. "Have *you* ever experienced any of those?"

Victor didn't answer.

"Didn't think so." Teddy fished in his coat pocket and pulled out some change. He gave it to the guy with the sign. Next, he walked up to the two mothers and spoke quietly with them for a moment before pulling out the pair of ten-dollar bills that had been blown miraculously into his hand just minutes ago. Each woman took the money with a sense of gratitude that, while obviously fatigued, radiated enough through to Victor. He knew that, had he been mortal, he would have choked up at the sight.

Teddy returned to him, a self-satisfied smirk on his face. "Let's go, Angel Boy." Without waiting, he walked off down main, and back toward the pier. Victor followed, keenly aware that Legion had noticed him and was watching, if warily.

"So," Victor said, trying to piece things together, "this is like some weird kind of reverse Ebenezer Scrooge thing, where the living teach the dead something about the Christmas spirit, then?"

Teddy stopped and looked point-blank at Victor. "It's amazing how dumb people with a college education can be." Victor opened his mouth to protest, but his companion continued without granting him the chance. "It's about me showing you that your pretty little world ain't all there is to it. There's a reason why people do things you angels frown upon. It's because we don't get to sit around on clouds playing harps while hot women fan us and stuff figs in our faces. It's because we don't even live as well as some *living* people do. I'm trying to say that you're clueless, kid, and that until you *get* a clue, you just ain't going to understand. Bad things happen to good people; sometimes street justice happens because we just can't wait for Heaven to clean up the mess." Teddy spun on a heel and stalked off down Main Street, leaving Victor behind, stunned.

"Hey, Teddy. Wait!" Victor teleported in front of Teddy, only to have the man walk right through him. Victor shuddered at the oozing spiritual darkness he felt as the man's filthy body passed through his; that was never a good sign. "I said *wait*," he repeated, falling in next to the man.

Teddy didn't stop, but instead marched toward the elevated freeway and turned right where Main passed under Alaska Way. As he did, Victor felt an unnerving pulse of energy from the man. At once, Victor realized he had pulled a knife from his jacket. Without looking at Victor, the vagrant raised the blade casually and shaved off a little of his scraggly beard with a single, clean stroke. Victor didn't bother to wonder how a homeless man had managed to come by such a sharp blade; the perpetual emanation of dark energy from the man held his attention firmly.

Teddy slipped the knife back into his coat and kept his hand on the weapon as he made his way north under the long viaduct that served Seattle's main pier area. The concrete overhead seemed to press down on Victor as though the whole viaduct was merely waiting to crush him. He could hear the ominous hum of power through the metal conduits as though they were breathing life into some sleeping beast at the far end of Alaska Way. What activity there was on the pier seemed cold and unyielding, and the idle boats gave the place the appearance of a graveyard. Victor scanned the area again, and probed at Teddy's thoughts, only to be actively rebuffed again. Flustered, he voiced his question. "Where are we going?"

The other lengthened his already determined stride. "Remember what I was saying about 'street justice'?" At once, a sense of darkness was clearly growing around him, and Victor detected at least one or two demons waiting in the wings. He put his mental shields up and prayed he wouldn't need to try out any of the spiritual self-defense techniques Rao had taught him. Still, he pressed on.

Some blocks later, they stopped across the street from a building Victor instantly remembered. A sign on the door read "Trend Modeling Agency." Lacey had walked through the front door of the place not more than an hour ago. He felt his nerves tighten. "What are we doing here?"

Teddy only smiled another cruel smile.

FIFTEEN

Victor ground his teeth. "If you hurt Lacey, I *swear—*"

"I ain't gonna hurt your girlfriend," Teddy interrupted. "Well, assuming she's not the one who comes out first. But you never know. Fortune can be pretty fickle."

Victor stared across the way, his senses casting about for signs of life in the building. Lacey's signature aura was still definitely inside, but a startling sense of blackness seemed to obscure his senses; he felt as though someone had thrown a thick, dark woolen blanket over his head and was holding it tight around his neck.

"What *is* this place?" he half-choked.

"A place to find babes," Teddy replied casually. "Sometimes, even the right sort. You wouldn't believe how much they're willing to do for you when they've imbibed few chemicals. We've had a lot more of those, lately."

Victor tensed at Teddy's remarks. "Like I said, if you so much as lift a finger against—"

"You can't do anything to stop the living, Angel Boy," Teddy said, cutting Victor off again. "I've done business with Heaven enough to know the rules. And 'final judgment' don't really scare me much. I've heard that line before. I'm here to teach you a few things they forgot to teach you upstairs, so just be a good kid and wait. Oh, and keep praying that whatever girl you left behind stays indoors long enough. We wouldn't want her to get hurt."

Victor growled, wanting to do *something* to the scraggly-looking man, but knowing that Teddy was right. Unless Victor could summon a gale to blow the man around, he still couldn't do much of anything to prevent him from doing whatever it was he had in mind. And so he waited as the minutes ticked by, anxiously focusing on Lacey's thoughts and feelings. He blushed when he felt her endure a stretch of feeling vulnerable, almost violated. Yet when he tried dashing to her side, something seemed to restrain him.

"Easy, boy," Teddy said soothingly. "I don't know what's got your panties in a twist, but Angels ain't all that different from us regular people. Your girl's in there, and you know what happens in modeling agencies. Don't worry. The guys in there are professionals."

Victor stepped into the street, looking for a break in the invisible barrier he sensed. He didn't even flinch as a car drove through him. He called over his shoulder, "You know these people?"

"Naw," Teddy said. "But a guy hears a few things if he pays attention. The girls here—they seem pretty high class. They're the kind that wouldn't give a guy like me even a *first* glance. That doesn't usually happen if the staff ain't high class to match. Betcha they've got some really rich clients. Girls like the ones in there don't come cheap. "

Victor hated the implications. "You make it sound as though they're involved in more than just modeling." He glanced at the muscular transient, who shrugged.

"You like to read into things *way* too much." Suddenly, he brightened and straightened from where he rested against a concrete pillar. "Here comes tonight's main attraction."

Victor spun, and watched as an attractive black girl emerged from Trend. She was wrapped in a stylish, teal coat that fell to mid-calf, but was still shivering despite the fur-lined hood cradling her head. She exited the building with nothing more than a glance at traffic, then hurried to the stop light to wait for a chance to cross.

Victor searched her thoughts. Frustration at an unexpected late night and a surprise call for a shoot that wasn't supposed to have happened, eagerness to get home to a warm meal and a hot shower, gratitude that she'd finished dealing with her creepy photographer, curiosity as to the new girl who'd also come in for a late shoot, anticipation of what would happen next in her favorite TV show. There was nothing in her mind to indicate she knew of Teddy's presence.

"Showtime," the vagrant muttered. Victor could sense the man tightening his grip on his knife as he waited for the young woman to cross the street just beyond him. The moment she was safely across, Teddy went into action, falling into step behind her as she hurried through the cold evening toward the parking lot. "I think it's time for you to leave."

"Hey," Victor called. "You! Girl with the teal coat! Run!" She gave no indication that she'd heard him. Victor focused on finding a way to even just distract Teddy; a growing sense of power and eagerness radiated from him as he closed on the girl. Victor managed to stir up a stiff breeze, but Teddy continued undeterred, and the girl, far from noticing her pursuer, merely pulled her hood closer around her head.

Teddy was within ten feet of the girl now. Victor flashed forward to hover right in front of the girl, drifting along with her and trying to connect with her mind. Her thoughts were everywhere, but he'd learned a little better how to navigate people's minds now. He looked for an opening, then merged into her train of thoughts.

You're in danger, he said, trying not to sound panicked. *There's a guy behind you with a knife. You need to get to safety as soon as you can.*

The girl's eyes widened ever so slightly, but she didn't seem to hear him. Instead, Victor saw a scene from her beloved TV drama play across her mind, drowning out his words.

I'm telling you, he repeated, *there's a guy. With. A. Knife. Behind you.*

The girl frowned and slowed her step, eyes confused. The hesitation was enough for Teddy to overtake her. Victor felt a shout of triumph from the transient as he came within arm's reach of the girl, and suddenly understood the lesson Teddy had said he was trying to teach Victor: in that moment, Teddy felt *powerful*, a feeling Victor could tell defied the man's every waking moment. The crazy homeless guy with unnatural senses was, for a glorious moment, no longer the victim.

"Run!" Victor screamed at the girl. But it was too late. Teddy's knife flashed, and the girl stumbled forward, her face a mask of shock. It was all over in a split second, and Victor found himself screaming. Before he could even right himself, dark shapes swarmed over him, clawing, biting, and shrieking.

Legion! they wailed.

Victor gritted his teeth instinctively, desperate to calm his mind and not give into the despair already threatening to overwhelm him. He thought of Lacey, of Heaven, and of everything Rao had taught him. Yet the demons continued to swirl around him, pulling him away from the girl.

Yet he refused to give in. Forcing himself to be calm, he called on Heaven's light to shield him. One by one, he pressed the demons back until, at last, they'd all fled, a clear desire for revenge trailing behind them. Victor straightened, triumphant but drained, and immediately searched for Teddy and his victim.

The transient was nowhere to be found, but the girl was still nearby, propped up against one of the dead-looking trees lining the street. He hurried to her, biting back terror. To his relief, she stood, still looking dazed, breathing heavily. She brushed at her coat as if to get rid of something dirty, then stopped. Victor watched her probe the garment and frown.

"How did *this* happen?" she asked, as she pulled part of the coat toward her face. Victor peered at the portion of cloth she held and winced. A long, clean incision scored the coat over her ribcage. He searched in vain for signs of injury, but he could tell the girl was clearly unnerved, verging on panicked. She scanned the area quickly, then broke into a trot for her car.

Somehow, she had survived the attack.

*

As soon as Lacey's shoot was over, she called for Victor to come back, who met her down in the lobby right as she exited the elevator.

"How did it go?" he asked. "Everything okay?" Something in his tone was off, and his eyes seemed unusually alert.

"Yes, why wouldn't it be?" Lacey said, stepping out. He didn't need to know how she was literally shaking in her ankle boots a couple times.

"Just wondering," he said, sticking close to her and staying just a bit ahead.

They crossed the lobby to the front door, where Victor walked right on through. With a sudden gale, the door quivered open a couple feet. "At least I can still open a door for *milady*," he teased.

Lacey's lips upturned. "Thanks. How was your time scoping out the city? Everything go okay?"

"Nope." They walked together down the dark and now desolate sidewalk, his hands stuffed in his translucent jeans.

"No?" Lacey looked up into his eyes with question. "Why not?"

"I met a guy."

Lacey laughed, trying to break the tension. "I thought you were straight."

He rolled his eyes. "Kinda not in the mood tonight."

Lacey sobered again. "What was his name?

Victor half shrugged. "Teddy. Either he's a fan of cuddly things or dead presidents."

"Teddy?" Lacey stopped in her tracks, her eyebrows pressing together. "Homeless guy? Scruffy looking? Black beanie?"

Victor nodded, eyes narrowing. "You know this guy? How does *everyone* seem to know a random transient?"

Lacey ignored the question. "What happened?"

"I have to say, he's acting like quite the suspicious character. He had a knife on him, and thought it would be funny, or a rush—or I'm not sure, because I'm not crazy—but he scared the heck out of a young woman. I thought for sure he was going to knife *her*."

"Is she okay? What happened?"

Not bothering to tell Lacey it took place just outside of Trend, Victor said, "She's okay. Her jacket was torn, is all. Thankfully."

"Victor, there's something not right about Teddy." She ticked off the reasons on her fingers. "First, the guy is clearly loony—we've both seen that. Then, he was the *only* witness to Jessica's murder. If that weren't enough, he," and she paused, fighting the images that filled her head. Setting her jaw, she pushed on. "He's so much like the man I glimpsed in that dream where Jessica died. The one who grabbed her. And now you tell me he carries a knife and nearly slashed a girl." She went quiet, but the look in her eyes said everything.

Victor nodded thoughtfully. "Definitely all adds up. But I think we need to be careful about assuming he's guilty of anything; we've only got circumstantial evidence because, trouble is, I can't read his mind. Makes it hard to confirm anything."

"Y-you can't read his *mind*?" she stammered, a cold fog expelling from her lips. "Well, why not?"

He shrugged. "Apparently, there's more I need to learn about the spiritual side of life."

"You're my guardian angel, Victor…"

He was surprised at how her desperate, pleading tone appealed to him. Like she really *did* want him to be around. "Yes, I am."

"Aren't you trained on things like this, before you come down to help me?"

Victor chuckled. "Give an angel a break. This is all new to me, too, and no, Heaven doesn't tell me everything. Something about it going against free will, I think. I'm sorry, we just can't know everything."

"Well," Lacey said, her eyes having a determined glint in them. "We need to dig deeper into Teddy. I have to know now if he's the murderer."

"I'm with you on that."

They paused in thought, though Victor's thoughts were mostly turned to the woman before him. He'd given up Heaven for her, initially. But now, he was there, and he missed Lacey every bit as much as he expected he would. And still, he'd gone to Heaven for her sake; he couldn't bring himself to think of just how close to tragedy they'd come the last time he'd seen her.

He wondered whether she ever thought of him. She'd certainly seemed happy enough to see him when he'd returned. How long would that last? Until they figured out who was killing girls in Seattle? And then what? Would he still be allowed to protect her? Would she even *want* his protection? And yet, the way she looked at him gave him hope; he wasn't about to let her down. Problem was, Lacey had a strong tendency to get herself in tight spots; Victor worried about that more than he cared to let on. He could already see her winding up in *someone's* crosshairs if she kept digging deeper into this thing. Seeing as Victor was already dead, however, he could take risks he'd never let *her* take. And that decided it.

He'd use his role as guardian angel to piece together this dangerous puzzle before the woman he loved could get herself *truly* killed, even if that meant he had to be away from her. He'd do some scouting, but first, he needed to know she'd be safe. That was more likely to happen if she were in public places. He had just the ticket.

"Lacey," he said, meeting her eyes, "How's your grandma doing?"

Lacey frowned slightly and sighed. "Showing signs of age, and feeling lonely. But otherwise, she's okay. Why?"

He smiled. "How do you think she'd feel about a little Christmas cheer, mall-style?"

SIXTEEN

Lacey pushed Nainai's wheelchair through Northgate Mall's arched grand entrance, out of the brisk cold. Her grandmother was dressed snuggly, with a puffy jacket, a red scarf around her small face, and a plaid blanket across her lap.

"Thank you for taking me out on a special shopping trip," Nainai said, smiling brightly. "I just love Christmastime. The holiday to spread good cheer. Although, it does make me miss your grandfather. Every Christmas Eve, he had a very special gift for me. You know what it was?"

Inside, they were greeted by sparkling wreaths hanging from high ceilings, white lights scaling tall walls, and the scent of warm cinnamon rolls filling their nostrils. "No, Nainai," Lacey said. "What did he get you?" She smiled at the scenery, continuing on. Shopping always felt so good, especially this time of year. Her Macy's card would come in very handy today.

"He always got me an angel," Nainai said in a sing-song tone.

"An angel?" Lacey repeated, distractedly perusing the many shops they were passing. Thoughts of Victor, who was—where was he, anyway?—drifted to mind over the word.

"Yes, it was always so special to open a small box, neatly wrapped with a bow, to find within an angel."

"Forgive me for my ignorance," Lacey said, "but what exactly do Buddhists believe when it comes to angels?"

Nainai gave a small laugh. "Baby girl, you didn't know? I'm not Buddhist."

Lacey paused her steps. "What do you mean, you're not Buddhist?"

With a sly smile, Nainai said, "I believe in truth, from wherever it may come. That is my religion. So I take a bit from here," she motioned with her fingertips, "and a bit from there, anything that brings enlightenment to my mind. What I know is there is a higher being watching over us all, a God. You see, there are many similarities between religions, and it's my belief that those similarities are tied together by truth. Buddhists believe in guardian angels, just as Christians do. I have no doubt they are real."

Lacey headed toward the food court in the distance, knowing a bite to eat was in order. She wheeled her grandmother through the crowd of people carrying flashy handfuls of shopping bags, deeper in thought, thinking her grandmother—despite her silly dreams and made-up Confucius sayings—was surprisingly wise.

They soon settled down at a table for two, Styrofoam to-go boxes of Panda Express before them, and the aroma of orange chicken a welcome scent. Lacey passed chopsticks to Nainai, and picked up her own plastic fork to dig in.

"You are funny," Nainai said, artfully plucking fried rice between her wooden sticks.

"What?" Lacey said, tilting her head, some long dark bangs falling over a cheek.

"Chinese-American girl eating with forks."

"Yeah, well, what can I say? Pa's a redneck. Be thankful I don't use a shovel," she teased. "I'm sorry they won't make it here for Christmas, this year." Seriousness spread across her face. "They don't—well, I don't either—have the means for that right now."

"Is Oklahoma far from here?" Nainai ate her rice in thought.

"Yes, it is. But Mom really misses you. She will see you as soon as possible. I promise."

"I understand," she said.

Enjoying their meals, they ate in a bit of silence. Letting her eyes drift around the very busy food court, lines snaking around lines, Lacey caught sight of someone familiar in their midst. At first thinking of Victor, by the height and coloring, Lacey realized it was the back of Jack Beals, in another suit, ordering from Sarku Japan. Her heart skipped.

As if sensing eyes on him, Jack glanced over a shoulder. Upon making eye contact, he gave a small wave of surprise. He pointed at the food place and motioned with his watch that he'd be just a moment. Lacey suddenly found herself surprisingly impatient.

*

Victor had painfully little experience with Seattle's homeless population. What did he *really* know about homeless people other than what you saw on TV or in brief glimpses on the street? Walking among them, on a dark December night, he plumbed the depths of his ignorance in new ways. Beyond the sense of desperation he saw in so many eyes, he could feel the palpable sense of hopelessness, of defeat and sorrow, more than he'd been capable of in life. He'd never comprehended just how valuable one's dignity could be until he saw so many people who had little to none. And yet, they survived, and some even thrived, taking a certain sense of pride in their hardiness, while still others simply enjoyed feeling free from what they considered the shackles of modern society. There were as many stories to be told as there were individuals, and Victor was stunned by the variety. Yet Victor had a job to do, and that didn't include anthropology.

"Teddy?" he called, knowing that no one else in the area was likely to hear him. His path had taken him to the tip of the peninsula, however, and he doubted he'd find many people wander around the water treatment plant at Lawton Wood even during daylight. He'd been at this for several hours now, but being an angel meant he didn't have to worry about fatigue or boredom. Still, it pained him to be away from Lacey, especially since she was out having fun with her grandma at the mall.

He sighed inside, reflecting on his memories of the mall at Christmas, but turned his thoughts back to his task. Rao hadn't told him quite a few things, apparently, and while Teddy didn't seem forthcoming with answers, Victor hoped he could find a way to persuade the man to divulge a secret or two—like how he could kick Victor out of his mind, and why a tramp claimed to have dealings with Heaven.

"Hey, Ted! Where'd you go, man?" Victor had made his way to the water's edge, eyes and ears alert. Water, he had noticed, seemed particularly hazardous, and not just because of drowning. Though Rao had only vaguely mentioned it, he recalled something about the forces of darkness having been given power over the water. He wondered if that had anything to do with why so many shady deals went down on piers and in seaside warehouses. Indeed, the hints of Legion were everywhere, and a general foreboding that was impossible for him to miss seemed to swirl around him.

"Don't overthink things, Vic," he told himself. "Just find this guy and figure things out."

He called again, but with no answer. The woods along the water were unusually quiet. Except for the faint, dull noises from the water treatment plant, there was nothing. That disturbed him. A flicker of light from somewhere in the woods caught his eye, and he teleported there immediately.

There, near the base of the hill, was a small campfire. That alone struck him as odd, but the collection of college students around it explained it pretty quickly. Their thoughts were superficial and vapid, and he didn't need supernatural senses to see the way they swayed, the bloodshot eyes, and the clouds of smoke they exhaled. Two couples were a short distance away from the fire, doing things that made Victor blush. The rest of the group hung around talking, drinking, and laughing. Victor wondered why in the world anyone would be out in the woods in December, but he'd done plenty of stupid things in his college days as well. He wondered just how much *he'd* attracted, back then, the kind of darkness these guys were. He shuddered to think. At least he'd never been into drugs or drinking. Frowning, he turned back toward searching for Teddy.

"So you know Rebecca's gonna be a model, right?" a girl said behind him. Victor paused, his interest piqued. He searched their thoughts and found an image of the same girl whose interrogation he'd broadcast to Lacey, that day on campus. Despite the dark presences, he lingered, waiting for them to continue. A guy in the group made an off-color remark about Rebecca's body, and those around the campfire laughed.

"No, seriously," the girl continued, taking a swig from a can, "she told me she got a scholarship for it."

"A *modeling* scholarship," the guy said. "What do they call it? Bucks for Boobs?" The group laughed again, but Victor snorted .

"We're all taking bets," the girl continued, pausing to hiccup, "on how long it is until she gets knocked off."

"Or knocked *up*," the guy retorted to more laughter.

"So anyway, she's supposed to start soon," the girl said, leaning in as though she were about to share some big secret.

Victor had a hunch Lacey would eat this conversation up. Surely, this could yield some advanced leads.

SEVENTEEN

"Nainai, the man I went out with the other night is here." Lacey pointed. "The one in the black suit."

"You will introduce us, yes?" Nainai winked.

"Of course. He's coming over as soon as he gets his food." She smiled.

Jack arrived with his meal on a cardboard plate, chopsticks in hand.

"Hi, Jack." Lacey stood, gesturing. "This is my grandmother, Chun Hua Ling. Grandmother, this is Jack Beals, my uh..."

He smiled, about to speak.

"Sit down with us," Nainai burst. "We're all Asian today. Even you," she said in respect to their food choices. "Look, and you use chopsticks! Better than my granddaughter."

Rolling her eyes playfully, Lacey smiled. "I *can* use chopsticks. They're just reserved for my sushi utensils."

Jack stayed standing. "I wouldn't want to impose. I'm actually quite busy. You wouldn't believe how this week has been."

True. Lacey could only imagine, feeling sympathetic. And yet, he had fit her into his schedule already, in spite of everything.

Pointing a wrinkled finger, Nainai said, "We'll keep it brief. Besides, it's been too long since I've had dinner with a handsome man. Now sit and humor a lady."

"Nainai," Lacey interjected, feeling slight embarrassment. "We can catch up with him another time. He's—"

The chair from the next table over screeched across the floor, Jack dragging it to their small table. He quickly sat in it with a smile. "I have a few minutes," he said, looking at Lacey. His smile was reassuring, and so she settled into her seat with a relaxed sigh.

A few minutes turned into more than twenty, with everyone's plate cleaned. Three fortune cookies sat between them all, waiting to be opened. "Shall I do the honors?" Jack asked, picking one up.

Lacey lightly laughed, pulling long hair over a shoulder in amusement. "Sure."

Jack set it back down, placed his hands over the cookies, and moved them around like a magician.

"You can't do that," Nainai said in protest. "The cookie you receive is yours. No trades."

"Why not?" Lacey asked.

"The messages will be mixed. Confucius say, 'Don't mess with someone's good fortune, or be cursed.'"

"Grandmother," Lacey chastised, feeling apologetic toward their guest.

Eyebrows shooting up, Jack said, "Oh, it's okay. *I* apologize. Look, I still know which one's mine. It has no panda on the packaging, see? And yours, Ms. Ling," he spoke to Lacey's grandmother, "has a mark right here, see?" He showed her the red ink smear on the corner of its packaging.

That seemed to calm Nainai, whose childlike smile returned. A seriousness then overcame her, as she leaned forward in her wheelchair and said quietly, "You are a man of details, aren't you? Your eye misses nothing."

Lacey thought of his apartment upgrades.

Jack stared back at Nainai with the same intensity. "Nothing," he said in agreement. "Nothing."

If two souls could speak with mouths closed, Lacey thought. Nainai and Jack's unbroken stares gave an air of something cosmic happening.

"Well, I'd better go." Jack stood, taking his leftover trash. "Hey, listen, Lacey." He touched her elbow. "I just thought of something. Can we talk a moment?"

"Sure." Standing up, she said to Nainai, "One moment. I'm just going to say goodbye to Jack, okay?"

Nainai was still surprisingly in her own thoughts.

Stepping a few feet away from the table, Jack's eyebrows pressed together in concern. "Hey, listen. First, I wanted you to know I really did enjoy the other night. I apologize that I haven't been able to catch up with you since—"

Lacey, you gotta see this. Victor's voice sliced through her thoughts, and before she could think, the mall, Jack, Nainai, and everything else disappeared from sight. All at once, she found herself standing in the woods, looking at a group of college-aged kids around a fire acting intoxicated. For half a minute, they bantered about nothing of consequence, before pairing off to further intoxicate themselves on love hormones.

Um, Victor said again. *Wasn't trying to show you* that, *sorry.* And in a flash, she was back in Northgate Mall, sprawled on her back, staring up into the face of Jack Beals. It was a beautiful sight, but she was mortified that he'd seen what had just happened.

"Lacey?" he asked, voice urgent. "Are you okay?"

She sat up, woozy and embarrassed by the stares she got. She could only guess she might end up as tabloid-level gossip before the night was out. She could already see the headline: "Washed up KZTB reporter's public collapse; drugs suspected."

She blinked several times, trying to clear her vision, and took the hand Jack offered. He pulled her up with surprising ease, and she wound up almost literally face to face with him. A thrill coursed through her, and she wanted to lean in for another kiss. But she'd already humiliated herself enough for one evening—no, *Victor* had humiliated her—and she just wanted to collect Nainai and make a hasty exit.

"Lacey?" He seemed unusually stiff as he studied her with slitted eyes. "I'm sorry if—"

Lacey shushed him, touching her forehead. "You don't need to say you're sorry. I'm fine now. Not sure what hit me. "

"No," he said, locking eyes with her. "I meant for not spending more time with you. And I *do* need to apologize." He brushed a hand along her chin affectionately. "I was about to tell you about the results of your shoot. I saw the images, and sent them to several clients. They *loved* them. *I* loved them, and I've seen a lot of pictures of some of the best models on the planet. We'd like to sign you, if you're still willing.

Lacey's heart skipped a beat. Despite all her reservations about the profession, she found she was simultaneously grateful and flattered. She had a job, *and* an attractive guy. She hadn't realized how much she'd missed either of them until that moment. "I'd be happy to accept. I'll stop by tomorrow morning, and we'll get started."

Jack sighed audibly, clearly relieved. Almost at once, however, he stiffened, his face darkening. "I'm sure you've heard the latest news about our model, Brittany."

Lacey nodded. "Oh, I completely understand. And don't worry about not catching up with me since the other night. You've got bigger worries than spending time with me. It's not your fault, Jack."

To Lacey's chagrin, Jack pulled away and looked into the distance. He still managed to seem handsome despite the deep furrows of worry on his face. "But Lacey, this *is* about you. I can't imagine what concerns must be running through your mind at a time like this, second-guessing whether or not you should sign with us, over fear of... *you know*." His hand dropped to his side.

"Yes," she simply agreed, letting him continue.

He pursed his lips. "I want you to know I'm going to do all that I can to safeguard our girls. Tomorrow I'm going to be holding a press conference. I've invited all the local media and beyond…"

"Okay." Lacey's brow wrinkled.

He looked at her meaningfully. "I would very much like it if you came."

She wouldn't miss it for anything. "Yes, sure. I will, definitely."

"Good," he said, quickly brushing her cheek with a kiss. "It will be held in Trend's Lobby at eleven o'clock. And Saturday after next, will you be my date at a charity ball? It takes place at the Hall at Fauntleroy. The mayor is hosting it. I'm sure you've heard of it. I'm going to ask him if we can donate a portion of the proceeds to the families of my girls who became victims."

Lacey nodded. Everyone who was anyone had heard of the Mayoral Charity Ball, a first of its kind in the City. "I already have the *perfect* red silk gown to go with it."

He smiled. "Of course you do. I have your number from the paperwork Geo had you fill out. I'll keep in touch." He kissed her cheek again, and with a charmingly boyish wave, sauntered away, Lacey's eyes trailing him until he rounded a corner and disappeared.

Behind her, Lacey heard Nainai take a deep breath, then exhale, as if she'd just finished an exercise. Lacey crossed quickly back to her grandmother. "You didn't tell me about the murdered woman," Nainai said, accusingly.

Lacey's eyes narrowed. "What do you mean? Could you actually hear us?"

"It was horrible, wasn't it? Pretty girl."

"Yes," Lacey said, still perplexed. It must have been something she'd seen earlier that day, at home, on her bedroom TV.

Nainai, nodded, sinking back in her chair in thought. "Long brown hair. Longer than yours."

"Oh—Brittany?" Lacey asked. "You saw her picture? On TV?"

Her grandmother's gaze was as still as could be, peering into the distance at nothing in particular. "Long brown hair," she repeated. "Beautiful."

Lacey snatched her phone out of her purse, and pulled up the Internet, quickly Googling Shayla's picture. A few similar results popped up under Images. Each one of them were of a twenty-something beauty with thick dark hair that went to the small of her back. "Wow," Lacey said under her breath.

"Beware," Nainai said at last.

"Beware what?" Lacey asked, feeling a sudden surge of anger over the cryptic declaration. "What's going on, Nainai? You're behaving strangely right now, and I don't like it."

Nainai tilted her head in her scarf, and just like that, she snapped out of it, scanning the mall with a wide smile. "You know, I always enjoy Christmastime. Such a time for good cheer. Your grandfather used to always get me the same gift every Christmas Eve. You know what that was?"

Lacey sighed, thinking about the medicine she had at home in a cabinet, for early onset signs of dementia. Suddenly feeling compassion, even a few tears wanting to break loose, Lacey forced a weak smile, and said, "No, what did he give you?"

EIGHTEEN

Just before dawn, Victor found his man. Teddy was holed up in a train car near the grain silo complex near Lower Queen Anne. Victor had made his way through that area earlier, but hadn't been able to sense the man. Even now, he only knew where Teddy was because he could see him.

"Congratulations," Teddy drawled as he rose from his sleeping mat and stretched. "You just woke up a homeless man early on a Tuesday morning. Your parents must be so proud."

"We need to talk, Teddy," Victor said, hovering over the man, trying to look ominous.

Teddy didn't even look at Victor but, instead, went to work tugging on his battered army boots. "Your 'angel of death' act ain't gonna work on me, kid. Like I said, I've been dealing with Heaven a long time. I know 'wrath-o-God' when I see it, and you ain't it."

Victor rolled his eyes. "So you know why I'm here, then?"

Teddy shrugged and rolled his shoulders and head, then rubbed his hands vigorously. "It's cold this morning. Real cold. I was just having this great dream about this one chick from Tacoma. Young, blonde. Nice legs."

It burned Victor that he couldn't grab the man's collar and make him look at him. "Let's cut the crap, Ted. The way the dice roll, there are more than a few fingers pointing at you in connection with the recent murders. We might as well do this the easy way."

Teddy laughed out loud. "Oh, *that's* rich," he said, slapping his knee. "Angel boy wants to play Sherlock Holmes, and comes here trying to scare a confession outta me. Funniest thing I've heard in weeks. You really *are* new in Heaven, ain'tcha?"

Victor crouched and gazed directly at the transient. "So you *did* kill them?"

Teddy returned his stare. "And why would I tell you something like that?"

Victor glared. "Then you're not denying it?"

Teddy shrugged again and rolled up his sleeping pad before gathering a few belongings into a worn hiking backpack. He stood, belched loudly, then hopped down out of the boxcar he'd slept in. "Ya' see, kid, there's a funny thing about truth. For a lot of people, they think truth is what you make it. And so they act that way—as if they're always right, no matter what anyone says to the contrary. Me? I've seen truth, and I've seen lies. Truth can be pretty weird sometimes. Thing is, it doesn't do any good to tell someone the truth when they've already made up their minds as to what the truth is. Ya' followin' me?"

Victor frowned. "So you're saying you *didn't* murder those girls."

Teddy locked eyes with Victor. "You're gonna believe whatever you wanna believe, Angel Boy. But it ain't gonna change the truth. Now, if you'll excuse me, I gotta bell to ring, over on First."

Victor watched him go, fuming. He reached out to Teddy's mind again, but the man shut down his attempts with contemptuous ease. "Nice try," he said, chuckling quietly without even looking back. "Best to just leave me alone."

As he watched the man go, Victor scrambled to come up with some way—any way—to get him to talk. Teddy hadn't exactly trumpeted his innocence, but something about what he said kept Victor from passing judgment. And yet, how to get any straight answers?

When a direct attack fails, Rao's voice said in his mind, *you attack from the flanks.*

Victor looked to the sky. *Since when did you become a military strategist?*

He felt Rao's customary smirk. *Since I finished my croquet tournament. I won, by the way. You should have seen it.*

Victor rolled his eyes and trailed Teddy. He wasn't about to let a night's worth of searching go to waste.

Help me out, cat. I mean, that's what we do in Heaven, right? Transparency and all that?

Well, Rao replied, *I could just* give *you the answer, but where's the fun in that? Use your brain, Vic. I know you picked one up at least since dying. Though, making Lacey fall over in a mall like that? Smooth move.*

"I wasn't thinking," Victor said aloud. He noticed that Teddy perked up and stopped.

"What was that, kid?"

Here's your chance, Einstein, Rao said. *Now. I'm heading off to check on my grandkittens. Ciao miao!*

"Ciao *miao*?" Victor muttered. "Where'd she get *that* stupid phrase?"

"You still talkin', kid?"

Victor blinked over to Teddy, an idea forming in his head. "My girlfriend. She's going to do some volunteer work at local homeless shelters." Victor hoped Lacey wouldn't make him a liar.

"And?"

Victor warmed to the topic. "And I was thinking that maybe you could introduce her to a few people. Help her see your side of society for a change. She's from… money… and I don't think she gets just how hard life on the streets is."

Teddy eyed him for several seconds. "You're pretty desperate, aren't you?"

"Have you ever loved a woman, Ted?"

The vagrant stiffened, then softened, turning his eyes toward the water. "You telling me this is some way to impress your girl? Not sure what she'd want with a dead guy. Not like you can give her anything in the bedroom."

Victor buried his face in his hand. "It's not like that.

"Clearly."

"Look," Victor said. "I'm not judging you. I don't know whether you killed anyone or not. Just… meet Lacey, and help her help people like you."

Teddy's face looked amused. "People like me?"

The angel sighed. "I'm not good with words. I'm just asking for some simple help. I'm sure I can talk to Heaven and get you something to make it worth your while."

Teddy's eyes glinted. "You making a promise?"

Victor looked up at the sky, and one of the unspoken impressions that came to angels filled his mind. He turned his eyes back to Teddy and nodded resolutely. "Promise." He extended his hand, and Teddy glanced at it, then gave Victor a look of incredulity.

"Oh," Victor said. "Right. Can't shake."

"Well, then, kid, let's talk about details." The other man's grin was thin but alarming. Victor saw cold calculation in the man's eyes, and hoped he hadn't unintentionally made a deal with the devil.

NINETEEN

"You volunteered me to do *what?*"

Victor had expected this, and had a plan. "You want to know who killed those girls, right?"

Lacey paced across her tiny living room, swiping furiously across her phone's screen, alternately frowning or raising her eyebrows as if impressed. Victor walked over and caught a glimpse of Lacey in a variety of poses and outfits. A surge of longing filled him. Lacey had always been beautiful to him, but to see her exceptionally done up and posing like that just blew him away.

She sensed him watching, and promptly hid her phone.

"What?" he said.

She glared. "Personal space," she said.

"You just don't want me to see you looking sexy, do you?"

She scoffed, but he could feel her embarrassment and knew he'd hit close to home whether she'd admit it or not. "If you insist on knowing, I'm reviewing the results of my shoot for the other night. I was asked to pick personal favorites for marketing purposes. But you were *saying*?"

Victor blinked. "I was?"

Lacey turned on her computer and slipped off her shoes while it booted "You said you had a surefire way to confirm Teddy is the guilty party."

Victor waggled a hand uncertainly. "More accurately, I've got a place where you can safely talk to him and see whether you're going to be any more convincing than I was."

She grimaced slightly. "You didn't happen to tell him who I was, did you?"

He shook his head. "Should I have?"

"No, but he'll know me. We've already spoken. He remembered me from TV, and knew what I used to do for a living. He wasn't easy to get information from even when I bought him a sandwich. He kept wanting more."

"Well, then my idea is perfect," he said, walking over to the window to stare out at the snowy afternoon. "We'll have a whole Christmas buffet waiting for him."

Lacey began checking her e-mail, noting she had painfully little these days and hoping Jack had sent her the formal offer she was sure he'd send. She felt a bit crestfallen when nothing from him was there. "Somehow," she said without looking back to

Victor, "I don't think that'll have quite the impact you may think it will."

"Well, we need to think of *something*," he said. "He keeps blocking me from his mind, and if he only wants you for your meat and cheese…"

Lacey rolled her eyes but couldn't help smiling a little. As annoying as Victor could be, she really had missed him. And she had felt safer at night since he'd been back. Though he might be a bungling idiot, on occasion, he was kind, honest, and even mildly amusing. His abilities as a ghost also offered her unique resources for tracking down the killer.

Finishing her e-mails, she checked her news feeds to see whether any additional murders had occurred. She was grateful she hadn't been dreaming of all of them, but was beginning to wonder whether she *should* hope to see more, on the off chance it gave her a lead.

"I'm sorry you had to see Jessica die," Victor said quietly, reading her thoughts.

Lacey softened slightly, and glanced at him. "I didn't actually see the death. Just the lead up. But that…" and she shuddered. "I could feel her fear, Victor. Her adrenaline. Like I *was* her."

His expression turned pensive. "And you think these dreams have something to do with our spiritual connection to one another?"

She half-shrugged. "That's for you to research. I'm pretty sure I won't find it even on Google."

He crossed to her. "So what *are* you researching?"

She smiled, and her fingers played over the keyboard. "Everything and anything I can with regards to this mysterious little scenario. Police reports, crime statistics, social media sites, anything I can find on those girls from the coffee shop. You name it. Somewhere in all of this, there's got to be *something* that'll at least point us in the right direction."

"And legwork?" he asked.

"You already know I've been doing that. I plan on doing as much as I have to."

"Nice to know. I look forward to seeing you on the runway."

Lacey didn't manage to hide her blush. She wasn't sure what it was, but something about Victor seeing her as a model was inexplicably humiliating. "Do you really have to keep bringing that up?" she muttered.

"Hey, I think you look *hot*," he answered. "Models are attractive for good reasons. You should be flattered. I thought girls like feeling pretty…" he trailed off suddenly, noticing Lacey's expression. "Oh," he said, sensing her thoughts. "You're not quite as happy about this as I thought you'd be."

She pivoted her chair around to face him, and locked her eyes on his. Her thin-lipped response was barely above a whisper. "Victor St. John, I'll have you know that I am a woman and a human being, *not* some object to be gawked at. I utterly detest the way women are objectified by marketing. And to have you taking their side? Is this all I ever was to you?" And she gestured at her chest, then her legs. "I thought I knew you better than that. I thought that you were actually a decent man."

She spun carefully back to face her computer.

"Lacey, no. I—"

"I think it's time for you to leave, Victor."

He touched her shoulder, knowing she'd at least see the gesture. "Babe, that's not what I meant—"

"Just go," she said quietly.

He made to reply, but he knew she was perfectly serious. He reached out to her mind, but she recoiled immediately, and he backed out, not wanting to offend her further. *I can finally read a woman's mind, and yet I* still *can't figure out what she really wants,* he thought ruefully. *Great.*

"I'll see you later," he said sullenly. Shoulders hunched, he made his way out through the nearest wall.

As soon as she saw him leave, Lacey slouched in her chair, hating the fact that she felt like crying. It had been hard enough to get excited about taking a job like this, even if Jack hadn't yet formalized things, but to have *Victor* give her another reason *not* to? It tore at her heart. She wondered whether she should just call Jack and cancel, and find some other way to figure out the murders, and hope to make rent and bills.

"How *could* he?" she murmured, a sob escaping despite her attempts to keep it inside. "I thought he really cared about *me*."

"Granddaughter?"

Lacey composed herself at once, quickly dabbing her eyes dry and straightening her hair.

"Yes, Nainai? I'm sorry if I woke you." She rose to go into the bedroom, but Nainai was already wheeling herself out.

"What has my lovely Lacey sad on such a beautiful winter morning?"

"Oh, Nainai, it's nothing. I'm just caught up in a few things."

Her grandmother's expression told Lacey her lie hadn't been very convincing. "You were arguing with him, weren't you?"

Lacey paused, unsure how to proceed. How long had Nainai been awake? How much of her discussion with Victor had her grandmother heard? Would the old woman think Lacey was going crazy, too?

"It's fine," Nainai said. "I already know how you feel."

Lacey's eyebrows scrunched. "You do?"

Nainai gave her a patient look. "Lacey, I think it's wonderful how you're so young, and spirited, and that you want to stand for this cause or that. I know you feel your worth should be about more than just the good looks you inherited from your grandmother," and the old woman gave a playful shake of her hips. "But it's not so bad to be pretty. There are *plenty* of women who would love to think they are, or already are but don't realize it.

"Your young man wasn't trying to say you were anything less than the intelligent, capable, beautiful person you are. We both know men can get hot and bothered about a nice figure, but you ought to see him the same way you want him to see you. He's a piano that plays more than a mating call, Lacey. Even before he died, I could tell he truly cared about you. I can see it even more clearly now. You're in his every thought.

"Don't go driving away a good prospect just because he has good eyes. You really *do* have a beautiful face and a truly excellent figure. Like I said, you got it from me. It's okay if Victor sees that, because for him, it's a package deal. Learn to accept him for who *he* is, too."

Lacey sagged into her chair with a sigh. She really had overreacted. While she still hated the fact that women's bodies were, essentially, used to sell things, it hadn't been fair to take it out on Victor. He'd made no secret of just how attractive he'd found her from the first time they'd met, and, if she were honest, it *had* been more than a little flattering to know that she'd caught his eyes.

"I'm sorry, Nainai," she said. "You're right about him." Something hitched in her brain, something her grandmother had said. She sat up straight and stared at the woman. "Wait—did you say something about knowing Victor's thoughts?"

Nainai raised her eyebrows. "Don't you?"

Lacey frowned. "Well, yes, but we have a special connection. Can you actually see and hear him?"

Nainai smiled enigmatically. "When you are as seasoned and wise as I am, you can perceive many things, even if it doesn't involve your eyes and ears. You can even see the future, because you know so much of the past. People think they're good at keeping secrets, but over the years, the attentive person learns how to figure out what *isn't* being said."

Lacey's eyes widened. "The other night, in the mall. You told me to beware of something. Can you tell me what?"

Nainai made to speak, but her face clouded over and her shoulders hunched slightly. "You know, it's awfully cold in here. It's not usually this cold in Tokyo."

"You're not living in Tokyo anymore, Nainai. Remember? I brought you here to the States?"

"Oh, that's right."

Lacey pursed her lips in thought. Her grandmother's memory was clearly fading, but there was something in what she'd just said, and in the possibility that her discernment (when she was lucid) might be better even than Victor's, who seemed to rely on actual mind reading. Though it was a stretch, it was worth a shot.

"Victor was going to have me meet with Teddy," she said softly. "I wonder…"

"Confucius say," Nainai interrupted, "that muttering granddaughters make for one-sided conversation."

Lacey faced her grandma. "Sorry, Nainai. I was just thinking aloud."

"Well think a little louder, then, so I can at least give you a penny for your thoughts."

Lacey smiled at that. "Nainai, I think I have an excellent idea for our Christmas dinner. You may even make some new friends."

TWENTY

Trend's lobby was already packed by the time Lacey shouldered her way inside. Various news outlets were there, clamoring near the empty set-up podium, a red-velvet rope keeping them at bay. KZTB was there, a new anchorwoman speaking into a camera. At least Lacey wouldn't be bothered by an old coworker and having to share pretend smiles and hugs of missing one another. Cathy was an editor, not a reporter, and she was the only one who held the title of "friend" in Lacey's book.

Lacey had contacted Victor within minutes of their argument, and had called him back to her place for a sincere apology. He took it in stride, as he always did, and eagerly agreed to her plan of bringing Nainai to meet Teddy. As an olive branch, Lacey had invited him to the press conference, and now, here they were.

Words buzzed in the air, over each other: "Murder," "Models," even "Mayhem," which was a bit too cheesy-dramatic for Victor's taste, who literally walked through the crowd. He took his place on one of the stools behind the podium, placing a hand to his chin as if he were considering the crowd with the air of a GQ cover model.

Very funny, Lacey mentally told him.

Honestly, though, don't you think I could pass for a pretty boy? He stood up and sucked in his cheeks like Zoolander, before doing a little model walk, swaying his hips. The elevator swished open and out stepped Geo, who did almost a mirror-image catwalk to the chair Victor was once seated in. Lacey stifled a laugh, covering her mouth.

Abruptly, Victor's face fell.

What's wrong, Victor? Lacey asked.

Victor's eyes scanned the room deliberately for several long seconds, but finally he shook his head. "There's a dark presence here. Like, it just showed up." His eyes lit, and he shot a glance at Geo, who was clearly faking smiles for the cameras. "Who's that guy?"

Lacey's gaze darkened. *Geo. Talent manager. Seems to run the place. I'd say he's Jack's right-hand man, but I get the sense they mostly just tolerate each other. Why? You think he's—*

"The source of the darkness?" Victor frowned, and focused his attention on the well-dressed man. "Maybe."

Lacey raised an eyebrow. *What do you mean, "maybe"?*

Victor floated over toward Geo and hovered around him, examining him from all angles (even doing a headstand) as the colorful little man dropped soundbites for reporters or posed just right for photos. He carefully dove into the man's thoughts, and tried broadcasting them to Lacey. At once, he was assaulted by a million different ideas, spinning inside the man's mind: shoot schedules, the need for new models, "stupid press conferences" and unwanted attention, Jack's plan to handle the mess, deadlines, fury that the new product line for spring wear hadn't arrived, and who would "have to pay" because of it.

"This guy has the mind of a woman," he said, turning back to Lacey. "Did you catch any of what I sent?"

Lacey subtly shook her head. *It was more like noise on top of noise. It wasn't at all as clear as when you showed me that vision of those girls from the coffee shop talking to the cops. What'd you get from him?*

Victor's shoulders sagged. "That he's a very busy, angry person."

Lacey tapped her foot impatiently. *And what about that "maybe" you mentioned? Is this guy a problem or not?*

Victor shrugged. "Timing-wise, it was almost perfect. And I can definitely sense dark things about him. But it's... it's almost like meeting with Teddy. *Something* is keeping me from pinpointing the source of this. But it most definitely appeared when *he* did," and Victor pointed at Geo again.

Though, you could read his thoughts, Lacey replied. *Keep an eye on him while—*

Her phone buzzed. She pulled it out of her slim red coat, thinking to ignore the call. But the ID said "Trend." She glanced around to see whether anyone in the room was calling, but saw no one she knew with a phone to their ear, so she decided to answer. "Hello?"

"Lacey." It was Jack's warm voice.

"Yes, hello."

"It's me. Jack. I'm on in a moment. I just wanted to make sure you're here."

She smiled, feeling her heart catch. "I am. I'll be in the crowd, standing to your right."

"Okay, perfect." She thought she heard a smile in his voice. "Wish me luck."

Her own smile widened. "Good luck."

The call ended without him saying goodbye.

Victor stood at the podium, translucent as always, a joker's glint in his sparkly eyes. "Ladies and gentlemen, thank you for coming," he lifted his arms, "to see me, the most studly studmuffin dead ex-boyfriend there is." When no one responded, of course, he said, "Please, hold your applause. No, I won't be taking any questions."

Lacey shook her head at him. Victor appeared beside her, arms crossed. "Just wanted you to see who Pretty Boy is up against, lest you forget."

Just then, Jack entered the lobby to the flashes of a hundred cameras. He was handsome in his fitted navy suit, the white dress shirt unbuttoned at the neck, no tie. All business, he straight away approached the podium. Lacey's smile was instant. Two large men, also in expensive suits, trailed behind him, taking their spots on the empty stools beside Geo.

In a red Hawaiian shirt and khakis, Geo was the only one casually dressed. His dark eyes looked glazed over in what appeared to be exhaustion, sitting beside the large men.

"Good morning, everyone," Jack soberly greeted. "Ladies and gentlemen of the press, and local law enforcement, among others. Welcome to my agency, Trend Modeling, the fastest growing modeling agency in the Seattle area."

He inhaled deeply and scanned the crowd for a moment. "I have invited you all here in response to heartbreaking news." His eyes shifted away as a hand rubbed his mouth. He looked back at the crowd, catching Lacey's stare. "As you're aware, we recently lost two of our very beautiful, very intelligent and very successful models, Jessica Simcox and Brittany Lareaux.

"Miss Simcox was expecting her first child when her life was so gruesomely taken, which makes her tragedy a double homicide. And Miss Lareaux was just starting her life's journey as a freshman at the University of Washington, interested in Political Science."

The press was quiet. All that could be heard were camera shutters as more pictures were being taken. Jack continued. "First, I want to give my condolences to their families. On behalf of myself and my staff, I can't help but feel some guilt over what happened. You entrusted your loved ones to our care. Miss Simcox's murder was a tragedy all on its own, but it wasn't until Miss Lareaux's life was brutally taken away, as well, that it gave us reason to seriously consider whether there may be a connection to Trend. We have no choice but to face the facts: that this agency has, for reasons unknown, been targeted by some maniac on the streets."

Lacey inhaled sharply. Victor glanced at her in concern.

Jack dabbed lightly at an eye, and took a moment to compose himself. "I want the families of the victims to know, as well as you, concerned citizens watching from home, that Trend will do everything humanly possible to keep our models safe. We've hired military-trained security guards," he pointed behind him to the two large men in suits, "to escort our models to and from their cars, no matter what time of day. You can say we're overreacting, but I ask you this: how well would any of *you* sleep if you knew people in *your* care were being actively targeted, and you stood by and did nothing?

"These guards, and more, will be surveilling and safeguarding this entire building twenty-four hours a day, so even after-hours emergency meetings or bookings won't be a threat for any woman. If necessary, I'll personally see to your protection. You will be safe in our care. Nothing is more precious to us than you. Nothing."

He paused and lifted a finger, eyeing the several cameras in the front row poised at him. "I have a message to the police." He pressed his lips together firmly. "The police have been failing us."

Surprised by the statement, Lacey eyed the room. Expressions were somber, flat. But then, that's how the media is trained to be—emotionless. She remembered. Yet a murmur arose from the various law enforcement personnel throughout the room.

Jack's finger shook as he reiterated, "The police have failed us. I'll say this—after now two murders, they should have at least offered to stake out Trend and provide protection. But even if the police offer their protection now, know that my private security will remain. They will remain, because these so-called defenders of law and order should be working *tirelessly* on the case so this doesn't happen to *anyone* else, but they haven't. Two murders is one shy of what constitutes a serial killing, and I will *not* have that. "

"Wow," Victor uttered. "He's not pulling any punches. Good thing they haven't lost any *more* girls, or he might be calling for military action."

Lacey gave him a muted scowl. *Be serious here, Victor. We're talking about murder.*

I am serious, he replied. *I know a thing or two about that, remember?* An idea occurred to him, but he knew Lacey was too focused on the moment to want to listen, so he filed the thought away.

Jack continued, his speech gathering momentum. "Whoever is guilty of the vile acts of violence against these women, know your days of freedom are numbered. You will pay. Justice will be serviced. You will be found. I promise you that."

Gripping the sides of the podium, Jack said with a slight lilt, "Here's another promise to the murderer: you'll never harm one of our girls again. And I'm not alone in my faith in that. In fact, our team has recently been joined by someone this community already knows and trusts for her intelligent and probing mind and no-nonsense attitude. I take her acceptance of our offer as a sign of good faith in the promises I've made this morning."

Lacey's heart pounded, knowing he was talking about her. She hadn't expected this; Jack hadn't sent her the formal offer she'd been waiting on, but she supposed this was it. She tucked some hair behind an ear, feeling her face burn.

"In fact, she's here with us, in the crowd, the very lovely and talented Ms. Lacey Ling."

In a commotion of murmurs, searching cameras abruptly whirled, finally landing on Lacey's face. She successfully hid embarrassment under a practiced, pleasant demeanor made for TV.

Jack smiled mildly. "As a further sign of solidarity, she'll be my special guest this Saturday at the mayor's ball, where we'll be raising money for the families of Jessica Simcox and Brittany Lareaux." He paused for a moment. "I'm really going to miss Brittany and Jessica."

He composed himself again. "Now, I understand you're the press, and therefore you're accustomed to refrain from things like laughter or clapping on camera," he said with a charming smile, "but let's give a hand for Lacey Ling, who will help give back to those hurting in our community."

Jack applauded loudly, and after a moment's pause, was joined by soft clapping that soon intensified into something sincere. Lacey allowed herself a blush for the cameras.

When the applause died, the media attention returned to Jack. He waited a beat before continuing. "I want you to know Lacey didn't expect me to put attention on her this morning. She was merely invited to attend, like the rest of you. She's a special person with a special talent. KZTB sure is missing a superstar. I want to publicly thank her for signing with us. She will be a bit of sunshine amidst what has been dark, dark clouds."

Lacey could crawl under the reception desk, and yet she loved the zing at her former employer. Only Jack's charm could get away with criticizing the police and the media, while simultaneously praising Lacey's "special"-ness.

Victor shook his head in awe. "I have to give it to him. He is gooood… Just don't forget to send me an invitation to the wedding."

Lacey internally rolled her eyes. *Be quiet*, she teased back, though she wondered whether she'd ever consider going that far with anyone. But Jack was definitely worth hanging on to for now.

"Just wait until I get back, at least," he said, walking slowly backward, eyes never leaving her face.

Her brow wrinkled. "Back from where?"

"Heaven. I need to do a little investigating of my own."

TWENTY-ONE

Lacey found herself pacing Trend's lobby in the wake of the press conference, grateful she was no longer the center of attention. She was impressed that Jack had gone to such lengths, both in assembling the media and in offering so much protection for his staff. While she expected companies to be concerned about their staff in situations like this, most places, eager to protect both their people *and* their bottom line, would have just offered staff training, offered stern warnings, and maybe installed some security cameras, or arranged for a few extra police patrols. She found it touching to see a man so willing to sacrifice for others.

She heard someone coming up behind her, and turned to see Jack striding across the polished floor. He smiled as soon as she met his eyes, and she felt her heart miss a beat. "Lacey, there you are."

She returned his smile and the embrace he offered. He quickly glanced around and she followed suit. Finding no one there, he leaned in to steal a quick kiss, only to pull away quickly as though he were a little boy about to get caught stealing his mom's cookies. Lacey couldn't help but smile at that, and she found she loved the feel of his lips.

"Oh, Mister Beals," she said in mock-seriousness, "I think you can do a little better than that. Besides, I think you owe me, after the stunt you just pulled."

He chuckled. "I suppose you're right. Let's try that again." He pulled her in for something more serious, and she let herself get lost in it, savoring the way it soothed her nerves. When they parted, she pushed him to arm's length and gazed into his eyes for a moment, before letting her face show the concern she felt.

"You could have at least warned me before throwing me to the wolves."

He raised his eyebrows. "Lacey Ling, given your history, you were a wolf among wolves. The way you handled the press after today's conference was a sight to behold. I think that if anyone ought to be running home with their tails between their legs, it'd be the reporters who showed up, not the former reporter who outshined them."

Lacey couldn't help but smile at that. Jack offered his arm, and she took it, mildly surprised. "What say we give you a little tour of the place, get you your keys and ID badge, then grab some lunch?

We can handle all the messy paperwork next Monday, then you can start for real on Tuesday."

She pecked him on the cheek, finding that he was very easy to forgive. "That sounds wonderful." He began to lead her away, but she stopped him and locked eyes. "Jack? I just wanted to thank you."

His eyebrows knit together. "Thank me? For what?"

"For everything," she said. "For buying dinner for a random stranger—that just happened to be me—for offering me a chance to better my situation and... and..." she glanced away, feeling a strange tremor and wondering why she was nearly fighting tears, suddenly.

He gently lifted her chin. "And what? Lacey, it's okay. If there's something you need to tell me, I'm all ears." His soft smile encouraged her onward.

"Thank you for protecting your girls."

His eyebrows shot up. "Of *course* I'm interested in my girls. Not only would I not have a business without them, but they're special to me. I've taken care to get to know every last one of them. You have no idea how much it hurt, with Jessica and Brittany."

Lacey swallowed hard. "That's what I mean," she said. "I-I actively *didn't* want to become a model. I didn't want to just be a piece of meat to show off for all the world to see. And I know a little about the business. I didn't want to just be 'product,' either. But this? All you're doing to protect the other models? It says you *care* about them. That they're real people to you."

Jack's face softened, and he pulled Lacey into a long, soft embrace. "Of course I do." He held her away from him, and gazed at her. "You know, maybe this is a little too forward of me, but I have a confession to make. When I bought you dinner, I didn't know you, it's true, but you looked like someone who'd had a rough day. That, and, well," and he actually blushed, "I couldn't help but find you more than a little attractive."

It was Lacey's turn to blush. "You, sir, are too good at that. *But*," she chewed her lip in thought, "I've still got a bit of an obstacle to really going ahead with this."

Jack frowned, worried. "What's that?"

"My grandmother. I can't just leave her alone all day. And from what I've gathered…" she let her words hang in the air.

He nodded thoughtfully. "That is a concern, yes." He rubbed his chin for a moment, then his eyes lit. "How social is your grandmother?"

Lacey laughed. "You met her."

He smiled. "True. Humor me—would she be okay with a visiting nurse?"

She looked across the lobby, cringing inside at the cost. "Well, that's not an option I'd considered…"

Jack touched her shoulder. "Let's try again. If money weren't an object, would you be willing to trust her to a visiting nurse?"

Lacey looked up at him in surprise. "Jack, I couldn't ask you to—"

He pressed a finger against her lips. "I've just hired military-grade bodyguards to protect my girls. I won't even tell you how much I'm spending on upgrading the security system. I learned that if I take care of my girls, they take care of me. I'm serious about signing you. I can see how much you love your grandma. I happen to know a few people; I'll get her the perfect nurse, and you won't have to worry about her for even a second. What do you say?"

Lacey felt her breath catch. This was all so fast. How would Nainai react? Would she feel she was being abandoned? What if she *did* get a nurse, but didn't like her? So many questions swirled in her mind.

"Lacey?" Jack's voice was warm and patient, and snapped her out of her spinning thoughts. "Trust me on this: she'll be fine."

Lacey's worries melted away, and within moments, she'd nearly forgotten she'd been verging on panic. She wondered why she'd freaked out. Jack's solution was sensible and elegant; of *course* Nainai would be fine. She smiled up at him, still fighting not to let her eyes mist up. "Thank you, Jack," she whispered. "You have no idea how much this means to me."

He answered with a crooked, boyish smile. "My pleasure. So it's settled. I'll make the arrangements this afternoon.

"Now, how about that tour and a little bite to eat? I don't know about you, but that press conference made me hungry."

*

Victor found Heaven simultaneously thrilling and slightly painful. He'd been with Lacey again, and the thought of leaving her in such a miserable place made his heart ache, even when he'd cleared the glorious pearly gates through which streams of angels passed. He'd come here on a hunch, and was about to find out whether he was right. With some digging around—which took surprisingly little time—he'd manage to locate whom he was looking for, and arrange a meeting.

Standing at a small but glorious fountain beneath a tree that reached to the sky, he kept his senses open, scanning for one particular angel among the myriad of others who were gathered around, conversing, hugging loved ones, laughing, and otherwise enjoying their existence.

He felt the presence before he saw her, and instantly, she was there. She was a head and a half shorter than Victor, but carried herself regally. The long drape of her luxurious black hair stood in stark contrast to her glowing white dress that looked more like something a girl would get married in than wear as everyday attire. Her eyes were a stunning hazel, and they sparkled with both intelligence and amusement.

"Well, brother," the girl said, "I hear you were looking for me."

Victor scratched at the back of his neck, wondering how to go about this.

"The memories of my death are... not something I'd prefer to dwell on," she said, interrupting his thoughts."

He nodded, slightly glum. "I don't blame you, sister," he said, still feeling slightly strange about addressing his kindred dead as siblings. "Can I call you Brittany?"

She nodded. "All my family on earth did." He felt a flutter of sadness from her at the mention of her loved ones.

"Thanks, Brittany. I'm sure you know what's been going on down there since you left."

The girl's face fell slightly. "I haven't been given many glimpses in The Pool," she said, glancing away and smoothing her dress. "Only a few views of my family, to assure me they'll be alright after... what happened."

Victor took her in a brotherly embrace, and she returned it gratefully. "I'm so much happier here," she said. "I just wish my family knew I was okay."

He nodded, thinking of Lacey, and knowing that Brittany would take his meaning and feel his empathy. "That's why I tracked you down."

"I know. It's weird that I know—that we all know everything up here. It's... kind of embarrassing at times, isn't it?"

Victor laughed openly. "Yeah, but you get used to it. I can tell you're still new by how formal you're acting."

Brittany blushed. "Is it really that bad?" But they both knew the answer, so she continued. "Okay. I'll share everything I remember, but I warn you, there were a lot of bad things that went on that night. Forgive me if I only grant you one look. I've tried hard not to remember it myself, but the other angels here—they've really helped me heal from that."

Victor nodded, remembering his own reception when he'd finally given in to coming to Heaven. "Okay. One look, and I won't ask any questions after that." They both knew he wouldn't have to; he'd memorize it the first time through.

Brittany's face grew serious, and she sat on the ground, leaning back against the tree. "Brace yourself."

He nodded. "Ready."

And there it was. The whole murder, with all the sights, sounds, and sensations, played out before him as though he were living it himself, just like Lacey had said. He wasn't prepared for any of it. Fear, adrenaline, the haze of drugs fogging the mind, blind groping for an escape route, a knife flashing again and again, a dark, vaguely man-shaped figure looming above, more terror. Then, falling into nothingness.

When it ended, Victor staggered and nearly toppled. He lunged for the tree and managed to prop himself up against it. Brittany's face was a mask of sorrow and remembered pain, trails of tears lining her beautiful cheeks. A small shudder coursed through the ground, as Heaven responded to the manifest sorrow. A sense of calm and love flowed into Victor, soothing the sharp touch of remembered trauma. He straightened, and held out his hand toward Brittany. She took it, and he pulled her up and into an embrace of gratitude this time.

"I'm sorry to have put you through that again," he said softly, peering at her, and feeling the same affection he did for his sisters.

She pursed her lips. "And I'm sorry you didn't find what you were looking for," she replied.

"I'm sorry, too. And I'm even more sorry for what you suffered during your last months of life. I won't ask you for anything else."

He felt her desire to help him, and he knew that, if he asked, she'd tell him more. But after the pain he'd already put her through, he couldn't bring himself to make her endure more. "Don't worry," he said. "My girl is pretty resourceful, even if she's still mortal. And I think there may be someone else up here I can talk to about this."

She gave him a knowing look, and he scratched at the back of his neck again. "Guess I have to bite that bullet sometime," he said sheepishly. "Wish me luck."

"I'm sure she'll forgive you," Brittany said with a kind smile. "This place has a way of bringing out the best in people."

"I hope you're right," he replied. And with that, he made to find the one person who, if she were here, would make Heaven a distinctly uncomfortable place for him.

Jessica Simcox.

TWENTY-TWO

Lacey wondered whether she was overly obsessing about finding the truth behind the various murders. Now she was wheeling her dear grandmother into the local shelter, a banner displayed outside advertising "The 12 Days of Christmas - Hot Turkey Dinners. Dec. 13 - 25." Wearing a black shawl around her head for some sense of anonymity, Lacey whispered to the handsome ghost floating alongside her, "You sure Teddy will be here tonight?"

Victor nodded. "Being that it's the thirteenth today, and Teddy mentioned he wouldn't miss it for anything, I expect to see him around here somewhere. And although he can't totally be trusted, he did agree to seeing you again. I hope you're right about Nainai being able to read him."

Lacey merely nodded as they ducked through the door and into the shelter.

Inside, the tables were filling with men, women, even some children, many bundled in worn jackets and scarves. There must have been over a hundred people. Lacey stood on tip-toes to peer around for Teddy. She'd never expected to feel sheepish over wearing nice clothes before, especially brand names, but it felt as if all eyes were suddenly on her and could see through her Michael Kors jacket to her Vera Wang top. Upon further scrutiny, she shook her head, again ashamed to realize the diners didn't care how rich or poor she looked; they were totally focused on the turkey meals before them, taking hearty bites, and some even moaning in happiness. The turkey looked okay, but the mashed potatoes were a tad too runny. Lacey would have made them thick, fluffy, with a sprinkle of chives. Again, she scolded herself.

Speaking to Victor again, she said, "Are you seeing my thoughts? I'm feeling so ashamed right now. Suddenly, my ghetto apartment seems palatial."

"I know what you mean," Victor said. "And that's coming from me, who's resided at the Great Palace in the Sky the last few months. It's easy to take so much for granted."

"I already ate," Nainai said, looking around the place as if it were a senior's buffet. "Why are we here? Hoping to put more meat on these old bones?"

A sudden shout caught their attention. "Well, if it isn't the rich brat, herself?"

Lacey turned in her pumps, away from her grandmother's chair, to Teddy, who was approaching her with an awkward smile that she couldn't interpret. Victor closed in, side to side with Lacey.

"And the Ghost of Christmas," he chuckled, speaking of Victor. "You know each other?"

Nainai's face flushed, and she scoffed. "Excuse me." She turned, looking up at Lacey. "You should have put more blush on my cheeks. I told you I look too pale!"

Lacey whispered out of the side of her mouth. "He's not talking about you. You look great."

"So did Angel Boy tell you I'm a mass murderer? You're looking at me as if I am. Just because Angel Boy saw me draw a knife on someone for kicks, huh?"

Lacey was seriously starting to detest Teddy more than ever before. "How can you be so flippant about that?"

Remember our objective, Victor mentally told Lacey. At least they had that little trick of privacy. *Let's not anger him.*

You're right! He's just such a sleazy buffoon, it's hard to bite my tongue.

But you will, right? Bite your tongue?

Of course. She gave him a quiet glance.

"A rich brat wouldn't understand," Teddy said. "Sometimes we need a little more entertainment than staring at fiery trash cans."

Nainai tsked him. "You are not a nice man. Not a nice man at all." She squinted her dark eyes at him in strength.

"I see you brought your poodle," Teddy said to Lacey, pointing at the old woman in the wheelchair, white hair puffing out of her shawl. "Does it bite? Hope it doesn't have rabies." He chuckled.

"Why? You haven't had your shots?" Lacey was amused by her comeback, the side of her mouth curling up.

"Good one," Teddy sincerely complimented.

Victor cut in before further contention. *Quick, ask him about Brittany. See what he says. See what Nainai does in response. Let's test our theory.*

Clearing her throat, Lacey pointed toward a table still open against a wall, in the distance. "Shall we sit? Have you eaten?"

Eyeing her and then Victor, he said, "I'm going to try an' get seconds. I'll be back soon."

Lacey saved him a spot at the table, parked Nainai to the side of it, and Victor opted to stand. Teddy soon came over with a plate heaped with food. "My lucky day. Not only seconds, but I think the kitchen maid likes me," he lifted his eyebrows toward the massive amount of food.

Surprisingly, as he sat, he asked Lacey, "Want some?"

"Oh, no, thank you," she said, shifting to a comfortable position on the hard plastic chair.

"Your loss." He grabbed a fork and dug in. "So," he said around chomping some potatoes, white frothing the corners of his mouth, as if he had contracted rabies. "I'm doing Angel Boy a favor by talking to you here, and in turn you can get to know some of us lowly peasants and how we make it through the holiday. So just so you know, I don't have to humor your pathetic investigation going on here, but Teddy can also be a nice guy, and it's close to Christmas, so I says to myself, why not? That's the charitable part of me."

Lacey caught her grandmother eyeing Teddy with intensity. Happy about that, at least, Lacey did manage to say "Thank you" to the rude vagrant. "I won't bother you too much," she said. "We can keep it brief." She glanced again at Nainai, locked in on him still. "Did you murder Jessica?" she asked quietly.

"Nope," he said, his teeth tearing into turkey. "And seriously. You're asking me that in public?"

Lacey grimaced. "*Absolutely* not?"

"Hey, in my book, no means no. Got anymore brilliant questions?"

Lacey folded her hands and continued. "Did you murder Brittany?"

"Once again, no." He spooned gravy on top of another piece of turkey before slamming it into his already-stuffed mouth.

"Do you know who did?" she quickly added, lifting her chin.

"Mmm…" His eyes shifted away a moment as if in thought. Like maybe he knew.

"Who killed them, Teddy?" She leaned forward in her seat, looking intently up at him.

"You take my advice and get into modeling yet?" he asked her, some turkey pieces spat out of his mouth.

Lacey recoiled with an internal cringe. Victor winced out of sympathy. Hoping Nainai was getting some kind of… prophecy, Lacey glanced at her, and found her gazing intensely at Teddy. What Lacey *really* wanted to do was get up and give her face a rigorous washing. All she had was a moist towelette in her purse, which she snatched out. As she wiped a cheek, she said, "I am in modeling, yes. Let get back to—"

"Good." He nodded. "Hey, look, I'm innocent, okay? It was fun at first, being all elusive and stuff with you two, but the game is only interesting for so long. You all, including the poodle, are starting to annoy me. A man wants to eat in peace, you know."

That rubbed Victor the wrong way. He had to speak up. "Hey, now, Ted, you'll sit here and answer any question Lacey has for you. You made a deal."

Teddy slowly stood with a maddening stare at the ghost. "I've done my part. That means you gotta pay up. But I don't got to do anything for anyone."

Victor retorted, "Yes, you do. Now if you have any other information, tell us."

Quaking, Teddy looked like he was about to erupt. Instead, he suddenly flung his tray full of food at Victor with a growl, mashed potato and gravy splatting and dripping down the wall. "I said, I don't got to do *anything* for *anyone!*" To all the other people, volunteers and fellow transients, it looked like a temper tantrum at nobody.

As if on cue, a couple of police officers entered the shelter, surprising everyone, as things became a hushed quiet. They strode right over to Teddy, and said, "Theodore Finn, you're under arrest for the murders of Jessica Simcox and Brittany Lareaux."

Teddy cursed loudly as the handcuffs were being put on. He wriggled in the men's grasps as he was forcefully ushered out. "Rich Brat," he seethed. "This is your fault, ain't it? You set me up. It's not over!" Struggling against the cops, he continued rambling all the way out the door. "You'd better watch your back! Teddy don't take kindly to traitors!"

Lacey stood in shock. "What just happened?"

Victor slowly shook his head. "Looks like Teddy's going to the slammer."

Nainai eyed her granddaughter. "I'm glad I already ate. That man would have made me lose my appetite."

Feeling suddenly all too conspicuous, Lacey pulled Nainai's chair away from the table and wheeled her through the dining hall, long stares following her every step. One person was heard saying, "That's that one reporter," followed by a growing murmur from the crowd. Turning her face away, she hurried out the door into the cold night, where Christmas lights were joined with flashing red and blue ones as Teddy was taken in for booking.

Lacey quickly helped Nainai into the front passenger seat, and put the wheelchair into the trunk. Driving away, Nainai broke the silence with, "I didn't even have a chance to eat."

"We ate at home, before we came," Lacey said, although she knew explaining could be futile. "And you just said you weren't hungry."

Nainai's eyes flicked back and forth in thought. "I did? Oh, that's right. That's why I'm not hungry."

"That's fine, Nainai. I'm glad you're not hungry. If you are, we can get you something at home." Nainai went quiet, leaving Lacey to her thoughts.

Victor sprawled across the back seat, and entered Lacey's thoughts. Immediately, he was met with a conflict of feelings and suspicions. *Do you want to ask Nainai what she thinks?* he intruded as softly as possible.

Lacey stopped at a red light. She didn't respond.

Is that a no?

Tapping her fingers on the steering wheel in hesitation, Lacey finally said, "What did you think of that man at… the restaurant." She knew that's what Nainai thought of the shelter, a big restaurant.

Nainai said, "Oh, I don't trust him. Has a murderer's heart."

"He does?" Lacey's eyes lit in curiosity.

"Yes, he is a man of many secrets." Nainai turned to Lacey. "Promise me you will not go around that man ever again."

"Uh…" The light turned green, and Lacey pressed the gas. "Only if you are sure, Nainai."

"I am definitely sure." Nainai sank back against her chair with resolve.

Victor tried entering Nainai's thoughts with success. Flashes of a scene came into his view. A brunette, her hands in front of her face in horror, as someone was stabbing her with a knife. An image of Teddy tearing viciously into his turkey followed almost at once, and Victor recoiled in surprise. "I just checked Grandma's thoughts," he said to Lacey.

"I have no doubts now. She sees things. Teddy was one of them."

Lacey huffed, unsure as to why she still felt little to no satisfaction. "So case closed? He's the murderer?"

Thinking the question was directed to her, Nainai said, "Yes."

TWENTY-THREE

Victor laid up in the living room expecting to spend some time watching late-night infomercials or reading some of Nainai's Chinese books. But as he lay there, he simply let his thoughts drift. Teddy had been arrested, but his spirit didn't feel settled. He knew by Lacey's rampant thoughts that she wasn't settled either.

It took a long time for Lacey to fall asleep. It was hard to believe that was it, the end of the mystery, that the killer had indeed been taken into custody. Eventually, she did fall asleep at nearly 3 a.m.

Lacey found herself sitting in a hospital waiting room, sweating under the sterile lighting and the faint odor of decay mingled with antiseptics. Apprehension clutched her chest, and she rose, looking around for something without knowing what.

A she wandered the halls, her anxious curiosity drove her on, and she began looking into patients' rooms as she passed by. She saw the usual assortment of people, but they were all bland, wearing the exact same hospital gowns, the same blank looks on their drawn faces; they struck her as a collection of factory-made robots waiting to be switched off at any moment.

Recoiling, she pressed forward, still burning to find an answer to a question she couldn't even articulate. She passed a doctor, and tried to ask him whatever came to mind, only to find her mouth was dry and no sound would come out. The physician looked at her with open pity, then passed her by.

Frustrated and sensing the leading edge of panic scratching at her mind, Lacey broke into a run. On and on she went, weaving down halls at random, flinging open doors and finding the same dying, robotic people. Then she noticed a long, dark hallway with a single, piercing light at the end. She halted, somehow knowing she'd find what she was looking for there.

Woodenly, she crossed its length to find that the light came from a small window set into the door of a patient's room. She made to open the door, but her hand jerked away as if of its own accord, and she found she didn't want to go in, or even look in. Then, she heard a sound that made her blood run cold.

The drone of a heart monitor flatlining.

Suddenly, there was a flurry of activity behind her. She whirled to see a troop of doctors and nurses scrambling toward her. She darted aside just in time to avoid being trampled as they flung open the door and poured into the room. Lacey felt as though she were sucked in behind them, and she found herself standing just inside the doorway, craning her neck as she tried in vain to get a glimpse of who was on the bed.

"She'll be okay," Victor said from beside her.

Lacey started and spun toward him, wondering how she hadn't seen him earlier. He looked even more handsome than usual, with his dark hair and those crystal-blue eyes that smiled at her.

"Victor?" she asked, clasping his lapels. "What's going on?"

His smile saddened. "There's only so much I'm allowed to say. But I can say she'll be happier where she's going."

"Where who is going, Victor? Tell me. Please."

Victor sighed, then pointed toward the bed. As if moved by an unseen force, the gaggle of medical personnel parted around the head of the bed, giving Lacey a look at the person laying on it. It was an old woman. The lady weakly rolled her head toward Lacey, and Lacey gasped at the tubes in her nose, and the bandages shrouding her head so thoroughly as to nearly hide her identity. But those eyes—simultaneously sad and accusatory—were unmistakable.

They belonged to Nainai.

"Lacey," the woman croaked.

Lacey was at her grandmother's bedside instantly, clutching her hand and pumping it gently as though she could coax a pulse back into her. "It's *okay, Nainai. I'm sure Mom will be here any minute."*

"Why didn't you warn me, Lacey?"

Lacey frowned. "Warn you of what?"

"Lacey..." The word turned into a hissing breath, and the woman's eyes fluttered shut for what Lacey knew would be the last time.

*

Lacey jerked upright in bed, heart slamming against her ribcage, breath rapid. She was out of bed and in Nainai's room before she knew it, and barely managed to keep herself from flipping on the light as she entered. She collided with her grandmother's bed, but the old woman didn't so much as twitch.

"Nainai?" She shook her grandmother's shoulder. No response.

"Nainai?" she repeated, feeling a small amount of bile rising in her throat. The woman remained motionless, and her usual snores were entirely absent. "Grandmother?" Fighting panic, she flicked on a bedside lamp. In the wan lighting, her grandmother's Asian features looked startlingly pale, her lips slightly blue.

"*Nainai!*"

There was a snort, a spasm, and a muttered curse as Nainai's eyes flew open. After a moment of obvious disorientation, her gaze settled on Lacey. Nainai's face fell instantly.

"For the love of Buddha," she muttered. "You're *not* Bruce Lee."

Lacey's shoulders sagged, and she put a hand to her chest, letting out the breath she hadn't realized she'd been holding. She flung herself at her grandmother and embraced her tightly. "I'm so glad you're still alive, Nainai."

"No thanks to you," the woman replied. "And if I *were* dead, it wasn't that bad. I was making out with Bruce Lee while he was kicking butt and taking names. We were in this romantic little village high in the Tian Shan Mountains, and he was just about to propose to me.

"And I wake to see *you* instead? That's more disappointing than finding my dim sum plate came from McDonald's. What's the meaning of this? And why is it so cold? My face feels like ice."

Lacey laughed despite herself. Her grandma was clearly fine if she was talking like that. "I'm sorry, Nainai. I—" She paused, wondering whether she should tell her grandmother the dream. Unbidden, thoughts of the morning news came back. But that couldn't happen to Nainai, could it? Still, in her dream, the old woman had scorned her for not warning her. But warning her of *what*? What would she even tell her?

"My dreams," Lacey began slowly, "were... not as pleasant as yours."

Nainai leaned back into her ample pillows and rubbed her eyes. "Well, you dragged me away from a hot young stud to wake me up at some unearthly hour. You may as well tell me. If you don't, I won't be able to sleep for curiosity, and I'll have to start quoting Confucius at you."

Lacey smiled a little. After a moment's thought, she gave in, and related her dream, including the one about Jessica Simcox. When she finished, Nainai closed her eyes in thought.

"So," Nainai began, "you're trying to warn me I'm about to die because you dreamt of someone else's death just before they actually passed."

Lacey nodded. "I thought the details may have mattered, so I shared."

Nainai shook her head. "They might, they might not. Confucius say, 'Some men are worth dying for.' Remember that."

Lacey's chest tightened as she thought of Victor and her own brush with the afterlife. "Please don't joke like that, Nainai."

The old woman's eyes snapped open again. "Bruce. Lee. Kissing. Engagement. Even an old woman can still fantasize, can't she? I'll joke however I please."

Lacey sighed and stood to leave. "Well, whatever happens, I'll be here to take care of you, okay? Please don't go dying on me yet."

Nainai smiled softly. "The cat said I've got a while."

Lacey halted. A memory of Victor's dead cat came to mind, then she cocked an eyebrow. "Black and gold tabby?"

Her grandmother nodded. "That's the one. My *real* lucky cat."

Lacey smiled again, and tucked her grandmother in for the second time that night. Maybe she was just being paranoid about the whole thing. She kissed her grandma's wrinkled forehead and switched off the light. "Goodnight, Nainai. You can go back to the Tian Shans and your kung-fu master."

"And don't wake me again before my dream ends," Nainai said sternly, wagging a finger. Lacey laughed and left, her grandmother muttering, "I was *this close*," as Lacey shut the door.

She made her way to the kitchen and whipped up a quick cup of soothing tea for her nerves, hoping it would help her sleep again. When she finally returned to her bed, she lay there for a long time, eyes wide open, trying to forget everything she'd seen in her sleep.

TWENTY-FOUR

To the chorus of angels singing *Hallelujah*, Victor was yanked out of his deep thoughts in surprise. He jolted up in the couch as a white light from the corner of Lacey's living room ceiling started to grow in intensity. Even as one the heavenly hosts himself, he had to shadow his eyes with a hand in order to withstand its brilliance.

"God?" he asked carefully, his voice just above a shaky whisper. "Is that… you?"

The singing intensified, filling his entire spirit with a feeling of majesty.

"I-I don't feel worthy to be in your presence." Victor pinched at his T-shirt. "I mean, you've accepted me back home, but I still feel like a work in progress, if you know what I mean. Of course you do; you're God." He got to his knees on the stained and shabby carpet, and pressed his hands together in a prayer gesture.

A sort of strange voice replied, "I have a favor to ask. Once you're back home, be sure to pet your spirit guide Rao on a regular basis, right behind his fuzzy ears..."

Bowing his head, Victor said, "I will try my best." Then his eyes flew back up to the ceiling. "Wait—what? Rao, that's you, isn't it?"

"Pay no attention to the cat behind the cloud," said the voice like The Wizard of Oz.

Rao suddenly appeared in front of him with an amused smile, her fangy teeth in full view. "You should've seen your expression."

Victor's face instantly straightened.

Rao floated beside him on the couch, the white light now gone, along with the sounds of the angelic choir. "Don't be mad at me, Pretty Boy. It was a teaching moment."

"Yeah? What'd you teach me?" Victor glared.

"God wants his angels on assignment to dig deeper, not just look at appearance only. You saw a shiny white light, heard some pretty music, and you thought it was God, right?"

Reluctantly, Victor conceded. "Right..."

"You can do this, Vic. You'll figure things out."

"I hope so. I mean, there's a bigger purpose to all this sleuthing around. You've mentioned it affects Lacey's destiny, her safety." His statements came across more like questions.

"It does." Rao's eyes became supremely serious.

"So, what you're trying to tell me is to not just judge things by appearance." He was mentally connecting the dots. "Does this have to do with

Teddy? And me and Lacey feeling unsettled about his being arrested? Am I right? It's about Teddy? He looks like he came from the bottom of a trash can, eats like one, too."

"Yes, you don't feel like he's guilty, do you?"

Victor had to slowly shake his head on that one. "No, I can't help it. Even though all the signs are there."

Rao just nodded.

"If it's not Teddy, *who* is it?"

"How did the talk with Brittany go?" Rao ignored the question.

"As good as can be, I guess." He shrugged. "Why?"

"Who you really wanted to interview was Jessica. Am I right?"

Victor raised his brows and gave a dark chuckle. "I can't say I was looking forward to it. But I am disappointed that I couldn't find her."

Rao raised up and down her lightly whiskered brows. "That's because she's not in Heaven."

A mix of horror and amusement bubbled up from within. "You mean my ex-ex-girlfriend is in *Hell*?" Imagining her in a sparkly red bikini while breathing fire at him made him nearly laugh.

"No, no. Nothing like that," Rao said, not laughing.

"Well, then? Where?"

Standing on all fours, Rao said, "Follow me. This is the other reason I came down to you tonight. I'll show you."

*

Victor entered the jail cell, nervousness tingling throughout his spirit. There, crumpled in the corner of the empty room, sat Jessica. Her eyes instantly widened at the sight of him.

"Victor?" she uttered. The left side of her face had a muddy streak.

"Jessica?" he stepped right over to her. "Y-you're alive?"

"No," she said standing, spreading her arms out wide. "I'm dead. Deader than dead. Can't you tell?"

"Not really." He looked down at his own translucence and back to her.

"Well, I am." She opened her jean jacket all the way. Slash marks emblazoned her pink shirt.

"Ouch..." was all he could say in his shock.

"Yeah, *ouch!*" she snarled, tossing some bouncy blond hair over a shoulder, showing off a matted-in-mud hunk of tresses.

"But... what is this place, and how come..."

"This is what they call Spirit Prison, Victor. I'm not surprised you've never heard of the place, seeing as how you were such a *good boy* you made it to Heaven." She stuck a hand through her chest and pulled it back out without consequence. "I'm nothing but spirit, too, only I don't have that glow you angels have. My hair, my skin—there's no conditioner or cream that can help me get that glow, either." She huffed. "I can't even wash the dirt off. I'm left looking the way I did right after death until I'm stationed somewhere. Yeah, get this—they're deciding whether I should go to Heaven or Hell.

They say this isn't Hell, just a holding place, but it is Hell to me."

Seeing that she didn't have a baby bump, Victor dared ask, "And the baby? Where is it?"

Jessica's brow scrunched over her fiery green eyes. "It's not an *it*, Victor. He was a *boy*. I would have given birth to him in just three more months, if it weren't for…" Anger and sadness flashed in her eyes, and she looked away.

"I'm sorry," Victor uttered. This was going worse than expected. He didn't expect to feel so much heaviness, so much sorrow.

When she looked back up, she said, "He's in Heaven."

It was Victor's turn to look down. When he met her eyes again, Jessica's expression was softened. If she were alive, he would have definitely expected tears.

And then as fast as that, she snapped, thrashing at Victor. Punches to his face and kicks to his gut did nothing but send heated ripples of hate through him. But that was bad enough. He took hold of Jessica's shoulders and did the only thing he could think to do. He hugged her.

She struggled in his hold before crumpling out of his grasp to the floor. "Why'd you break up with me? This never would've happened if we were still together." She looked up at him with pure anguish.

Victor fell for the guilt trip for a moment, hating himself, but quickly snapped out of it. Sitting down with her, he said, "You and I are too different." He quickly realized that was the same exact line Lacey had given him, but it was true. Besides, he thought to himself, there was that little thing about being a gold-digger that turned him off.

Her face straightened, and she said with acceptance, "You're right. Look at you. And look at me. You were always the do-gooder. I'm sure you were fast-tracked to your Heavenly mansion."

The word mansion made him cringe. That gold-digger thing again. "You know that's a metaphor, that scripture about mansions in Heaven. Hey, listen," he put a hand to her muddy cheek, "for what it's worth, I really am sorry this happened to you. Nobody should have to experience what you did."

She eventually shrugged and said, "How did *you* die?"

"You didn't hear?" He remembered her sitting in at his funeral in a large black sunhat. "I was murdered, too. Poisoned."

Jessica gave a dark chuckle. "If only I could have been poisoned."

"Jessica," he said, drawing her eyes to his again. "I don't know how much time I'm given here to visit you. I have some questions. I'm on assignment from Heaven to help close your case on earth. Think you can help me?"

"I don't know. Do you think you can help *me*?"

He didn't expect that response. "How?"

"For all the hate I hold in my heart, I wouldn't care to be sent to Hell." She looked to her right, batting her eyes in emotion. "I've done some terrible things, Victor. Things you can't imagine. I probably deserve to live with others like me for the rest of my life, in eternal torment. But this Prison is also an opportunity for a second chance, I'm told. And I have a baby boy waiting for me up in Heaven. I have to make it there, if only for him, so he can have his mommy."

That tugged at Victor's heart like almost nothing before. He gulped, taking a moment to compose himself. "You're better than you think you are."

Jessica looked away as if not believing it. Peering back into his eyes, she said, "Do we have a deal?"

"Deal. Who murdered you?"

TWENTY-FIVE

Jessica repositioned into sitting Indian style, her Ugg boots splattered in mud. Victor mirrored her. "It's not that simple," she sighed.

"Not that simple? Is this another rule of the afterlife? You can't just tell me who murdered you?"

"Yeah, I had a visit from some cat who told me, and I quote, 'Never divulge to a handsome visitor in blue who was responsible for your death.' That it was 'important to the case' for you not to know yet. It would 'ruin everything' if I just blurted it."

"Rao," Victor muttered. Glancing down at his blue shirt, he said, "She gave me a compliment?"

"Excuse me?" Jessica was perplexed.

"Nothing. Never mind. Go on." He should have known. If Rao wasn't allowed to say whodunit, why would Jessica? "What *are* you allowed to tell me?"

"Ask me about me," she said with some apprehension in her pouty pink lips.

"Your favorite subject," he said without thinking.

Jessica scowled.

"I mean, this is pertinent to the case?"

"Yes," she said hotly.

"Okay, what's your favorite color?"

Rolling her eyes, Jessica scolded. "OMG, you must be the worst ex-boyfriend there is. It's pink—duh—and that's *not* what I meant about you asking me personal questions."

"A little help here?" He put his hands up.

"Ask me why I'm such a terrible person." Her voice shook.

"I don't know if I'm comfortable..."

Jessica's stare could've sliced through him.

"All right," he said, "I'll rephrase. Why do *you* think you're such a terrible person?"

Jessica's chest puffed out with a deep breath. "Okay, remember how I followed you to Tokyo?"

"Stalked." The word shot out of his mouth, and he instantly felt bad again.

"Yeah, sure. Whatever," she admitted. "Well, my college funds were running low. The loans and Daddy's money were about down to zilch." She pinched the air in emphasis. "I-I was poor," she nearly choked out in embarrassment.

Victor gave a crooked smile. "That doesn't make you a bad person, being poor."

"No, dummy, *listen*. I'm not done." She huffed again. "I needed money fast. When you rejected me, I ran out of options. Desperate, I went to a modeling agency called Trend."

"I've heard of them." Victor nodded.

"Other girls on campus were having success through them. It was supposed to be my ticket out of being broke as a joke. It was a successful plan at first. I was one of—no, I was *the* top model there. In my first month, I made a ton of money."

"Okay," Victor nodded, seeing how this might actually go somewhere important to the case.

"But there was suddenly a dry spell, for some reason. Geo, the demented photographer and booker, wasn't scheduling me jobs anymore. It made no sense. I was the best they had. Why were they booking girls uglier than me for jobs I could've easily done? Do you see what I mean?"

"Hmmm…" Victor feigned sympathy, biting his lip. "Strange."

"Anyway, Geo pulled me aside one day, a day I stomped into the agency to demand answers. He told me that he just didn't have any interested clientele. He blamed it on the market, a seasonal thing. Didn't make sense, because summer wasn't over yet, and I totally have a body made for summer. Right?" she said, demanding confirmation.

"Uh, you're a beautiful woman. Yes."

"I know, right? So, anyway, he pulled me aside and told me he knew of a better job offer. If I wanted to make more money than at Trend, that I needed to talk with these two girls from school—Rebecca and Emily. They could hook me up."

Victor's brows perked up. "Some sorority girls?"

"Yes," Jessica nodded, going on, "Anyway, I should have never listened to Geo. I knew he was off his rocker, and not to mention, so super jealous of me."

"What did it lead you to?" Victor asked, his blue eyes anxious. "Meeting up with Rebecca and Emily?"

Shuddering in her jean jacket, Jessica finally confessed. "Prostitution."

*

"Prostitution?" Lacey said, brushing her hair as quickly as she could. Victor was behind her, arms folded and nodding. Morning light had broken through the small bathroom's window just a half hour earlier, when Lacey sprang out of bed after getting a text from Geo at Trend.

"Crazy, right?" Victor said.

"Is that… how she got pregnant, I'm assuming?"

Again, Victor nodded. "She doesn't know by whom. She was often drunk or drugged up to get through her 'sessions.'"

"That is so tragic," Lacey said, setting down the brush in exchange for lipstick. She rubbed it across her full lips, and added, "You say Geo had something to do with it?"

"Yep." He paused. "That's a great color on you."

Lacey grabbed her tube of mascara and started brushing the black stuff on her lashes, accentuating their almond shape. "I-I'm shocked."

"Why? Red has always looked good on you."

Lacey turned to peer at him over a shoulder. "Not about the makeup. *Jessica*."

"Oh. Right. And the fact that Rebecca and Emily somehow play a part in this big puzzle is surprising, too, right?"

"Yes," Lacey said. "It's always the people who fly under the radar who are most guilty, it seems. Of course those girls would blame Teddy. Of course." Her thoughts drifted back to Geo. "And Jack's photographer just seems to get creepier in retrospect. He *did* sound jealous of Jessica... and Brittany. We need to follow up on this. I'll confront Geo today, once I'm done with my job."

Victor shook his head and stepped over to the window, peering out. "I don't know if that's a good idea."

"Why? What are you thinking? Too obvious?"

"Yes. That's why you have a ghost as your teammate, remember? I am the figurative fly on the wall." He turned back to her. "Let me do some digging around. I'm not sure how long I'll be. Just sit tight."

Lacey huffed, not liking to be left out of the excitement. "What can I do? Anything? Oh, maybe I should confront Rebecca and Emily again."

Victor pursed his lips. "And you know where to find them?"

Lacey nodded, and skillfully applied her eyeliner. When she finished, she turned her head to either side, examining her makeup. "It'll have to do," she said before quickly stashing her cosmetics and making for the living room. "Those girls were regulars at the little cafe I used to work at," she called back to Victor. "The only problem is that I might be in the middle of a shoot at their usual time. Maybe I can get Geo to bump things back a bit while I wait for our ladies."

Victor shrugged. "Suit yourself. Just don't go doing anything dangerous. Again."

Lacey leveled a flat stare at him. "This is why I'm not looking to marry anytime soon, Victor."

He screwed his face up. "Because you'd rather gamble with your life?"

She threw her hands up. "Because I don't want a man mollycoddling me as if I'm some baby just because he's my husband and feels the need to protect me. I *don't* need protection."

Victor folded his hands behind his back and looked at her wordlessly until several unpleasant memories of their last time together flitted through her head. "Okay, fine," she huffed. "I can use a little help now and again. Just don't treat me like I'm ignorant or incompetent."

Victor drifted to her, stopping so close their noses nearly touched. "Lacey Ling, I've dated stupid, incompetent girls. You are *nothing* like them. When I bought that ring—"

"From Wal-Mart online," Lacey muttered.

"Yes, when I thoughtlessly bought a ring from the wrong place, I did it because I knew I'd found someone extremely intelligent and capable."

He paused, gazing thoughtfully at her. "Heaven is a place of unspeakable beauty, Lacey. You'd fit in perfectly there. One thing we learn very quickly, in Heaven, is that, with so much *ugliness* in this world," and he gestured around them, "things of beauty are to be cherished, sought, and, yes, protected.

"Your beauty," he continued, "is more than just that makeup, or what you wear. Your beauty is in your heart, your kindness. Your willingness to sacrifice yourself for the good of others—which is exactly what drives you to investigate murders."

He looked longingly at her. "You don't know just how valuable you are, Lacey. And if I fail as your guardian, especially through neglect, then they might as well damn me. Because Heaven wouldn't be Heaven if I knew I couldn't see you there, or if you got there because I let you suffer."

Lacey found she couldn't breathe. A single tear pooled in her eye, but she wiped it away before it could damage her mascara. For a long moment she looked at Victor, remembering the tender moments they'd shared both when he had lived, and then again after he had died.

At last, she caught her breath. "Thank you," she said softly, reaching up to stroke his ethereal face. "Thank you for believing in me."

"Always and forever, Lacey." His smile turned impish. "Now go tear up that runway, and show them how Lacey Ling does things. And good luck finding your girls. I'll let you know what I find."

She smiled and nodded once, resolutely, before turning for the door.

Lacey would show the modeling world just how things were done.

TWENTY-SIX

"No, no, and, let me check again... no," Geo said, eyeing the clipboard he was holding.

Lacey was posing on a box, in one of Trend's studios, a fake palm tree overhead while a beach ball hid the box from the camera. White sand had been piled up around the scene, and a fan, just outside the camera's view, played at her hair and the loose beach attire she was in.

She still struggled not to squint in the intense lighting, but the diffusers and a little additional makeup under her eyes made it easier, and even she was pleased with the shots she'd been in this morning. Things had gone well enough that, when the time arrived that she'd wanted to leave to intercept Emily and Rebecca, she'd asked Geo whether she could cut out for an hour or two. Needless to say, he wasn't helping her pack.

"Look," she said calmly, "I've got another appointment—"

"Honey," he snapped, "I *know* you've had other jobs. How many of *those* jobs just let you walk out whenever you liked? I don't know about you, but in my world, deadlines matter. Do you have any idea just how much inventory we have to get through? Or how far we are behind?"

Lacey put her hands on her hips. "Look, I'm fine working extra hours to help with the deadline. I just need two hours off. Change my clothes, quick trip into town, come back, and get prettied up again. How hard can that be?"

Geo stalked directly toward her and jabbed a finger at her chest. "You leave, and I'll make sure Beals fills your spot by tomorrow. We picked you because we saw professionalism and talent. Right now, you're proving us wrong. You sure you want to do that, honey? Maybe Jack Beals is a nice guy, but he's the face of Trend. He doesn't have to deal with the ugly side of what makes a business actually work. When do you see *him* behind a camera? Or rearranging props, or directing a crew? I don't think he appreciates how much I do as his little work whore."

Lacey narrowed her eyes at him, and Geo stopped, face flushing. He cleared his throat loudly and refused to meet her gaze. He snapped his fingers in the direction of some of the studio crew. "Mike. Steve. Clarissa. Let's get set up for the Tuscan shoot. I need every last grain of sand *gone* in ten minutes. Suck it up with your mouth if you can't find a vacuum or broom. Chop, chop!" He clapped his hands twice and headed for the dressing rooms.

"Ling," he called over his shoulder, "you're doing that shoot, too. You and the other new girl. Let's get to it."

Lacey perked up. "Other new girl?"

Geo didn't answer, but, instead, power-walked with his usual hip sway off the set, leaving Lacey to fume slightly.

No matter, she told herself. *I can play this game better than he can.*

*

The dressing room was controlled chaos. A dozen girls in various states of undress scurried about, several parked in front of mirrors, peering at themselves while hastily applying makeup. The whir of hairdryers competed with the call of commands, summoning girls to this studio or that. The air seemed to have more hairspray than oxygen. Lacey had seen this kind of thing on television, but it was different to be *living* it. She felt so crowded, but noticed that no one seemed to have time to care about personal space or comfort. Hairstylists tugged, twisted, and yanked some girls' heads around, while the girls themselves sat stoically in chairs. Other girls were able to shed formal gowns quicker than on prom night, and replaced them with swimwear in mere moments; some didn't even bother to step behind the privacy partitions in the process.

The sheer energy of the room was both dizzying and exhilarating, and she wondered what she had gotten herself into. Then she remembered so many days on the newsroom floor, or in various press conferences; the same level of vitality had marked her time as a reporter. Switching into "business mode," she immediately went to work, reporting directly to the stylist Geo had assigned her.

The moment she sat in her chair and began undoing her blouse, she heard a gasp. Her eyes whipped up to see a stunning redhead—her hair still being styled—sitting next to her. It was the girl from the coffee shop.

"You work *here*?" the girl asked. "I thought you were just a barista."

Lacey searched for the girl's name for a moment, then realized that she wouldn't have known it had Victor not eavesdropped on the girl's conversation with the cops. Instead, she smiled and waved. "Yep. Little career change. The coffee shop was just for fun after I left my last job. Hi," she said, extending a hand. "I'm Lacey."

The girl's eyes narrowed thoughtfully while her stylist twirled her red locks around a curling iron. "Lacey?" At once, awe crossed her face. "Lacey— like, that reporter woman from KZTB? Lacey *Ling*?"

A few heads turned briefly in her direction, but Lacey ignored the looks; she'd gotten used to them long since. She nodded.

"Oh... my... *gosh*! I can't believe that *Lacey Ling* was serving *my* mochaccino! And now I get to *model* with her! Oh, Emily is going to be *so* jealous."

"Emily?" Lacey tested. A stylist stepped up behind her and pressed against her lower back, a gesture telling Lacey to sit taller. Lacey complied instantly, her head tilting back enough to allow easy access to the hair pins.

The redhead nodded. "Emily, my friend. She always came with me to the coffee shop, so you met her, too."

"I'm sorry," Lacey said, as her stylist went to work on a coif, "I didn't catch your name."

The girl blushed. "Oh, sorry. Rebecca. Just don't call me 'Becky'. That's what my Dad always calls me, and it makes me feel like a little girl again."

"Rebecca, it's a pleasure to meet you."

Rebecca nodded, earning a frown and a rebuke from her stylist. "So how long have you been working here?"

Lacey closed her mouth and eyes as a makeup artist powdered her face. When the artist finished, she replied, "This is my first day."

"Really?" Rebecca said. "Mine too. But I bet you didn't need to apply for their scholarship to get in. I'm sorry I didn't notice it at the coffee shop, but you are *gorgeous*."

Lacey smiled gently. "For a plus size, I suppose."

Rebecca scoffed. "You are *nothing* like fat. Not like these thunder thighs," and she gestured at her legs. I practically had to beg to get in here."

Lacey allowed her stylist to turn her head, and waited patiently while some styling work was done. When she was able to look at Rebecca again, she replied, "You said something about a scholarship. Aside from the fact that you're beautiful, I imagine you must have the GPA to back it up if you're getting a scholarship."

Rebecca opened her mouth to reply, but Geo stormed in. "Let's go, let's go, let's *go*! Tuscan shoot in three, Studio A; San Marcos in seven, Studio B. Let's *move,* people!"

Both Lacey and Rebecca's stylists quickly applied finishing touches, and both of them were handed their new outfits. They both donned them quickly and, while Lacey buttoned up Rebecca's dress, the college student glanced over her shoulder. In hushed tones, she said, "Hey, maybe it's super forward of me, but we're having a party tonight, up on the north end of the peninsula. You could *totally* come join us. I mean, if you wanted. I mean, I know you're *Lacey Ling.* I still can't believe I didn't recognize you sooner."

Knowing Nainai would be safe with her new nurse, and unwilling to ignore an investigative opportunity that had dropped right in her lap, Lacey nodded and smiled. "Actually, that sounds fun. You can count me in."

*

The rest of the day was a drawn-out blur. Lacey was poked, prodded, and primped more times than she cared to count, as she moved from studio to studio, changing clothing and makeup the way couch potatoes changed the channel. Dinnertime had passed when Geo finally called it, and Lacey was ready to drop into bed. She'd heard how demanding modeling could be, but nothing had prepared her for the endless spells of standing perfectly still under glaring light, or wishing you could sweat but being mortified of it at the same time, nor the apparent disregard for personal space. As she tottered across the street toward her car on cramped legs, she wondered how long she wanted to continue this.

"Hey, Lacey!"

Lacey finished crossing, then pivoted to see Rebecca waving at her from across the street. She smiled and waved back, though the move hurt her face, and it bothered her to realize that every part of her ached at least a little. It had definitely been a long day of work. Still, she held her smile until the perky redhead had cleared the crosswalk.

"So, uh," Rebecca began, glancing everywhere but at Lacey, and tucking a strand of hair behind her head, "did you, uh, still want to, you know, go to that party I mentioned earlier?"

Lacey smiled again. She wanted nothing more than to drive carefully home and sleep for ten hours, but this was a lead she didn't feel she could pass up; Rebecca seemed to know a startling amount about more things than she rightfully should. "Sure. Should I just follow you? I'm parked right over there," and she gestured a little further down the pier. "Where are you parked?"

Even in the dark, Lacey could see the redhead blush. "Yeah, I don't have a car, so…"

Lacey grinned. "Don't worry. We'll take mine."

Rebecca's eyes whipped up. "Are you *serious*?"

Lacey nodded and headed for her car, her fellow model trailing her like an affectionate kitten.

TWENTY-SEVEN

Standing outside Lacey's dressing room, Victor felt mortified, which, he noted, wasn't a terribly hard place to reach as a guardian angel. He'd followed Lacey to work, and then watched her shoots, telling himself he was there to find the photographer Lacey called "Geo."

Without thinking through the implications, he'd followed her to the changing areas after her first shoot. He was out the door against in a flash, wondering whether he'd be allowed into Heaven again after seeing what went on in there, and with so many babes.

Eventually, he managed to convince himself he was overreacting, and after a brief conversation with Rao, was assured that he hadn't inadvertently put himself on the "naughty list" with the Big Man. He was just coming to terms with his mistake when the little, flamboyantly-dressed photographer stormed out of the dressing room, still calling over his shoulder. "Let's go, let's go, let's *go*! Tuscan shoot in three, Studio A; San Marcos in seven, Studio B. Let's *move,* people!"

A gaggle of cronies trailed in his wake. Victor picked out their thoughts easily. Two were interns, both desperate to make a good impression so they could land a job somewhere, one was a new hire who practically *sweat* desperation and was so concerned about not offending Geo and losing his job that he almost couldn't walk straight. Only one of the photographer's entourage seemed to have any real experience, and they were simultaneously nervous, bored, and eager.

Geo, for his part, was a tornado of thought. Victor wondered whether Geo were actually even male. He shook the thoughts away and followed the man through the hall and into a lavishly-appointed, if small, office on the second floor. A desk, buried under a mountain of photos of more women than Victor had ever known in his life, occupied the center of the room. Behind it was a kneeling chair, something Victor had only ever seen pictures of, but never actually used. Clocks and calendars fought with autographed images of various celebrities and a 48-inch television for wall space. A disheveled row of binders seemed ready to burst off the shelving behind the desk, and, to round out the chaos, a pair of potted plants and a parakeet rounded out the scene.

"Not sure how you can work in this, dude, but hey. More power to you. I know a guy who can get you a good deal on some used parakeets." He laughed, remembering the warehouse full of them that Lacey's former boss had once owned.

Geo froze, his eyes narrowing suspiciously. He cocked his head ever so slightly and, at once, his mind seemed to blank. Slowly, he turned his head to either side, then straightened

Victor would have held his breath had he had any to hold. Something seemed to slither through him, and he felt as though he were suddenly standing naked in Seattle's Winterfest Ice Rink. Something inside warned him to leave, but he had no idea why, other than the fact that things had just turned creepy. Cautiously, he drifted toward the door, but stopped when Geo jerked open a desk drawer, causing a cascade of photographs to spill onto the floor. The images caught his eye and froze him in his tracks. Staring back at him from the dull, matte prints were dozens of girls in various states of undress and a variety of poses, all of which made him cringe more than anything he'd stumbled across in the dressing room. Without fail, all of them looked dazed, and most had desperation clear in their eyes. He found he was able to feel every moment of whatever sadness they'd endured in whatever events surrounded the various photographs, and his heart sank lower than he thought possible.

Cries and moans echoed through his mind, and the whole room seemed to turn gray. "Save us," he heard in his mind. "Please. Anyone." And suddenly, he was in a hundred different, filthy hotels rooms, feeling as though his mind were nothing more than a cloud of smoke, vaguely aware that his body was being put to a use he didn't want to think about. He tried to pull away, but every face of every girl seemed to twist a strand of sorrow and disgust around his mind that bound him like steel cables. He sank to his knees as the room began spinning. He heard a hiss of static, followed by slurred voices. Barely able to raise his head, he wished he hadn't. Geo had turned on the TV. Darkness oozed from the screen as scenes of unspeakable perversions played out across it; Victor felt powerless to look away.

Legion.

The sibilant whisper was as chilling as it was unwelcome, and already he could sense the demons being drawn to the room, even during the daylight. From the corner of his eye, he saw Geo swiftly shut the door and mutter a few words that sent shivers through him.

"You know," Geo said, as though he were remarking on the color of his shoes, "something always struck me as a little... off... about that Ling chick. Jack made a mistake hiring her, and he'll regret it, even if I have to see to it myself. For now, whoever you are, enjoy the show. And my friends. "

The little man stepped into Victor's field of view, but not enough to block the TV screen. Victor felt small, strangled, and hopeless. The television played mindlessly on, showing the inner light of one beautiful girl after another being carelessly extinguished by men who seemed to care nothing for them as anything but easy pleasure. Geo pulled a small plastic baggy from his back pocket; Victor didn't have to read the man's mind to know what the powdery white substance inside was.

"Oh, don't worry," Geo said. "This is for the girls. You don't think they do that because they really *like* it, do you?" He chuckled darkly. "Jack likes to sell this place as a friendly modeling agency, but there are times when I have to... compensate for his lacking."

He leaned in close and looked Victor straight in the eyes. "It's funny what making a deal with the devil can do. Like let you see careless angels who think they're so sneaky just because they're no longer physical. Oh, the drugs help, but between you and me, there are better ways to get high."

A woman on the TV moaned, and then cried out a name. Victor's insides clenched; he knew that voice. There, on the screen, was none other than Jessica Simcox. Gone was the gorgeous, self-satisfied woman who had once captured his eye only to tear out his heart. Any bad feelings he'd harbored after the way she'd once mistreated him evaporated. He couldn't hate her; not when he saw, heard, and felt what he somehow knew to be part of the final hours of her life. He trembled, and Geo smirked.

"Seems like you might know more than one of our little dolls, hmm? Well, let's take a little sashay down memory lane." He fetched a remote and pressed a button twice; Victor saw a "repeat track" icon flash on the screen.

Unable to turn away, Victor began weeping openly, vaguely aware of Geo bustling around the room, arranging things and muttering in a strange, guttural tongue. The hosts of Legion flitted through the wall, and what sounded like a jail cell door slamming closed echoed through Victor's mind.

Geo reappeared before him. "Didn't they ever tell you why Heaven has such strict rules, little Mister Angel? It's because it derives strength from goodness and structure. Well, in my world, that's all relative. And now that you're seeing the flip side of things, maybe you'll want to think again about who you work for. After all, He didn't stop any of this from happening," and he gestured toward the screen.

Victor heard him open the door and step into the hallway. "Oh," he called back. "In case you think of following me, well, I'm too busy to be bothered by avenging angels today, so you just keep watching my little version of daytime television. Because, guess what? One day, it might be your cute little Miss Ling who ends up there. Toodles." With that, he shut the door.

Rage hammered through Victor, and his jaw clenched hard enough to bite through steel. "*No!*" Surging to his feet, Victor hurled himself toward the door, only to find himself unable to turn, as though he were swimming in tar. Pictures of Geo's horrible deeds were everywhere.

And at once, Legion was on him.

TWENTY-EIGHT

"Wow," Rebecca said for probably the hundredth time since she'd first seen Lacey's Lincoln. "I *love* this car. I can't believe I'm riding with *Lacey Ling*! That is *so* cool!"

The adulation had worn Lacey's nerves thin within the first thirty seconds of the twenty-minute drive. Though she'd long since become accustomed to the status of being a minor local celebrity, the way this girl *fawned* over her had graduated from "merely annoying" to "if I weren't so nice, I'd have shoved you out of my moving car by now." Still, something deeper was bothering her. She hadn't heard a peep out of Victor since he'd taken off; that wasn't in line with his "faithful puppy" act, though, if she thought about it, he *had* been gone for the better part of a day when he'd been tracking Teddy down. Biting back her concern, she returned her thoughts to the girl rambling beside her. Lacey *was* kind, though, and took it in stride, trying not to panic as the redhead gave nothing but last-second driving directions.

Her lack of familiarity with the Lawton Wood area demanded she pay close attention to the road; that did nothing to help her nerves. Though she suspected the place was probably lovely during daylight hours, it felt forbidding and constricted now, with hints of houses hiding behind trees and hedges, and tight streets winding through a never-ending maze of conifers. Lacey found she was having difficulty breathing.

"Oh, oh!" Rebecca called suddenly. "Turn here. *Here.*"

Lacey resisted the instinct to crank the wheel hard, knowing she'd probably wind up colliding with a tree if she turned so tightly. Instead, she slowed the car, and, noting she'd missed her turn, carefully reversed and made her way onto the choked side street, though she realized the road wasn't actually any tighter than any other road in the area.

"Okay," Rebecca said, leaning forward in her seat and gesturing, "just follow this road around and we'll park. It's a bit of a walk after that. I'm glad you've got your coat."

Lacey turned a critical eye on her passenger. "Walk? Where are we going?"

Rebecca swallowed, but feigned a smile. "You'll see. It'll be great. And *totally* what we need after today. *Ugh.* Can that Geo guy get *any* worse? His face is probably online under the definition of 'creeper'."

Lacey blew out a breath. "Tell me about it."

Moments later, a parking lot next to what appeared to be some kind of Native American museum came into view. "Here we are," the redhead said.

Lacey parked, noting a handful of other vehicles of various makes and models. Given that the museum was clearly closed, she surmised the other vehicles probably belonged to whomever Rebecca intended to meet her. Parking, she emerged into the frosty evening and pulled her hood tight around her head. She grimaced; there was something even more chilling in the air than the usual December cold. Even the moonlight seemed strangely subdued, though when she looked at it, it wasn't hidden behind any clouds. She wondered whether she should call Victor. No—she wasn't about to go back on everything she'd said about being able to handle herself. And besides—she'd be with a group of college kids. Not four months ago, she'd literally chased down a murderer and come out okay in the end. Shuddering again, she told herself she'd be fine.

The ginger hopped out of the car as well, and waved toward an opening in the fence edging the parking lot. "C'mon. I can't *wait* to introduce you to everyone. They'll be *so* jealous." She hurried toward the fence, then stopped suddenly. "Oh—um, can I ask you a favor?"

Lacey avoided rolling her eyes. "What's that?"

"Could you, you know, act like we're BFFs?"

Lacey officially felt used now. "Let's go meet your friends," she said flatly.

The sorority girl had the decency to blush, and led them on into the woods.

"Where are you going?" Lacey asked after a minute.

"Just to our little hangout. It's pretty cool."

Stepping over frosted brush and twigs, Lacey pushed some branches out of her way. Soon the glow of a campfire came into view. They headed straight for it. The distant sound of laughter mingling meshed into indiscernible words echoing in the night.

They came to a circle of friends, two other girls and two guys. A ramshackle old home was nearby, the small porch's overhang cracked and bowing. Lacey wasn't too surprised a bunch of young twenty-somethings might find the location "cool." Although she was still in her twenties, she'd passed this particular phase long ago, if she ever actually had one.

"Hey, it's Rebecca!" The girl Lacey knew was Emily sprang up from her seated position beside the large, crackling fire. She rushed over and nearly tackled her in the hug. "I was starting to worry you wouldn't make it. I was going to send the guys to look for you. And, oh—" She halted at the sight of Lacey. "You brought... barista girl?"

That's what she thinks of me as? Lacey asked herself, playing off the inadvertent insult.

"Yes," Rebecca replied evenly. "Don't you *recognize* her?"

Emily squinted, her eyes gleaming slightly in the firelight. Something in her gaze seemed off, and the pall of smoke that hung on the air was already threatening to make Lacey cough; she wondered what these kids had been up to.

"Yeah," Emily said finally. "It's… our old barista. I guess that's cool." She staggered slightly as she crossed to her redheaded friend, and then, out of the corner of her mouth, testily muttered, "*Rebecca*, this is *our* secret place." From the looks of it, Lacey got the impression the girl thought Lacey hadn't been able to hear her. The reporter-turned-model brushed a hand through her hair and shot glances at the others, still sitting, who were whispering to each other.

Rebecca shrugged and turned a knowing smile toward Lacey that seemed to say, "I guess we've got our own little secret, too." Lacey forced a smile in return and tried to relax. She hadn't known quite what to expect, but it hadn't been barely-veiled hostility.

"She's cool, guys," Rebecca said, trying to act casual. "She works with me at Trend. She models, too."

"She *does*?" Emily said as if truly surprised, and that rubbed Lacey the wrong way, but she bit her tongue as it didn't really matter what they thought of her. But somewhere, oddly—must've been deep, deep within—she found she did care. Emily added, "Okay, um… let's just relax." She slipped something into her pocket that Lacey couldn't quite see.

For a long moment, the crackle of the fire was the only thing that broke the silence of the night. Emily mostly glared at her friend and stole quick, unpleasant glances at Lacey, but the guys couldn't seem to take their eyes off her. Lacey hated when anyone did that, especially men. She stood her ground, resisting the urge to shift her weight. As long as she convinced herself she was in command, she could hold the initiative here. At last, one of the guys, a pale kid with long blond hair and black skinny jeans, piped up, "Hey. You're that reporter chick."

Lacey shrugged like it didn't matter. She had to act, play the part of being one with them now, if she wanted to win their trust and learn about this alleged prostitution business going down. "I'm doing the modeling thing now. I'm not into reporting. Kind of burnt out with that. So how's it going?" she said, taking a seat on an empty log beside him. He sat up at once and edged closer to her. Lacey braced herself, waiting for him to decide it was time to make a move. Thankfully, he kept his hands to himself.

"Okay," Emily said. "Well, welcome." She forced a smile again but was clearly wary.

Rebecca, right away, sat beside Lacey, perking up again. Emily took her place next to a dark-haired guy wearing a hoodie and puffy winter vest. He seemed a little old for her, in his early thirties at least, and he gazed at Lacey too long for comfort. "Does Geo think she's cool?" he asked Rebecca.

The ginger nodded vigorously, and reached behind her, popping open a small cooler Lacey hadn't seen until now. She drew out a couple of bottles and handed one to Lacey. "Ice cold. But then, what else would it be out here?" The blond guy laughed, but everyone else sat in strained silence.

Lacey shook her head. "Someone's got to drive us home tonight."

Rebecca paused in thought, then nodded. "Right. Yeah. Good thinking. Hey, everyone? Lacey's our designated driver tonight." The guys murmured something like approval, but Emily merely shifted on her log, burrowing into the older man as if trying to prove a point.

At last, the dark-haired guy broke the renewed silence. "Emily. Pass the goods."

"You gonna share 'em?" the blond guy asked, laughing at his failed attempt at humor.

"Hold on, hold on," Emily said, stealing a quick look at Lacey again. "Rebecca," she said, "are you *sure* Geo's good with her? I mean, you know…" She let her words hang in the air.

Rebecca rolled her eyes. "*Trust* me on this one. She's *so* cool it's not even funny. You just need to get to know her a bit. She won't tell anyone about this place." She glanced at Lacey. "Right?"

Lacey drew an "X" across her chest. "Cross my heart and hope to die. Stick a needle in my eye."

It was Emily's turn to roll her eyes. "OMG," she said, and Lacey had to contain a laugh that the girl had actually spelled it out. "That is *so* junior high."

And you're not? Lacey retorted mentally.

"Fine," Emily said in a huff. "But none for *her*," and she gestured at Lacey, then, in a sugary tone, said, "Can't hurt the designated driver, can we? Besides, she can get her own from Geo."

Lacey wondered what had happened to Emily since the last time she'd seen her. The girl had been so nervous and shy that the person before her seemed to be someone else entirely, merely wearing an "Emily" mask. But when the brunette pulled a small pouch filled with white powder from her jacket, things started to click. She decided a little play acting was in order. "Hey—no fair. He never gave *me* any. Pass it over. I want to take it home."

Emily glowered at her, and even Rebecca seemed a little less enthralled. "I said pass some over," Lacey repeated. "How do I know you didn't talk him into giving you my share?"

Emily clung tightly to the bag and turned her glare on her friend. "I thought you said Little Miss Espresso was cool. What's going on?"

Rebecca chuckled nervously. "She's new. Newer than me. Maybe Geo just forgot to give her some? I mean, maybe he hasn't, you know... set her up with... clients."

"*Shhhh.*" Emily came up off her log, fangs bared and claws out. "Shut *up*!"

Rebecca scowled in return, and muttered, "Well, she's going to get them sooner or later. Not my fault Geo's not doing his job right."

"I said *shut up.*"

The two friends stared each other down, neither giving any sign of relenting. Thick moments passed until the dark-haired guy cleared his throat loudly. "Gotta pee. Be right back."

The rest of the evening passed with less apprehension than it had begun with, especially as the beer flowed freely and the bag of powder made the rounds. The dark-haired guy pulled out a guitar and, with their inhibitions gone, the U of W students sang loudly and stupidly. The guys made off-color remarks about the girls, and the girls fired right back. Lacey, still in possession of herself, pretended to laugh along, even while she cringed inside, especially when the dark-haired guy and Emily decided to find out, at length, how one another's tongues tasted. They retreated into the teetering shack to crude jibes from the blond guy, and Lacey was more than happy to let them go. When Rebecca and the blond guy began getting cozy themselves, Lacey nearly decided to walk, but aside from the fact that she still hoped for some useful information—which hardly seemed forthcoming—she worried that if she left now, she'd be at least partially responsible for four intoxicated college students on the road.

I just hope no one pukes in my car, she thought sourly. So she stood and stretched, and paced around the fire while Rebecca nuzzled the guy.

In the middle of their fun, the blond guy spoke up. "So, whatever happened to Shayla?"

Lacey froze for a moment, then continued walking, eager to hear more, but concerned that showing obvious interest might deflect the conversation.

"Well," Rebecca began slowly, "she, uh, went home for Christmas break."

"That's not what she told me," the guy said. "I mean, she wasn't going to leave until the twenty-third."

"Do we really have to talk about Shayla right now?"

"Yeah." He moved away from Rebecca just enough to look at her. "She kisses *way* better than you."

Rebecca gasped, and drilled a fist into his arm.

"What?" he asked, laughing. "She totally does. I mean, it's like she took classes for it and got an A."

Rebecca hit him again and pouted. "You are so stupid."

"Then prove to me you can earn an A-plus."

Before Rebecca could take him up, Lacey sat next to them. "So what *did* happen to Shayla? I never got to meet her."

Both her companions stopped and stared at her as if she'd appeared out of nowhere. Then the guy's eyes widened, and he smiled to match it. "I bet *you* got an A-plus in that class."

Rebecca pouted again, but looked torn. She flicked her gaze at the blond guy, then back to Lacey again. "Okay, *fine*. I wasn't supposed to tell you this, but since you and I will probably get the chance now that we're working for Trend, I guess it's okay.

"Geo sent her, and a bunch of other girls, on a Christmas cruise. That's what he called it. She told me how he arranged for them to all meet at someone's house, and then they were going to take a bus down to the port and get on the ship."

Lacey frowned. "Why not just go straight to the pier? It's right there."

Rebecca huffed. "*I* don't know. That's just what she told me, alright? And I asked to go, and Shayla was all, like, 'Nuh-uh. Trend models only.' And I was like, 'Well, fine. I don't need your stupid cruise anyway.' But she decided to rub it in by showing me the place they were going to meet, before the cruise. I totally shouldn't have gone. That place was *so* nice."

Lacey perked up instantly. "Wait—you saw the place Shayla was supposed to go to meet up for the cruise?"

Rebecca rolled her eyes. "*Duh*. I just *said* that."

Peering hard, Lacey asked, "Do you think you could find it again?"

Rebecca's face fell, and she looked down as if in thought. Lacey wasn't sure how well the girl could think, though, as glassy-eyed as she looked. The blond guy squirmed on his seat, obviously impatient to get on with his teasing and with his clear expectations for time with Rebecca, but Lacey had to know.

"Maybe in the morning?" she offered. "After you've slept on it?"

Rebecca squinted, clearly uneasy. "Maybe," she said slowly, then turned pleading eyes back to Lacey. "Can we not talk about this anymore? Let's just have fun."

Lacey faked an accommodating smile. "Sure. Sorry. You just made it sound like so much fun, you know? I thought it might be nice to get a sneak preview of what Geo has in mind."

"Well, if you *really* want to know," Rebecca said, standing slightly, then repositioning herself in her male friend's lap, "you could just talk to Geo.

Just don't go in his office; that place is a *mess*. It's no wonder he keeps it locked. I went in there once, and it just gave me the creeps, all those pictures everywhere. I mean, he's so neat and tidy at work, but a slob in his own office."

"I know, right?" Lacey agreed, hoping to stimulate the conversation. But Rebecca was already leaning in on the blond, and he obliged her fully, despite his earlier remarks. Conversation died in the pyre of a backwoods makeout, and Lacey sighed and turned for the woods, where she could be alone with her thoughts.

She'd spent plenty of time in the forest of the Puget Sound; you couldn't really live in the greater Seattle area and not be at least somewhat a part of them. There was, however, a distinct difference between the beautiful, filtered-green light that made summer daytime walks so serene, and the ominous, skeletal fingers that clawed at the sky as she looked overhead just then. She told herself it was just her mind playing tricks, but something inside her said otherwise; she still hadn't figured much out about anything—who actually killed anyone, what Teddy's part in this really was (and was he actually as innocent as he claimed?), why she'd utterly gone off script in a job interview, and so many other things. But at last, she had a lead—Geo. His office was easy enough to access, she was sure, locked or not. She hadn't been an investigative reporter for as long as she had without learning at least a few of the finer points of breaking and entering.

Knowing that Rebecca wouldn't need a ride home

for a while, she set herself to planning. She had a killer to catch.

TWENTY-NINE

The following morning passed in a blur. Lacey felt like the love child of a clothing rack and a Formula One race car as she bounced from studio to studio. By the time what passed as a lunch break rolled around, she could barely see for all the camera flashes she'd stood through, notwithstanding the diffusers. While most of the girls filed out the dressing room door in search of local eateries, Lacey stayed behind, surreptitiously keeping an eye on Jack Beals' head photographer while she pretended to slowly change back into her street clothes. When the moment was right, she caught his eyes.

"Don't even ask," he said.

Lacey turned innocent eyes on him. "What do you think I was going to ask?"

He waved it away. "You want me to tell you you're skinny, beautiful, and God's gift to mankind. That's why you're not eating, isn't it? I'm so sick of these girls thinking that anything but water and tree leaves is going to make them balloon. Besides, you could weigh five hundred pounds and I could *still* make you look good enough to sell clothing. Even before Photoshop."

Lacey adopted a defeated look. "So you really *do* think I'm pretty?"

He turned and headed for the hall. "I told you not to ask. As for me, *I'm* going for lunch."

She swallowed hard, hoping her gamble would pay off. "But what about Jack's e-mail?"

"What e-mail?" he called over his shoulder, but he pulled out his phone and began scrolling through it. She'd expected that, and moved to part two.

"The one about my new keycard? Said you'd have a spare somewhere." She crossed her fingers, then quickly finished lacing her shoes and hurried after him. He sighed heavily, and gave her a half-suffering, half-disgusted look when she fell into step beside him.

"You mean to tell me that you couldn't keep track of a simple card for even twenty four hours? How often do you get locked out of your car, or apartment?"

Lacey's shoulders slumped, and her face fell just the right way. "It was an accident. I promise. I'm usually good…"

He stared flatly at her. "You're a real piece of work, Ling. You're just gorgeous enough that I don't tell Jack to toss you. But mark my words—you'd better tread lightly around here. And don't even *think* about asking for any perks any time soon."

She nodded sullenly but held her tongue. "So... can I get one? Like, now?"

His jaw fell. "Do I look like the genie of the lamp? *Hello*! 'Geo. Get me a new keycard. Geo, get my lunch, but make it non-fat, dairy and gluten free, and entirely organic. Geo, paint my nails. Geo, I want a new apartment because mine's just so lame.' For the love of *Mike*, woman, did you not *hear* what I said about treading lightly?"

She sulked further. "Just thought I'd ask," she muttered. "I think I'll go grab a pizza and a pint of ice cream."

"It had better not be on your face when you get back," he warned. "And if I see *any* pizza grease on my inventory after this afternoon, I'm coming after you."

Lacey rolled her eyes. "I got out of kindergarten a long time ago, Geo."

He sneered but left Lacey in his wake as he power-walked his hip-wiggling figure down the hall. Lacey waited what she thought was an appropriate amount of time, then stole after him. The tour Jack had given her was still mostly fresh in her mind, and the building wasn't terribly complex, but she couldn't quite recall which door Jack had pointed out as belonging to the chief photographer. And so, she let Geo give her a little reminder.

She turned a corner and stopped abruptly, and ducked back around the corner as he wheeled around to face her direction. But instead of coming back her way, he went up a flight of stairs. She broke cover and hurried after him, stalking him carefully until, at last, he stopped in front of a door, shoved a key into a lock, and shoved his door open. Lacey bit her lip and waited. Geo was in and out again in moments, palming a small white object that may have been a key card. He bustled back toward Lacey, who dove into an office just in time to escape notice.

When he had passed, she scanned the hall and, finding it clear, hurried to his office. She tried the knob—still locked, but not surprising. She fished a set of lock picks from her purse; she'd carried them for years, just for instances like this. Constantly scanning the hall, she defeated the lock in short order and pushed open his door. Before she even stepped in, every hair on her neck shot up, and her muscles tensed of their own accord. Her breathing suddenly became shallow, and she felt herself getting tunnel vision. She had no idea what was going on, but she knew she needed to get in and out as quickly as possible. And so she forced herself into the room.

What she saw inside nearly made her vomit.

*

Victor was no more. At least, he didn't *want* to exist anymore. Sorrow and pain such as he hadn't thought possible were all he knew, and he was somewhere deep and dark that showed a gleeful resolve to keep him perpetually smothered. He couldn't really think about it—couldn't think about anything, really—but he didn't want to. He just wanted to wink away into a faded memory. But he couldn't. And that was the worst torture of all.

From somewhere very far away came a faint... something... that seemed vaguely different than the monotonous, chaotic misery he'd become. It meant nothing to him, but it caught his attention just enough to form a thought: I exist.

The sensation came again, or so it seemed, and from his abyss of despair sprang another thought: I hope.

If only he could remember what that word actually meant.

THIRTY

Lacey knelt beside Victor—or at least she was pretty sure the translucent being shriveled on the floor in his T-shirt and blue jeans was her ex-boyfriend—and let the tears flow. She wanted to scream his name, but bit her tongue for fear of giving herself away; but between seeing Victor and the scores of filthy photographs strewn everywhere, it was all she could do *not* to scream and light the whole place on fire.

Instead, she somehow reined herself in, keeping her eyes fixated on the shrunken figure before her. "Victor?" she asked carefully. "Victor? Can you hear me?" He gave no sign of recognition, and she reached out to pick him up, only to be reminded that she couldn't, as her hands passed clean through him; they suddenly felt like ice. Shivers racked her, which only made her sense of being strangled all the worse.

She pushed it away, but the sensation eagerly crowded back on top of her.

"Victor, *please*," she hissed. "We need to get out of here, *now*. Geo could come back at any time. And this place is *wrong*." She reached for him again, but with the same results. Then she remembered something. A time, not four months ago, when she *had* been able to feel him. She thought back to her stay in the hospital, when Victor had been there every waking moment. And it was in one of those moments that she felt how much he truly *had* loved her. They'd shared a kiss that she hadn't forgotten— one that, despite him being immaterial, she had been physically able to *feel*.

It was almost nothing to go on, but it was something, and it would have to be enough. She leaned down, closed her eyes, and drew as deep a breath as she could manage. Then she kissed him. Or tried to, anyway. Her face wound up on the industrial grade carpet of Geo's office. Worse, her entire head felt as though she'd dunked it in an arctic lake, and her vision swam slightly. Somehow, she knew time was running out for both her and Victor.

She gritted her teeth. *Think, Lacey.* And then, like a man emerging from a fog carrying a lantern, it came to her—she had felt him during a moment that she truly cared for him. Calling to mind every good time, even warm kiss, every kind gesture he'd made for her, she felt her hands and head and even heart warm. She closed her eyes and let it flow over him, remembering how he'd saved her life before the autumn had even started to turn the leaves in Seattle. Then she leaned in again.

This time, there was still no feeling, but she caught something in the recesses of her mind; it was the scent of Victor's cologne on a warm summer's evening. If was the feel of her pressed up against him as they looked out over the sound at sunset. And she saw in her mind his face, turning toward her, his eyes slowly blinking open as though waking from a coma.

Lacey? His voice was the barest breeze in her mind, but it was definitely his.

"Victor?" she said, wishing she could shake him, or hold him, or pick him up off the floor and carry him away from this… this… she didn't have a word for it, but kept her focus on him instead. "Come back to me. It's Lacey. I'm here, now. Please, come back to me."

The face in her mind peered through her, but eventually, his eyes came into focus.

Lacey? Lacey, is that really you? All at once, he sounded tired, enormously depressed, and afraid. It made her tremble, but she kept her thoughts happy and trained on him.

"Come on back, hon. I need you." She felt a tear well in her eye, and felt her words in her heart. "I really do. Please don't leave me."

What seemed like a ray of sunlight blossomed in her mind, and she watched as it washed over Victor. His frame filled out, and his eyes came open for real and began to glint as he slowly craned his neck to look at her. She barely refrained from hugging him, but he reached out a ghostly hand and stroked her face. She still felt nothing, but the gesture was comforting. "Can you move, Victor?"

He wrinkled his brow in thought, and made to stand. He managed it, a little shakily, and then glanced around the room. Almost instantly, the light that had been growing in him began to die.

"Lacey," he croaked.

Not knowing what to do, she placed herself directly in front of him. "Keep your eyes on mine, Victor. I'm going to back out of here, and you're going to think of nothing but me and how much you love me. Got it?"

He nodded weakly and followed her into the hall. He halted momentarily at the doorframe, as though he were fighting through a wall of tar, but after a brief struggle, he broke out into the hallway. Sagging, he placed his hands on his knees; she found it strange that he wasn't panting like a dog, but remembered that spirits needn't breathe.

"Wh-what *happened*?" he said, a note of despair ringing in his voice.

"I don't know," she said, sucking in a deep breath herself, "but we don't have time for that. Just stay here. I need to get something super quick." With that, she dashed into Geo's office, snatched a few handfuls of photographs out of the cluttered pile on the floor, then all but sprinted back into the hall, leaving the TV showing whatever smut was on it; she had actively avoided looking as soon as she'd heard the moans and screams. She hazarded a glance at the photos she'd grabbed—yes; they were plenty enough to paint the ugly picture—and shoved them carefully into her jacket pocket, and pulled the door closed behind her, double checking to ensure it was latched.

"Come on," she said, breaking into a fast stride for the stairs on the far end of the building; she wasn't going to chance another meeting with Geo this close to his office. Victor fell, uneasily, in beside her, and while he actually looked alive again, his face was stricken, haunted.

"Everyone's out for lunch," she said, avoiding the questions she desperately wanted to ask, "but I don't know how long that will last. I'm already on his black list, and I know he's eager to shove me out the door as soon as he can find an excuse. I can't let this go when I'm *this* close."

She gestured at her bag. "I'm taking these to Jack; it's not enough to convince the cops, but I'm sure he'll know what to do when he finds out his right-hand man is involved in a prostitution ring." She shuddered at the thought. "I can't believe Jessica got pulled into that. That's... that's *terrible*." They reached the stairwell door, and she pushed it open.

She felt, more than saw, Victor's shudder. He mumbled something.

Lacey glanced at him as she jogged down the stairs, Victor drifting sullenly, and half-listlessly, nearby. "What was that?"

"She was on TV," he whispered.

Lacey frowned. "Who was on what T—" she halted abruptly, comprehension dawning on her. She turned to Victor, and the confirmation was clear in his sad, deep eyes. Jessica Simcox's humiliation had been captured on film. Lacey's throat tightened, and she whipped out her phone, scanning the stairwell for any sign of anyone else. She unlocked the phone and hammered a number in, and paused until it rang. "C'mon, c'mon," she breathed. "Jack, please."

"This is Jack," said his voice on the other end of the line.

"Jack, I'm *so* glad you—"

"Sorry I couldn't take your call. Wait for the beep. You know what to do. Ciao."

She ground her teeth and growled, shoving her phone back in her bag. "I'll just have to find him myself," she murmured. Pursing her lips, she finally took a moment to think. She twisted to face Victor, and immediately felt her breath catch. Though he still had somewhat of a glow to him, his expression was still one of unbridled sadness. She'd seen him on his bad days, back when he was alive, but those days were rare; and he'd never really had one, as best she knew, since he'd died. Or, at least, certainly not since moving on to Heaven. She stepped to him and placed a hand over his cheek.

"Victor, what's wrong?"

He answered only with another look of unfathomable sorrow.

"Please," she said. "Let me help you."

He shook his head slowly and looked upward. "I… I don't think you can. I don't even know if *I* can." He turned those sad eyes on her again. "I—I can't feel Heaven anymore. I think I've been cut off."

Lacey gasped. "But, *how*?"

His eyes unfocused again, and he hung his head. "Maybe one day I'll tell you what happened in there." He paused. "But probably not. For now, I need some time alone, and in a place of peace." He locked eyes with her, and his face grew blurry through Lacey's tears. "I'm going to have to leave you for a while, Lacey, while I figure out what's wrong with me. This—this is… 'bad' doesn't even begin to describe it. Some guardian angel I turned out to be."

With that, he turned toward the nearest wall. She called after him, but he only shook his head once more, slowly. Defeated. He stopped just before disappearing through the wall, then glanced over his shoulder. "Thank you, Lacey," he said simply. "You saved me. Hopefully, one day, I can return the favor." And then he was gone.

Lacey stood, staring at the wall for a long time, breaking her stare only when the door clicked next to her and a secretary gasped in surprise at seeing a speechless model with her eyes glued to the wall. Lacey made a hasty apology and moved aside.

Her hands curled deliberately into fists. Fists she would, if necessary, use to dispense justice. She would see to it that Geo would *rot* for his crimes, both against Heaven and Earth.

And against the man she had once loved.

THIRTY-ONE

Lacey spotted Jack just outside the lobby mere minutes after Victor had left her. *He left me.* The thought made her heart hitch, but she kept the sadness from her eyes. Would she see her guardian angel again any time soon? He had looked so... lost. What was Heaven doing? Why was he feeling disconnected from God? The same questions attacked her mind even as she knew she needed to chat with Jack. Like, now.

"What's wrong?" Jack asked, hurrying to her and taking her gently by the shoulders. His jaw was set, and his searching eyes seemed to carry a determination to understand.

She shook her head. "It's... it's nothing. Nothing I can talk about here, anyway. But we *do* need to talk about this. And the sooner the better."

Jack's forehead bunched. "My office, or," and he glanced around the lobby, which was beginning to fill with people returning from lunch, "no. My car. They can handle things without me for a while."

She thanked him with her eyes, and he led her to his car and held the door for her. For the next hour, they drove the streets of Seattle while Lacey unloaded everything that had happened to her. She told him of Geo, the smut, the drug deals—even the creepy feeling she got when she was around him. The scowl on Jack's face grew deeper and deeper until Lacey thought it might be permanently etched there. When she finished, she could see rage seething in his eyes. He slammed a fist into the steering wheel so hard she worried he might break it, and yet, he managed to keep from even swerving in his lane. At once, he pulled over into a pierside parking lot and parked the car.

Lacey thought he might start cursing Geo, or frantically dial the man and fire him over the phone. But instead, he turned his eyes toward the water, as if to draw strength from the beauty of the Sound. A tense, protracted moment passed, and when he finally spoke, his voice was cold and determined.

"It would appear that some things need to change. *Immediately.*" He twisted in his seat to face her, and his eyes said everything else. He placed a reassuring hand on her knee. She smiled softly at the gesture; somehow, she knew that he truly cared, and that as long as she had Jack Beals on her side, she'd never be alone. In the wake of Victor's departure, Jack's unspoken pledge became all the more valuable.

Things had moved quickly from there. Several fast-paced phone calls, and a hurried drive back to the office to corner the squirrely photographer. Yet, when they arrived, Geo was gone. The last anyone had seen of him, he'd been running out the back door, clinging to a pair of briefcases, with papers and printed photographs swirling behind him. Jack and Lacey followed the trail as far as a half a block away, but it disappeared as if by magic, leaving them in the chilly December afternoon with only some educated guesses and a promise from the police to search for him.

The rest of the afternoon blurred by, and between the police reports, the small swarm of law enforcement that descended on Trend's office building, and answering more questions than she thought possible, she and Jack finally slumped into a heap against the wood paneling that lined his office wall. They sat there for some minutes, neither speaking, both lost in their brooding thoughts. At last, Lacey broke the silence. "They'll catch him."

Jack nodded solemnly and grimaced. Lacey felt like she should say more, but she'd spoken so much she had no idea what more *to* say. Then Jack began chuckling. Slowly and quietly at first, but the sound rolled and grew until he was rolling on the floor in a full-on guffaw. Lacey, stunned, sat and watched as tears streamed down the man's cheeks. When he paused for a split second and made a ridiculous face, Lacey found that she couldn't help herself, and soon, she was rolling on the floor, too.

"W-what are we-we even *laughing…* about?" she managed to ask through a series of snorts.

"I don't even know," Jack returned, and then burst into more laughter.

When they happened to bump into one another, their laughter subsided quickly as they met one another's eyes. Though a few rippling chuckles still bubbled out of Jack, and Lacey's smile was so wide it hurt, she saw her reflection in his eyes and found she couldn't laugh for lack of breath.

"By golly," he said in a goofy 1950s voice, "I think we might just need some real stress relief after today."

Lacey somehow managed to nod.

Jack picked himself up, then offered Lacey his hand and pulled her to her feet as though she were a feather. She stopped a breath away from his face, her hands on his chest. His smile never faded, but his gaze was intent, and she heard the blood rushing in her ears. Her lips quivered and pursed of their own accord, and his eyes flicked between her mouth and her own eyes.

"Let's… let's cool down for a bit, shall we?" he said, breaking the moment and edging just slightly away. "It's been a really long day, and I think we could use it."

Lacey's heart began to come down from turbo-mode, but she found she savored the prospect of spending more time with this man she realized she may really want to know better. Lamely, and for lack of a better response, she nodded.

His smile widened again. "I've got the perfect place."

*

Winterfest was the perfect place for a date, to give Lacey's mind a small break from the investigation—and from Victor. Hosted at The Seattle Center and other small venues nearby, it was advertised as "a wonderland of sparkling lights, child-sized diversions and spirited entertainment." Jack was obviously not feeling the magic, as he fell on his butt for about the twelfth time, ice skaters as young as four whizzing by him. Lacey laughed before doing an elegant pirouette in her usual competitive spirit. She was no Kristi Yamaguchi, but Lacey Ling could hold her own. For a moment, her thoughts drifted back to earlier in the day.

"Are you always so perfect?" he asked, pushing himself up to a wobbly stance on a pair of rented ice skates. He looked so... human... dressed up as he was, despite the formality of his trench coat. She thought it was great that he wasn't beneath renting things. To his credit, he'd even accepted a mismatched pair, for lack of anything else in his size—and he didn't seem to mind that one skate was pink with purple stripes. He looked dashing, with his dark hair gelled and a cozy red scarf around his neck.

She glided up to him and stopped abruptly. "Yes," she said, laughing some more, a wide smile hurting her cheeks, "I am always perfect."

She hadn't felt this happy in a long time. Maybe Jack could potentially be more than just a good distraction. He pulled Lacey against him, holding her tight to catch a sense of stability. Lacey lifted her chin and pressed her lips against his. He happily reciprocated, and when they finally broke the kiss, he said, "Oh, Lacey, there are so many things I want to do to you. You have no idea."

She arched a brow, understanding the steamy hot implications. "Give it up," she teased. "You'll never beat me at skating."

He smiled, showing a line of white teeth. "Clever." His green eyes glanced up at a clock on a wall. "Unfortunately, I'll have to take you up on your challenge another time. My bum is sufficiently bruised, and I have to get up very, very early tomorrow for a meeting."

Playfully frowning, Lacey said, "So soon? I was having so much fun. I haven't felt like a kid in such a long time." But she was prepared for a short date, since he'd told her at the start of the evening of his schedule; trouble with Geo didn't erase his many other responsibilities. Plus, she guessed it would be best, anyway, to be there for tucking in Nainai; she'd declined letting the hired nurse do it.

He offered her another warm kiss, adding, "Same here."

*

The evening ended with hot cocoa and donuts—it seemed a little juvenile, but Lacey was in a playful mood, and so was he. But as the evening all too rapidly drew to a close, and Jack opened the door to his Porsche and helped her in for the ride home, she was faced with a humiliating realization: there was no way around it now. Jack would see her ghetto apartment. She tried to beg off the ride by pointing out that her Lincoln was still parked across from Trend, and that, really, she was fine driving herself home. "After all," she teased, "you need to go soak your hiney after all those bruises."

He'd laughed, of course, but insisted that her car would be fine, and that it would be his honor to escort her home for the evening. "After what you've been through today," he said, his smile turning sad, "it really is the least I could do." And so, what choice had she but to accept?

THIRTY-TWO

They pulled up to the complex to the throaty purr of his vehicle, which seemed to rattle the windows of the dented white van he parked next to. By now, it was after ten p.m., and the shadows in the alleyways stretched along the cracked sidewalk. A police siren wailed uncomfortably nearby, and the crunch of her boots on the snow seemed so loud that she felt like a deer in the woods, waiting for the wolves to hear her and run her down. She shivered in her coat and chewed on her lower lip, wondering whether she should have taken him to a different address in a nicer neighborhood, and then walked home. But here they were, and Jack turned off the car and was looking at her expectantly. She answered with a nervous giggle. "Well, um, thanks for everything."

The words tasted lame in her mouth. This wasn't how she wanted her evening to end. She wanted to run off with him on a quiet winter's night drive, followed by cuddling under a heavy blanket in front of a roaring fire with a couple steaming mugs of tea or cocoa. They'd stare into one another's eyes, nibble on one another's lips, and—

"Lacey?" Jack's voice cut through her thoughts.

She shook her head clear. "Oh. Um, yeah. Sorry, just got lost in my thoughts."

His answering smile and the twinkle in his eye suggested he had a very good idea what she was thinking. For a moment, she hoped he would start the car again and whisk her away from this dumpy hole and into a place that didn't give her cause to fear the things that went bump in the night. Instead, he said, "Your grandmother is probably wondering where you are. I think she'd appreciate to know you were home safe. C'mon. I'll walk you to your door."

He unbuckled and was out his door in a flash, and by hers before she could even think. He pulled it smoothly open and extended his hand to help her out. She took it graciously, and, despite her nervous humiliation, she found his nearness delicious as he pulled her up and gazed down at her. "You and I, Lacey. We make quite the pair. I feel as though I'm someone else when I'm with you."

Her response was lost on a wave of smoke. A couple of guys on the balcony above laughed loudly, tossing vulgar remarks back and forth between each other like they were twelve-year-old boys in a cussing competition. She looked up, and he followed her gaze, scowling.

"This is home sweet home," Lacey breathed, feeling her heart beat hard over the grand reveal.

Jack gave her a sidelong glance filled with concern. "Like I said, I'll walk you to your door. Which," he added quickly, "I would've done no matter where you lived, by the way. But around here? It's just, you know." He surveyed the area meaningfully.

"Yeah," Lacey sighed. "I understand. But I'm fine, really," she said, carefully slipping her hand into her purse to feel bulge of the Glock 9mm concealed inside. She hated the fact that toting her gun had become a habit lately.

"Wooo!" one of the guys up in the balcony called, leaning over it, twin tails of smoke streaming from his nose. "Hot car, bro! And hot *babe*! Jared— look at *that*!"

"How much did it cost you?" the other called. "How much did *she* cost you?" The guys laughed, and Jack reassuringly grasped Lacey's hand.

"Just ignore them," he said out of the side of his mouth. They're high, and any real attention we give them will only make it worse." Lacey nodded subtly.

"Hey," the first guy called. "You have some drugs I can buy off you?" He laughed as though his wit were amazing.

Lacey and Jack continued to ignore them as they hurried across the parking lot and up the stairs to her apartment. They paused at the door, and he caught her eye. "I don't know how I feel about you living in this neighborhood," he said. "How did you wind up here?"

Pulling the keys out of her purse, she sighed. "I guess I should have had an emergency fund, huh?"

He gave her a big hug, kissing her forehead. "Let's get you inside." Still no smiling.

Lacey put the key in the door knob, jiggling it slightly, as was the routine, but was surprised to find the door swung slightly open without her even turning the knob. She squinted at it, wondering whether the lock was broken. Something crashed inside the house.

"What's going on in there?" Then it hit her, and she glanced up at Jack with terror. "*Nainai.*" Lacey whipped her gun out of her purse and slowly stepped inside, Jack following closely behind.

"You have a *gun?*" Jack said.

Lacey didn't answer, but silently rounded the wall separating the entry from the kitchen. She flipped the light switch, but was rewarded with only darkness. Her heart leapt into her throat. Nainai falling down didn't tend to damage her door locks and her lights. She readied her gun and swallowed hard. She took comfort in her quick glance at the darkened kitchen; everything was as she'd left it, down to the tea kettle sitting on the cold electric stove.

"Why do you have a gun?" Jack asked, staying a few feet behind her, watching her back.

Something crashed again, then slammed against a wall. She darted out of the kitchen, and a split second later, a shadow scurried out of one of Nainai's rooms and slipped into Lacey's. Glass shattered in the darkness, and her blood ran cold. "*Nainai*!"

Something feral drove her forward, heedless of whatever danger may be awaiting her. She thrust forward, ready to dispense justice. "Careful," Jack called, rushing after her. She burst into her bedroom, finger on the trigger, and saw someone— some*thing*—on her window sill.

"Stop!"

Whoever it was hesitated, and in the darkness, Lacey noticed something oddly familiar about them. A gravelly voice cut through her. "I told you to watch your back, Rich Brat. You got lucky tonight."

"Teddy?" But he was gone before she could pull the trigger. Lacey and Jack raced to the window, in time only to see him disappear down the alley and around a corner. Jack lurched toward the window, but Lacey grabbed his arm and hauled him back inside. "Let him go. We'll call the police, and they can track him down."

Not wasting any time, she whirled and bolted for her grandmother's bedroom, frantically rifling through her purse, hoping to find her phone. But even in the dark she could see dresser doors toppled on top of each other and clothes strewn about. Finally managing to get the phone light working, she flashed it around. There, in the middle of the ocean of chaos, Nainai sat stock still, and island of bewildered fear, her expression frozen except for the rapid blinking of eyes. She dropped her gun and rushed to her grandmother, wrapping her in a tight embrace, burying her face in the old woman's neck and letting the tears run free. The flashback of her dream about Nainai's death scratched fervently at her mind.

"Oh, thank God you're okay," Lacey said. She set her gun on the nightstand and wrapped her in a tight hug. "Are you okay?" she kept asking over and over. Tears brimmed her eyes.

"I'm okay," Nainai said, patting Lacey's arms still holding her tight. "But if you didn't come home just now, I don't know what would have happened.

Tears spilled down Lacey's cheeks. "I'm so sorry."

"Lacey?" a man said behind her.

She yelped and snatched her gun, whirling to point it at… Jack. At once, he put his hands in the air.

"Don't *do* that!" she hissed, lowering the weapon and clearing the chamber.

Jack stumbled back and clutched his wool jacket's chest. "Easy, girl," he said, his eyes flashing at the weapon.

"You're safe," she said. "I've got this."

"Clearly," he said, obviously surprised by such resolve in a woman.

"Teddy did this," she growled, climbing off Nainai's bed, gun still cradled in her hand. She set her gun on a night stand.

"Who?" Jack said, stepping forward in the dark. "You knew that guy?" His eyes flashed at the gun again.

Lacey looked at Nainai, then panned the light around the room. He'd been very thorough in his destruction. "Yes. I underestimated him. He was supposed to be in jail." She stared at the window, a cold draft fluttering her long bangs. "I can only guess that the police must've released him for not enough evidence or something."

"Lacey, what is going on here?" Jack said, stepping beside her.

She turned to him, and they shared a long, concerned gaze.

"Tell me," he said.

But there was too much to tell. And she didn't need to worry him with it.

Jack cupped her face in his warm hands and gave her a kiss on the forehead. "This isn't a safe place for you and your grandmother. I want you to come home with me tonight."

She wanted to shake her head no, but found she couldn't. Finally, she uttered the word "But…"

His voice soft and tender, Jack said, "No 'buts', Lacey. I can't let you stay here after what I've just witnessed."

"I said I'd call the police. They… know the area."

But the resolve in his eyes was unmistakable, and she had to admit that the offer had its own appeal. She had no fear for herself, but the vision of Nainai dying in a cold, sterile hospital bed, her last act a look of accusation in Lacey's direction—it was too much.

She swallowed hard and quickly dabbed her eyes dry. "Just for tonight. I don't want to be any trouble. We'll start looking for a new place first thing in the morning."

He raised his eyebrows. "I think it'd be better for you to rest. In fact, you take tomorrow off. I happen to know your boss, and I'm pretty sure I can persuade him to let you call in sick without getting in any trouble." He winked. "I'll go bring the car up. You get your stuff."

Lacey gave him a tremulous smile, then nodded once. Jack was right. She turned back to her grandmother. "Nainai? We're going to spend the night elsewhere."

THIRTY-THREE

Jack's place was a black diamond glittering on the shores of the Puget Sound, perched on the aptly named Sunset Hill. It was one of the finer homes in the neighborhood, a study in rugged rock work, wrought iron and dark wood paneling, giving the place an image closer to "medieval castle" than "upscale beach house." Lacey felt the breath go out of her as soon as she stepped through the massive front door, pushing Nainai in her wheelchair. Cherry wood flooring played tag with Mediterranean tiles up and down halls that seemed to stretch on forever. Art that probably cost more than the coffee shop she'd worked in lined the walls. Leather furniture in deep maroon was arranged around a living room with a ceiling that soared up on towering windows that gazed out over the water. A thin ribbon of moonlight danced on sleepy waves.

"Like it?" Jack asked.

Lacey nodded stupidly.

"Then you're going to *love* this." He snapped his fingers, and a fire roared to life in a real stone hearth on the far end of the living room. Lacey spun, eyes wide and jaw slack. Her host laughed. "You should see your face," he said. He snapped again, and the fire went out. Then he crowed like a rooster, and the fire kicked on again.

Lacey narrowed her eyes, and, after a little searching, noticed he was hiding his left hand. "Nice try, smart guy," she said. "Let's see what's behind your back."

He grinned and stepped aside, revealing a switch. "You're just too smart for your own good. Can't hide anything from *your* gorgeous eyes."

"Oh, listen to him flatter you, baby girl," Nainai crooned. "He's got the tongue of the devil, that one." Her eyes twinkled. "I think that means I ought to keep him."

Lacey rolled her eyes. "You'll have to excuse my grandmother. She can be a bit, shall we say, overly flirtatious."

"I made out with *Bruce Lee*, little girl," Nainai objected. "This old gal still has it."

Jack's laugh was a happy sound, and Lacey felt the tension begin to drain out of her. "No, she's wonderful. I'm happy to have her here. I'd like you both to stay as long as is necessary. In fact, if it's any comfort, let me show you my security system." He made for the front door but Lacey intercepted him.

"No, that's okay, Jack," she said, meeting his eyes, then quickly glancing away, feeling herself blush like a schoolgirl. "We trust you.

"I think we really ought to get Nainai to bed. She's had a pretty harrowing night, don't you think?"

Jack studied her for a moment, an odd smile on his face. He flicked his eyes at Nainai, then back to Lacey. "Think a couple of young kids need a chaperone, Nainai?" he asked.

Nainai hooted once with laughter. "If she doesn't plant one on you soon, I'm going to have to do it for her."

Jack laughed again, and Lacey's face flushed hotly, though she couldn't but giggle. With that, they put Nainai to bed. Lacey was decidedly pleased with the accommodations, including the low bed and walk-in shower. Tucking the dear old woman up to her neck in what Lacey was sure was 400-thread-count silk sheets, she kissed Nainai's cheek. "I love you, she said.

"I love you too, baby girl." And just like that, a bit of her memory faded. She eyed the room suspiciously before saying, "I'm so happy you're a reporter."

Lacey paused, her mouth drawn open. She simply said, "Why's that?"

"So you can afford a lovely room like this for me." Nainai smiled childlike, and then added, "Still not enough Asian inspiration."

Rubbing the white hair off Nainai's forehead, Lacey said, "I'm happy you like it, but this is my friend Jack's house."

There was a faraway look on Nainai's face before she said, "Who's Jack?"

"I'll have you meet tomorrow," Lacey said sweetly, and switched off the light.

Dementia was a mystery, making some nights harder than others. Tomorrow, maybe she'd remember who Jack was, and without any prompting at all. Making her way to the kitchen, Lacey wondered if Nainai had even the faintest memory of meeting Jack from the mall's food court, the other day.

With Jack having an early meeting the next morning, there was no time for staying up late, kissing by candlelight to the taste of sweet champagne. Besides, her worry over what had happened to Victor would keep her from enjoying any more fun distractions. What *had* happened to him?

THIRTY-FOUR

"You look absolutely stunning, Lacey Ling." Jack held out a hand for her to accept.

She emerged from the black Porsche in a red silk dress purposely falling off her shoulders. Happy that she'd succeeded at twisting her long hair into a pretty French twist, she knew she could take the compliment seriously. She hadn't been this done up since KZTB's 30th Anniversary of Good Day Seattle. The cool evening prickling her skin, she was happy to hurry up the steps with Jack, leaving a valet to appropriately park his car in a farther away spot.

The contemporary appeal of the Hall at Fauntleroy was beautifully juxtaposed by its classically exposed red brick, which gleamed in the setting sun. From somewhere close by, the marine scent of the Puget Sound salted the air. Lacey didn't have a moment to even think to breathe it in, however, since the media were poised, filming and flashing pictures as attendees arrived. The drama surrounding Trend had the dubious benefit of making them the "hot couple," and they spent at least as much time in front of cameras as the mayor and his wife. "Jack" and "Lacey" were called out so much it made Lacey half-expect a red-carpet and Hollywood stars.

From somewhere in the blare of flashes and confusing shouts, one voice yelled above the rest, "You're next, slut!"

Jack didn't even blink but the words pounded against Lacey's temples. "Did you hear that?" she asked, her eyes flashing around the scene at the many clamoring bodies, not seeing any familiar face.

"Hear what?" he asked, offering a wave at a camera crew.

"Nothing," she muttered to herself. *People could be so heartless*, she thought, shaking her head.

The moment the doormen opened the front doors, Lacey happily slipped inside, into the warmth and away from the public. Jack gave Lacey his elbow to hold once more, and she was surprised by the great comfort that offered her. Now under the lights of the grand charity event, she had a good view of her date. Looking up at him, he met her eyes, the greenness in them deep under his brows. He smiled and said, "Thank you again for saying yes to being my date."

"Thank you for asking me," she said, catching a hint of his cool-scented cologne from his tux's lapel.

They were quickly ushered by a man greeting them by name. "Follow me to your table, if you will," the young man said, taking them into the dining area. White Christmas lights adorned the many tall windows. Trees strategically placed in corners were also wrapped in the lights. At the head of the room was a set-up stage with a podium, the podium bearing the sign with the name of the event—The Inaugural Winter Mayoral Ball. They were escorted to a light-blue linened table to the rear-left of the hall, and Jack pulled out Lacey's chair.

She gladly sat, and as Jack took his seat, he apologized. "It's not the best spot, but I suppose I should be grateful for the invite at all." He picked up his navy cloth napkin and draped it over his slacks. The rest of the hall was filling up quite fast. Many were standing, mingling between tables. Her research earlier that night showed the cost of the plates was out of this world—for a good cause, of course. Lacey felt fortunate Jack could spend a thousand dollars on each plate without it being a burden. The last thing she'd want to be to a man was a burden. A waiter came over with a wine menu right away, and Jack ordered for them both. As the waiter moved away, he set his hand over hers and smiled gently. "I have to say, despite what it might seem, I'm not a very social person. I keep to myself a lot."

Lacey nodded. Even in his quiet moments, however, he had an air of calm confidence. "I'm very much the same," she said.

Glancing over the many utensils, plates and various glasses, Lacey felt at home. If there was one thing she knew for sure, it was table etiquette. So, when the festivities began and she was given her Caesar salad with juicy cherry tomatoes and fresh grated parmesan aplenty, she happily grabbed her salad fork and elegantly dug in.

Lacey caught Jack staring at her. She turned to him, still chewing her bite. He was so very handsome—his cheekbones, his jawline, those green eyes that had an amused sparkle. He said, "I'm sorry I haven't had more quality time to spend with you. This last week, with you at my place—I know you want to get a place of your own soon, but… I have to admit, it's been really nice having you so close. And I'm happy your mouth is full, otherwise I know you'd protest." He lightly chuckled. "But I want you to know how truly interested I am in where things are going… between us."

Chewing a juicy cherry tomato, Lacey nearly choked in surprise. She turned her face away from Jack as she, as covertly as possible, coughed it up. She was suddenly feeling like her chandelier earrings were dragging across the floor, and her heart rapped unpleasantly. "I'm sorry," she said, apologizing.

Putting her head in her hands, she closed her eyes, trying to compose herself. Her thoughts became hazy, and she wondered if maybe she'd just had some bad dressing. *I can't be that scared of commitment*, she scolded herself.

"Are you okay?" Jack's voice entered her mind. "Was it what I said?" His hand touched her back.

She opened her eyes and took a sip of water. The feeling passed, and she was back to normal.

Shaking her head, she said, "I'm sorry. I don't know what overcame me. That was bizarre."

"Hm," he simply said, and there was silence for the rest of the meal.

In the wake of dinner, tables were quickly cleared out for dancing. Lacey's head on Jack's shoulder, she was still puzzled by her reaction from earlier at dinner. They swayed to a slow song played by a live band.

"What do you think of me? Of us?" Jack spoke into her ear.

Lacey liked the feeling of Jack's warm cheek against hers. "I like you," she said.

Jack pulled her in tighter, and they swayed together, just letting those words linger. He finally asked with a tentative pause, "I have something to show you. Come with me out to the patio."

"Uh..." Lacey peered out the nearby window. It was dark out. No other guests were outside. "It's a cold night."

Breaking their embrace, Jack slipped his jacket's suit off and draped it over Lacey's shoulders. "I'll keep you warm. It will be quick."

Holding hands, the two slipped into the hall and out an exit. Even with Jack's suit coat, Lacey shivered, the air turning her breath into white fog. "What is it you want to show me?" she asked.

He brushed a hand under her chin and leaned down for a kiss. It was warm and heart-fluttering. He slowly released her bottom lip, and said, "Okay, I'm ready now." Jack slipped a long black box out of his pants pocket, and Lacey immediately thought of that scene from Pretty Woman, where Richard Gere snaps a jewelry box at Julia Robert's fingers, and she does her signature laugh. This was different, though. "But…" she stumbled, speechless. "You don't… have… Wh-what is this?"

He opened it up to reveal a necklace of multiple sapphires. "That is beautiful," she said, raising a hand to her chest in concern, "but *way* too expensive."

Before she could protest further, Jack slipped behind her and put it around her neck. He stepped back around to take a good look at her. "It's not nearly as beautiful as you, Lacey Ling, and I've made beauty my business." He gently spun her around and met her eyes. "I've made it a point not to mix business and pleasure. I have a very strict personal policy against getting involved with my models. But the more I've gotten to know you…" and he looked away, his breathy steaming in the air.

At last, he continued. "I've been unable to sleep. I told myself, 'Jack, policies have their time and their place." He looked at her again. "I feel like a different person around you, Lacey. A better man. I-I haven't been able to concentrate on much of anything since I met you except for wondering when I'd see you again. I don't see that changing."

He blew out a breath and raked a hand through his hair. "Geez," he said with a little chuckle, "It's never been this hard before."

Lacey felt something quiver inside. "Go on."

"I know it's fast, but... but I'd like it very much if you and I saw each other exclusively. Will you... be mine?"

That was a surprise.

"Jack, I don't know what to say." This time the haziness and heaviness didn't overcome her. She was simply stunned, and thinking about Victor, oddly. How she'd known him for just a few months before he was ready to propose. How he seemed like the perfect match so early on. How he had wooed her in a tux at a high-class social event, too, and she had given "love at first sight" a chance. Suddenly, she wished he were standing beside her, making snarky remarks about her date, just to know Victor was actually there.

Bursting her memory bubble, Jack asked, "What do you say, Lacey? Will you be mine?" When she paused to find her tongue, his eyes glinted with a knowing sadness, like he was already expecting the worst.

Tilting her head, her long bangs fell across her cheek like a curtain closing on a play. "I can't," she said. "I'm sorry."

Surprisingly, his eyes turned cold, his face darkening. He pressed his lips together for a long moment as he looked down. When his gaze met hers, he said, "I don't get it. I thought we had so much in common. I thought it'd be a no-brainer, that you'd automatically say yes. It's not a marriage proposal, Lacey. I simply want you all to myself, and *then* maybe down the road..."

She shook her head, and put a little distance between them. "I'm sorry. I'm not ready for a commitment of any kind. I'm sorry if anything I've done has led you to believe that. If so, then it's my fault."

"Yes, yes it is," he said, tilting his strong jaw. "I took you out on a fabulous first date, fast-tracked you right into my agency, invited you and your grandmother into my home to *live*, and made you my 'plus one' at the biggest charity event of the year. Do you know how much I've invested in you in this short amount of time? And you *still* say no?"

Fingering the back clasp of her necklace, she felt embarrassment and sadness both wash over her. "You're right," she said, struggling to get it off. "I don't know what I'm thinking."

"Is there anything I can do to knock some sense into you about this?"

Those words, both classless and vulgar, grated on every one of Lacey's nerves. Giving up on the reluctant gold clasp, she shook her head. "Excuse me, Jack, but this is not a matter of you needing to 'knock' sense into me." His face was hard and immovable as she continued. "Either a woman feels ready for something or she doesn't. I don't." Her heart felt a dull pang over what she was about to utter, but there wasn't really any alternative now. "I think the best thing, under the circumstances, would be for us to stop seeing each other."

He gave an incredulous guffaw, releasing a large cloud of icy air. "That's rich," he said. "Wow."

Lacey slipped his suit coat off, and handed it back to Jack, who wrung it slightly while gazing down at the ground. She folded her arms against the frigid air. Not seeing any signs that Jack had anything else to say, she pivoted in her heels and headed for the entrance.

"Lacey—wait," he blurted as she pushed through the door. "Wait." He jogged over to her. "Listen, I don't know what just came over me, but I don't like it. I'm sorry. Let's just pretend we never had a... disagreement. Keep the necklace, stay at my place. We don't need to push things to exclusivity. I see that. I was being a jerk."

Still fuming, Lacey just walked into the building to where it was warmer. "You were being more than a jerk," she said. An usher by the front door eyed them but said nothing. How she wished she had her car to take her home. But to where? Jack's house, of all places? Knowing Nainai was there, too, settled in for the night, she could feel nothing other than trapped.

"I'm sorry," Jack said again, touching her arm, but she moved away. "Hey, do you think we can at least pretend to enjoy the rest of the evening? I'll feel like a complete screw-up if we left the mayor's party, especially since some of the proceeds go to the families of Trend's victims."

Finally, he'd said something that made a little sense. If for no other reason, she could stay for that. She sucked in a deep breath and said, "I'll do it. For them, not you."

As they entered, the mayor was clinking a wine glass at head of the hall. Instead of using the microphone, he called out. "There they are, right now."

All eyes turned to Lacey and Jack's reappearance.

"Please, join me up here." The mayor waved them over, his white hair and pearly teeth gleaming. He picked up a framed something from a table beside him.

Jack clasped Lacey's hand and put on a smile, leading her past everyone to the front. As they approached, Lacey suddenly felt heady. And then, she realized that, right there in front of the massive crowd of philanthropists, she was about to see another one of Victor's visions.

You leave me in the lurch, she thought bitterly, *then have the gall to embarrass me in public?* But the vision came on anyway, and she gave herself to it, if only because it meant she could be with Victor in some way. Clapping faded into a light murmur as the view before her suddenly changed from regal ladies and gentleman smiling to some meager room with a young woman in her underwear, on a bed, chained to the headboard. The blond hair to her shoulders was unkempt, as if it hadn't been brushed in days, her eyes holding a glint of resigned sadness.

Lacey, Victor whispered to her mind. *I'm so sorry I had to go like I did, but I believe in what you're doing, and you needed to see this. Maybe you can still help these girls, even if I can't help you. Do you know who this girl is?*

Yes, Lacey said. *Shayla.* It felt like the right answer. Shayla was alive, but not unharmed; Lacey knew she could do something about that if she were smart and quick, and that washed away any embarrassment over her lapse. If she were on the floor in front of the mayor and half of Seattle's finest, so be it.

Yes, Victor said, and suddenly Lacey could feel her ex's great grief and disgust ripple through her spirit. And carrying those emotions on top of her own, made her heavy like never before. In her mind, she was actually starting to sob as she watched the vision before her, of a young woman, hope and a sense of worth gone.

Where is she? Lacey asked.

She's somewhere in Queen Anne, I think. Smaller place. I'm not sure whether I can lead you there, sorry, but I'll try. There was a brief pause, and suddenly a clear image of the home materialized in her mind, along with the full address, and even directions, as though she were looking at a map on her phone. The image was so sharp she knew she'd remember it when she woke.

Okay, she said. *Let's go.* She readied herself to wake up from the vision, to collect herself after her "fainting spell" and apologize to everyone, followed by a very quick exit from Fauntleroy. But she wasn't waking up. *Victor, hurry and release me, so we can go get some help.*

I'm trying, he said. *I don't know what's happening.*

271

The vision faded, like a flicker, and in that split second she saw Jack's face over hers. There was a loud wave of shocked murmurs. And then she was back to seeing Shayla.

It didn't work, Lacey said. *Just release me however you did before.*

That's what I'm doing. His voice was just as surprised and frustrated as hers.

More flashes and flickers jerked her back and forth between scenes, akin to a TV's fuzzy signal or radio stations garbling together.

What's going on, Victor? It started to make Lacey nauseous, like being subjected to a never-ending fair ride. *Does this have to do with you being MIA recently? Talk to me. Or—or talk to your cat.*

*I can't get in touch with Ra*o, he said, and his voice sounded pained. *I-I don't know what's happening to me, Lacey. Give my mind a moment to settle. Maybe we need to just wait a few minutes, or I don't know.*

Lacey felt herself grimace. *I just know my head's starting to pound, and this is no time to be getting sick.* The flickering stopped, and Lacey drew in a deep breath.

She watched as Victor stepped closer to the chained-up woman and perched beside her on the bed, giving Lacey the kind of view she'd have if she were sitting beside a friend. Pale blue eyes flickered up and rested straight ahead, feeling like they were gazing into Lacey's eyes.

Is she sensing you? Lacey asked.

I don't know, he said.

Tell her everything will be okay, she said softly. *That help is on the way.*

"Everything will be okay," Victor said aloud to the trembling girl. "Help's coming." Shayla tilted her head, as if discerning something, blond strands lying across an unwashed cheek.

Ask her if she sees you, Lacey thought.

Victor's face closed in closer on hers. Lacey could see clearly the tired red cracks in the whites of her eyes. "Can you see me?" he tried. The pale blue eyes narrowed in thought.

"Can you see me?" he asked again. "Can you hear me?" Victor turned his thoughts back to Lacey. *They've doped her up on something. I think she senses me.*

Shayla's mouth opened a touch, and her glazed eyes seemed to focus ever so slightly on Victor, before widening in hazy alarm. She brought her arms across her chest in a protective gesture, as much as her chains allowed. "Who... are you?"

THIRTY-FIVE

She sees you!

The sound of a door opening interrupted the moment. The vision flashed to Geo entering through an orange door. And then Lacey was released unexpectedly. Touching her head and blinking, Lacey sat up with a start. Shiny black interior, leather seats. New car smell. She was in Jack's Porsche.

"Rise and shine," Jack said, placing a hand on her knee. She was seat-belted in, and he was driving her somewhere fast and smooth down the dark streets.

Victor! Lacey called. *Victor!*

There was no response. Lacey touched her head again, consumed by worry.

"That was quite the show you gave at the ball," Jack said. "I was just about to take you to the hospital." He glanced at her. "Are you okay?"

Nodding, Lacey said, "Yes."

"That's the second time you've fainted in front of me. I'd like to think it has to do with your attraction to me, you know, taking your breath away. But something else is the matter."

Still feeling faint, Lacey peered out her window. Bushes and trees whizzed by beyond Jack's window. To her right was the Puget Sound, dark and silent in the night. *Victor!* she tried again. His silence troubled her more than it should. What could she do now?

"You're still looking really pale." Jack shot another glance at her, this time rubbing the back of her neck, where some of her French twist had come loose. "You look almost... afraid."

Should she say anything to Jack? How could she, without it sounding completely irrational, though? Thinking it over, she came to one option that wouldn't make her sound completely loony, or divulge her secret relationship with Victor. She turned to him, and said, "It's just... I was just thinking about Geo."

"Yeah, what about him?" Jack's eyebrow arched, and he resumed looking ahead, his car smoothly zipping around curves.

Lacey wondered at his response; not a week back, he'd seemed ready to kill the man the next time he found him, after Lacey had shown Jack the proof of what Geo had been up to. She sat up and shook her head clear. "It's just... I have a feeling the cops haven't found Geo. And some girls are in danger."

Jack gave a sidelong glance, surprise clear in his eyes.

She decided to take a leap, even if it meant a little stretch of the truth. "In the stuff I got from Geo's office, I saw a picture of a girl with blond hair to her shoulders and these really pale blue eyes. I realized I remember that girl from when I worked at the university…"

"Yeah?" Jack said, now clutching the steering wheel with both hands. "You worked at the college?"

"Yes, just briefly." She shrugged in her red dress. "Her name was Shayla; Shayla Anderson, and she's been missing over winter break. I've pieced some things together tonight."

"Missing?" Jack asked, once again interjecting while shooting her a funny look. "She's not on Christmas vacation or something?"

Lacey remembered Rebecca and Emily thinking so, and the media hadn't actually run a story on her missing, but she decided again to call it as she saw it, somehow. She needed help. She needed Jack on her side about this, even if he had freaked out at her earlier, especially now that Victor was MIA again. She almost smiled at the thought of an angel having to fight a fuzzy "reception." She paused. "Yes, she's missing."

"I think I see where you're going with this," he said. "With what you found on Geo, to do with drugs and pornography, I mean. But how do you know this girl is missing? I mean, how solid of a case do we have here?"

Lacey understood; making accusations without evidence was frowned upon in polite society. Unfortunately, her evidence happened to be supernatural. Though there was no denying its validity, she had no idea how she'd persuade the police that she'd gotten a solid lead from a friendly ghost. She punted instead. "I still have ties with KZTB. Someone I know was tipped off about this young woman, Shayla, missing. What my contact gave me was undeniable. I'd say it's a solid case." The lies were really starting to pile up, and she hated that fact. But pressing her full lips together, she soothed herself with the thought that a couple of lies were worth it to rescue Shayla. "I can't ignore that. Especially if Geo is involved."

Jack stayed silent, simply rubbing his chin a moment, his brow furrowed in worry.

"Listen, Jack," she said, "I recognize the place Shayla was at in the photos. I think if we just go there tonight, we can maybe help free her."

Jack shook his head immediately. "This isn't something you or I should be dealing with. This is something the police are trained to handle." He glanced at the back seat, to where her purse sat, and said, "I know you pack heat, but this is way over our heads. Let me make the call to the authorities, okay? And you and I can head home to my place, tuck in Grandma and catch a Netflix marathon of crime dramas—our favorite."

She managed not to scoff but instead kept her voice flat. "I'm sorry, but that's not an option for me tonight," she said, dismayed at how little Jack really seemed to know her. How could he ask to snuggle in front of a film in the wake of a break-up, to say nothing of the fact that Lacey was trying desperately to liberate a girl from a fate worse than death. Netflix was not on the schedule any time soon. "I can't relax until Geo is taken down and Shayla's freed."

"And you want to do this yourself?"

"Not completely. I'm not opposed to calling the cops."

Jack drew in a deep breath and blew it out. "Okay, I have an idea. Here's the deal—we'll head over to this place where you think Geo is holding Shayla. I'll do some of my own investigating, and once I can see things with my own two eyes, then we can call the cops."

Lacey hated how men underestimated her, but if that was the deal they had to make in order for Jack to cooperate some, she was game. "Okay, deal. Here's the address."

*

The sleek luxury car pulled up to the home's sidewalk like a panther, purring. "Why don't you stay here?" Jack said to Lacey.

Lacey unbuckled and went for her purse in the back seat. "You don't need to worry about my protection."

Jack gave a frustrated smile. "Of course not," he said. "But Geo might just open the door to me. You? No chance in Hell, since I'm sure he believes it was you who sicced the police on him."

"Well, I did," she replied grimly. "And if I see him again…"

Jack's smile hardened, and he slipped out of the car. "Just… just stay behind me. I still want you, and I'm not about to let someone break you, especially if you're just being careless."

Lacey ducked out of the Porsche and felt her collar get hot. She wanted to fume at his stupid arrogance, but she kept it together, gritted her teeth, and nodded, pretending to be an obedient little girl; still, she walked beside him to the front door.

The house looked like any other house on the block, but the memory of Victor's latest vision was still crystal clear, and she knew they'd arrived. Overhead, an unexpected cloud bank crawled ominously across the sky to hide the winter moon, sending shivers through Lacey. Jack shot her a sidelong glance. "Afraid of the dark?"

She wanted to punch him but said nothing. Instead, she stepped to the side of the peephole to ensure Geo wouldn't see her when he came to the door. Jack raised his fist to knock, then hesitated and fumbled with the doorknob. To Lacey's surprise, it clicked, and the door opened with a giveaway creak.

"So much for sneaking in," Jack muttered. "You'd think, for a guy on the lam, he'd at least lock his doors at night." He pursed his lips in thought. "Maybe he's not home."

Lacey answered only with a fiercely determined look.

"Okay, okay," he said, half-chuckling. "You're a force of nature, little lady. Let's go inside. And this time, I insist on being first."

Lacey scoffed quietly but gave him the benefit of preserving his warped sense of manhood. What had happened to the guy whom she thought she'd been getting to know? Where was the kindness? The nobility she'd seen?

Knock it off, Lacey, she told herself. This was no time to think about her love life. Setting her jaw, she marched in after Jack, her gun held low, but ready.

The two of them crept through the house, scanning the darkened living room, kitchen, and hallways. Nothing looked out of place, and the interior was clean, if not spotlessly so. Were she to have visited this place under normal circumstances, she would have thought she were in about as average a home as one could find, for the area. Almost too soon, they completed their sweep of the house. Nothing resembling a prostitution ring, or even a frat party, could be found.

"Seems this friend of yours gave us the wrong address," Jack said, sounding bemused. "I think we ought to quietly lock up, then take off before *we* get picked up by the cops for breaking and entering."

Lacey chewed her bottom lip. She was *sure* this was the place. But, was Victor wrong? *Had* he shown her the wrong house? She looked at Jack. "Is there a basement?"

Even in the dark, Lacey could see the roll of his eyes. "Did you *see* a stairwell?"

She frowned, feeling frustrated and foolish. "No," she began slowly.

"Then," Jack said, striding up to her and taking her arm, "I say we go home, take care of your grandma, and spend a little time together so I can make it up to you for tonight's little slip." He moved away, tugging her along behind him.

"But—"

He stopped, and turned a hot glare on her. "Look, Lacey," he said sufferingly, "it's getting late. I'm tired, a bit cranky, and really rather embarrassed that my date passed out and started babbling on the floor in front of some of the most influential people in this city. I'm trying to be nice, since I'm a nice guy, but I hate to say you're kind of pushing that.

"I've already humored you, so let's go do something enjoyable, rather than chasing dead leads."

Lacey jerked out of his grip. She was done with him. "Fine," she said flatly. "You go home. I'll get Nainai in the morning. But I *swear*, if I find you've done *anything* to her that I don't approve of—"

"As if she'd even remember it," he muttered.

Lacey knew her answering smack would leave a nice welt. "You make me sick," she said. "Get out. I'll handle this myself even if it means I have to search every house on this block myself."

For a moment, she wondered at the rage in his expression. The muscles in his neck strained, and veins appeared in his forehead. Despite the lack of light, his eyes seemed to practically glow, though she knew it was just her imagination; still, she felt an unnerving headache boiling to life inside her skull. She braced herself to block any attempt he might make to hit her. Nothing happened. Instead, he swallowed hard and took a step backward.

"Fine," he said with a cold calm that disturbed her even more than fiery anger would have. "Fine. You want to play burglar, you go right ahead. But don't blame me if the cops just happen to show up while you're in the middle of your little games, especially when I offered you a nice, safe night in a warm house.

"And you know what?" he added. "I need your keycard on my desk first thing tomorrow morning. I hope the college takes you back." He spun for the door.

"What *happened* to you, Jack?" Lacey said, taking an unconscious step toward him. "Where is the guy who bought me dinner? Who treated me so kindly? Who, just earlier tonight, I was starting to think about getting serious with some day?"

A howl of laughter pealed from him. "Oh, *now* you tell me," he said. "You couldn't have just said yes earlier, when things were going so well. Well, now you get to see the wrath of Jack Beals."

"My *gosh*," she whispered, backing away as he turned toward her. "You're acting like a man possessed."

Jack barked another laugh and strode toward her. Without warning, Lacey went blind as a burst of light filled the room.

"What is going *on* here?" It was a familiar, nasally voice. Geo. "Jack? *Ling*," the photographer spat. "How did *you* find me here?"

Still dazed, Lacey didn't see Geo's lunge. He tackled her around her midsection, blasting her to the floor. Her head rebounded off the tile, and stars exploded across her vision. He slapped her hard. "You little slut," he said, his face practically pressing into hers. "If it hadn't been for—"

The blast of a gunshot deafened her, setting her ears ringing and drowning out anything else he might have said.

THIRTY-SIX

Geo collapsed on her like a sodden mattress, and several seconds passed before she realized she was actually screaming.

Heaving herself out from under the lifeless form of Trend's late photographer, she rolled onto all fours and struggled to get upright. She found herself facing the main hallway. In the light, she noticed that the coat closet door was wide open; a square of pale, fluorescent light radiated up from the closet floor. Vague sounds of weeping women wafted from below. "He had a trap door," she whispered. "Thank you, *Victor.*"

She scrambled desperately toward it, ears still burning, only to jerk to a stop as a powerful hand seized her around the waist and spun her around. "We're going home," Jack said. "*Now.*"

"Let *go* of me," she said, flailing. But it was in vain. He seemed to have the strength of five men.

She kicked, clawed, and bit, but his grip was iron. After a few moments' struggle, he hefted her over his shoulder like a sack of potatoes. She hammered ineffectually on his back. To her surprise, however, he turned away from the front door and began carrying her toward the coat closet. She watched in amazement as the door swung shut on a hungry gust of wind that seemed to come out of nowhere. Suddenly, she was dumped unceremoniously on the floor in front of the coat closet. Her bruised head slammed against the door jamb, and she winced, grabbing the spot instinctively.

"You know," he said conversationally, "we were going to be something special, you and I. I'd gotten tired of the same old pretty faces coming and going every day. And vice, well, it has its virtues, but even that gets old when it's the same girls over and over and over. I wanted to make a fresh start. Maybe… get a girl that was mine, and mine alone. And you really had something special about you. Heavenly," he said, as if trying out the word. "You really did bring out the best in me, and that was something I've really, really missed."

She struggled into a kneeling position, wondering whether she could bolt past him. He cut her off, crouching on the floor and peering at her as though she were a curious animal, and he, a collector of fine beasts. He opened his mouth to speak. But without warning, his hands lashed out, and before she could even blink, she felt herself falling.

The fall ended with a sickening snap, and fire roared through her right leg. A ragged cry ripped from her lips, and her vision swam. She felt a dangerous cocktail of panic and anger clawing her mind. Her throat was thick with rising bile. When her eyes were able to focus, she realized she was in a basement room that felt uncomfortably familiar. Then it struck her—the place looked all too similar to the room she had seen Shayla in. She was in a narrow corridor serviced only by a fluorescent light that had one foot in the grave. Half a dozen doors lined each side of the hall, and each door had a number on it. On the far wall hung a rack full of products she knew tended to be used only in certain unsavory industries.

She wanted to puke.

"Welcome to our little funhouse," Jack called from above. Lacey looked up to see him smirking down at her at the head of a ladder built into the wall beneath the trapdoor. "What do you think?"

"Victor," she breathed, wishing desperately he were here.

"Oh, about that," he said. "Geo told me about your old boyfriend. "Kind of a pansy, from the sound of it. He couldn't believe how naïve and stupid the guy was. A little smut, a little voodoo, and he had your friend all locked up, almost without even trying. Funny thing is, we never knew Heaven had gotten that close to our business before then. I guess they're either getting sneakier, upstairs, or lazier."

Lacey stared up at him. The air around him seemed to shimmer darkly, and she blanched. "What *are* you?"

"What are we?" he asked, then laughed. "Wouldn't you like to know? I guess your wannabe guardian angel didn't tell you much about how things on this side work. Then again, from what Geo said, he was pretty clueless himself."

Victor, she pled in her mind. *Where* are *you?*

"He won't be able to hear you," Jack said, picking at his nails as he casually crouched over the hole. "Geo was useful, while he lasted. If nothing else, he knew his magiks, and was able to keep certain... holy eyes... from peering too close." Jack's mocking smile turned to a scowl. "But mortals get sloppy sometimes. Geo got comfortable, and getting comfortable, as a mortal, means getting yourself killed. The fact that *you* found him out with such a paltry effort on your part tells me it's time for me to find a new assistant. And new girls, since maybe you alerted the cops without me knowing it. But Jessica and Brittany were easy enough to replace after they ran from me, and the rest of the girls are all just waiting in their pretty cages like fat cows for the slaughter, now. Oh, and I may need to get... to get a new Lacey Ling. And that, my darling, is the biggest shame of all. You were going to save us from this."

"What *are* you?" Lacey repeated, trying to sound insistent but feeling a cloying terror tightening her chest.

Jack sighed. "You really want me to do the whole expository thing? Come on, Lacey. I've seen more movies than that. In fact," and he leveled a pistol at her. "I've already talked too much."

Lacey tried to jerk out of the way as he squeezed the trigger, and felt pain erupt in her right flank. She found she couldn't breathe for the agony, and curled up into a ball. Above the renewed shrill ringing in her ears, she thought she heard Jack curse.

Fighting against blacking out, she inchwormed herself away from the trapdoor. Somewhere in her mind, she knew his second shot wouldn't miss. She knew she *shouldn't* fear death, but after what had happened to Victor, she knew that dying *here* would be a one-way ticket to a very warm place.

Overhead, she heard a strange rumble, and nebulous, muted crashes and shouts. When she was able to force her eyes open, she noticed the trapdoor was no longer covered by her captor. Desperate, bleeding, and dizzy with pain, she only knew that she had to get out. Dragging herself across the carpet, she made her painful way back toward the ladder. When she reached it, she gazed up in dismay. Her right leg was ballooning by the moment, and she knew it wouldn't support weight.

She didn't even want to think about the bullet wound.

Lacey, get up. Quick!

"Victor," she whispered, wincing at the way breathing felt like being knifed in the ribs.

Quick. Do whatever you can. Here—this might help.

Miraculously, the pain dulled to a merely intense throb, and her vision cleared as a surprising jolt of adrenaline—and, she was sure, something else—surged through her. She grasped the lower rungs of the ladder and slowly hauled herself to her feet, taking care not to put any weight on her right leg. The adrenal rush continued, and, rung by rung, she was able to grit her teeth and perform the impossible. She emerged from the trap door in surprising time, but nearly fell back down the hole at what she saw.

Teddy lay on the floor in the foyer, looking for all the world like a junkyard dog who had gotten into a fight with razor wire. Foam spilled from his mouth, and a wild mix of fear and fury was on his face. Jack towered above him; he wasn't panting. He raised his gun toward the vagrant. From across the room, Teddy caught Lacey's eyes. "Rich Brat," he called, almost happily. Jack stiffened, and spun. His face contorted in rage at the sight of Lacey, and he swung the gun in line with her face, only to miss his shot as Teddy crashed into the back of Jack's legs, toppling him.

"Get *off* me," Jack roared, seizing Teddy by the collar and hurling him halfway across the room. The vagrant rebounded off the wall with a thud, and Lacey gasped to see the man-size dent in the drywall. In that instant, she knew that Jack Beals, CEO of Trend, was literally possessed. Suddenly, so many things made sense. Frantic, and feeling her miraculous second wind fading fast, she scrabbled out of the closet.

He snarled at her, and rather than simply firing, charged her.

Jack froze abruptly, then snarled. He jerked violently, and, like Teddy, began to foam at the mouth.

Lacey, get out. Victor's voice was unnaturally calm but unmistakably urgent.

Lacey perked up at the voice in her mind. *Victor? You are still here! Oh thank—*

Please, Lacey, no talkie. Just walkie. Front door is even open for you. You're welcome.

She made to argue but thought better of it. Raising herself painfully to her knees, she fumbled toward the front door. She knew she'd never be able to outrun Jack, and she had no way of getting home, but she trusted Victor—now more than ever—and did what she could.

As she made her slow trek across the living room, Jack continued to thrash and shriek as if grappling with some unseen opponent. Lacey felt— she had no *idea* what she felt, but she knew something monumental was going on in Jack's immediate vicinity.

Teddy had gained his feet again, and, though his face was already purpling, he howled and bull-rushed Jack from behind, dropping him a second time. The two men rolled on the floor, but Teddy was surprisingly agile and held his upper ground as he drilled punch after punch into Jack with one hand while his other hand fought for the gun, finally wrestling it free. He leapt clear of Jack and drew a bead on the man, his hand hovering tight on the trigger.

Jack loosed a shriek unlike Lacey had ever heard, and the sound—a swirl of unspeakable tormented sorrow—seemed to pierce her very soul. He frothed and writhed on the floor, all the while under Teddy's skeptical eye and ready weapon.

"Shoot him, Teddy!" Lacey cried. She found she hated Jack. Thoughts of inflicting on him the kind of wounds he'd caused who knew how many women roared in her mind. He deserved an agonizing death and an even more painful eternity. "What are you waiting for?"

Teddy's face was grim, but he shook his head and only continued to watch. "Trust me on this, kid. We need to stay calm."

"Stay *calm*?" Shocked and furious, she began clawing her way toward him. If this homeless bum wouldn't dispense justice, *she* would. "Give me the gun," she growled, noticing that her voice had suddenly turned deep and gravely. Her vision went red and dark, warm feelings caressed her mind. Yes, she would be justice today. For Jessica, for Shayla, for Brittany.

For *herself*.

"You've already been shot once tonight, Rich Brat," Teddy said, still calm despite the fact that he was panting and covered in a clear sheen of sweat.

"*SCREW CALM!*" Hatred welled inside her, and she stood with a sudden strength she'd never known, as if all at once she was being filled with a kind of power she felt she'd always deserved but had been denied all her life. She would kill Teddy if he stood in her way of ending Jack. The man's eyes grew with terrified surprise as she reared up, ready to strike, and only vaguely aware that Jack already lay motionless on the floor.

"Lacey," a voice said, "I love you."

Suddenly, between her and her prey, the spirit of Victor St. John stood, eyeing her with a quiet resolve. Her first instinct was to tear him to shreds, but the way love—real love—sparkled in his angelic eyes made her pause. The sensations of acceptance, devotion, and honesty were so real that tears sprang, unbidden, from her eyes. Here was Victor. Faithful, loyal Victor who, despite having walked away from her in his darkest hour, had returned to her in *hers*. How could she ever hate him? Part of her mind fought to push forward through this pathetic angel and pulp the vagrant who had kept her from vengeance, but...

"Victor?" she said. Her voice sounded almost normal again.

"Come out of her," Victor replied, staring straight into Lacey's eyes. "You've already been cast out tonight. By the authority vested in me, I command you to depart."

Lacey flinched as if struck, and felt as though part of her were being torn away. Then it was over, and she collapsed in a heap. The last thing she saw before drifting into a peaceful, blissful sleep was Victor kneeling over her with a smile on his face.

THIRTY-SEVEN

Lacey awoke in the hospital, sometime later, and groaned. The last time she'd been here, she'd been poisoned. She wasn't sure she felt any better now, especially when she tried to sit up only to feel a sharp pain through her right leg. She hissed through her teeth, then looked down at herself. Her right leg was in a cast, and, through her thin hospital gown, she could feel a small blanket of bandages all over her ribs and lower chest. She wondered where the bullet had actually struck her, but was too tired to really ask. Still, with her waking came hunger, and she didn't hesitate to summon a nurse, who graciously took her order and gave her a thorough once-over, now that she was awake.

As the woman left, a thought struck Lacey, and she gasped. "Miss? What's the date?"

The woman turned and smiled. "It's the twenty-first. Your wounds aren't as bad as we expected, and while you'll be wearing that cast until early February, I heard the doctor say she may be willing to release you in another day or two." She smiled warmly. "So you should be home for Christmas Eve, if that's what you're asking."

Lacey smiled; she could think of no better gift than that of Christmas with Nainai.

*

The sun was about to set outside Lacey's apartment. Tonight was Christmas Eve, and she'd make certain things were festive, no matter how her budget apartment and events of the past several days had conspired to stop her. Glancing around, she smiled at the meager decorations from the dollar store—the green-foil wreaths, crinkly red bows, and a cheap angel statue sitting on her kitchen table. A renewed sense of appreciation bubbled within as she happily worked on frying chicken over her electric stove while sitting on a tall stool to rest her leg. The chicken sizzled and crackled in the deep skillet, bringing back memories from her childhood.

Fried chicken, not honeyed ham or turkey, was the tradition—and not from the redneck side of the family. She always thought it was funny how East Asians hit up the KFCs to celebrate the happiest time of the year. With her grandmother sitting in the living room, watching the American tradition of *It's a Wonderful Life*, it made the fried chicken feel all the more special. She took in a deep breath and sighed. She'd gone through so much recently, she was grateful to start recovering from the emotional whiplash of it all.

"I wish I could have been loaned my body, if just for tonight," Victor said, *poofing* beside her.

Lacey eyed him, certain she knew what he was implying. He surely wanted to celebrate with a little bodily romance of hand holding and hugging during the season of love.

He continued, though, surprising her. "You don't have a Christmas tree, and that's a shame... I would have carried and set one up for you, if I could."

Oh, so that's what he meant.

Knowing what she was thinking, he said with a smile. "I mean, snuggling by a fire with you would've been amazing, too. Only, you don't have a fireplace..."

She laughed, carefully forking out golden-brown, sizzling pieces of chicken, and laying them on a plate. "I'm happy, Victor, with what I've got." She gestured with her fork. "I have Nainai and you with me, some good food and a warm shelter. What more can a girl ask for?"

"Wait a minute—" Victor paused, glancing around his shoulders, as if in search. "Is this the Lacey Ling I know? The one who buys all the latest Apple products? Spends more on her shoes than I did on my old car? Who scoffed at her Wal-Mart engagement ring?"

Lacey laughed again. "Okay, Mister—I'll ignore the mention of the ring. But I want you to know that I have learned something through this whole investigation." Her deep brown eyes went serious, threatening to tear up. "Girls trapped in situations like Shayla, and Brittany and Jessica were trapped in—they are the ones who really have it bad. Even Teddy. I'm not ashamed to admit that through getting to know him, I learned a thing or two more about myself. Maybe I have been a rich brat..."

Victor's brows raised in further surprise.

"So," she went on, "who cares if I'm neighbors to the cast of Cops? Who cares if this chicken was from the frozen section of Walmart, and who cares if I couldn't afford Nainai a gift?" But with that last declaration panging her heart, tears spilled from both her eyes.

Victor wished he could hug her. The best he could offer was a sympathetic stare with his sparkly blue eyes, and said, "She loves you. She'll understand."

Lacey sat a moment in thought, wiped her eyes with a sleeve, and turned off the stove. She carried the plate of chicken to the table, and glanced at her grandmother still sitting happily in her wheelchair, whose gaze was set on the TV.

The very humble-looking angel with dark hair, stunning eyes, and his trademark t-shirt and blue jeans, followed Lacey. The two of them sat together, staring out the kitchen window for a long while.

Victor broke the silence first, as fresh snowflakes fell from a placid, grey sky. "How did so much go wrong, Lacey?" He studied her thoughtfully, and she felt a sense of... maturity... in him that she'd never felt before.

She placed her hands on his knees, holding them where they'd be had she actually been able to touch them, and continued looking at him, and he, in turn, placed his hands on hers. "But in the end, it went right. Or, well, right *enough*." She bit her lip. She had so many questions for Victor, but she couldn't get past the way she'd wanted to attack him, that night at Geo's house.

"I can still read your thoughts," he said gently. "And yes, I've been given answers to your questions. You don't even need to ask."

Lacey trembled, wondering whether she wanted to know, but she closed her eyes and inhaled slowly, then let her breath go, before nodding.

"Jack Beals was, as you probably guessed, possessed by a devil. A minor one, apparently, but a devil nonetheless. Apparently, those are stronger and more cunning than demons like... the ones I had to face right after I died."

Lacey opened her eyes and nodded, while Victor looked pensively toward the sky. When he turned back to her, he went on, "Jack's... guest... had learned how to mask himself from most angels. Even Rao had a hard time seeing him. I guess we all knew something was going on—that's part of why she sent me in the first place—but Heaven's 'intelligence agency,' since I can't think of a better term, sometimes takes a little time before it sees everything. Sometimes, we have to go straight to The Top for answers."

Lacey thought on this, and nodded for him to go on.

"Jack, long before you knew him, was actually homeless—just like Teddy. In fact, that's part of why Heaven bargained with Teddy in the first place."

Lacey's nose wrinkled. "What do you mean 'bargained with Teddy'?"

Victor smiled easily. "See, there are certain things angels just aren't allowed—or are unable—to do. Like fight Jack physically. So while Teddy's not the kind of guy you'd expect to greet you at the Pearly Gates, he has a good enough heart, even if he's about as mercenary as they come."

"Really?" Lacey ran a hand through her hair in bewilderment.

"Yes, we misjudged Teddy a couple of times. It wasn't he who broke into your apartment. Jack hired someone, and Teddy was merely called there to check on things."

"Jack did *what*? And it *wasn't* Teddy?" Lacey couldn't be more surprised.

"Yeah, I'll get back to Jack in a sec." Victor nodded with an expression that told Lacey the worst was yet to come. "So even *I* went to Teddy out of desperation. When I figured out you were in danger, I tracked him down and sent him to Geo's house. It's a blessing and a miracle he arrived in time. I caught the tail end of that.

"But yeah, Teddy will have to make a few changes if he ever wants to play croquet with Rao—don't ask—but he's a far better man than he seems. Ask me again, sometime, and I'll tell you the whole story."

He stood and started to pace, then sat again.

She wasn't satisfied, but she let it go. Teddy *had* helped save her life, and she owed him at least thanks for that. "You were saying, though? About Jack?"

"Yes. Jack was down on his luck. Got into a lot of hard drugs, heavy drinking. Et cetera. Flirted with suicide several times, and the day he was about to do it, well, it seems that's the day his devil finally made a deal with him."

Lacey's brow wrinkled. "I thought you Christians only believed in one 'Devil'."

"With a capital 'D', yes. But... you learn a few things in Heaven that you don't pick up in Sunday School. Like how all those Bible stories of people afflicted with devils were probably true. And probably a lot more frightening than we think.

"Long story short, Jack's deal was the usual contract—wealth, power and fame in return for his soul, and as many souls as he could bring along with him. He was prodded into the modeling business, and railroaded to the top of the food chain at Trend. Turns out, it was the perfect way to fulfill his side of the bargain.

"See, he started coming in contact with an awful lot of women. Some of them... had insecurities, and he played on those. Started recruiting college girls to come work for him, and then bought them with scholarships, parties, easy drugs, and fast times. Once they were sufficiently drugged up, he'd edge them into prostitution."

"Like Jessica," Lacey said, nodding.

Victor's face fell, and Lacey saw an inscrutable sorrow in his eyes. "Yeah. Like that."

He looked away again. "Well, Jessica… decided she didn't want to live that life anymore. I could tell that her pending motherhood got her thinking differently about life, and she ran for it. She was set to tell the cops.

"Jack got her first."

Lacey winced, remembering her dream all too vividly. "And my vision of her death? Of Nainai?"

Victor shrugged. "Apparently the connection we forged, just after I died, has opened you to the occasional vision of the future. As for the dream about Nainai, I would say that was simply a terrible nightmare. You've been worried about her a lot lately. "

Lacey mulled that thought for a while. "Yes. Hmm. And you? Were you…"

"Was I able to get back? Yeah. Not long before I found Shayla. Time doesn't work the same on the Other Side as it does here. If you'd been a spirit as well, hanging out with me, you'd know I was gone for a *long* time."

She held out her hands, pleading. "Doing what?"

He sighed heavily, then winked at her. "Yeah, I can still do that even if I don't need to breathe. It's good for expressing emotions, even after mortality ends." She smiled a little, too. He sobered again. "I was… healing, for lack of a better word. I'm not going to tell you what I saw and felt in Geo's office, but let's just say it was… bad. So bad that I ended up being sucked into it and getting lost; it was just so…

infuriating to see it, that between the anger and my shock, I couldn't think clearly enough to pull myself out. After that, the demons had their way with me, and they're none too kind to angels of light who fall into their hands. I was so tainted afterwards that I couldn't talk to Heaven at all; my mind was so... so fouled up with anger over that... stuff... I experienced that there was no way I could feel what they were trying to say, including answers to my calls, even though they could hear me just fine.

"They sent Rao right away, and she had to walk me through... a process to get me back on track and out of that black hole I was in." He shuddered visibly. "I almost relapsed into fury when Rao showed me where Shayla was, finally, and when Geo walked in, I did actually make myself scarce; there was no way I wanted a repeat of that night."

Lacey wanted to hug him but knew he could see it in her face, and without speaking, they both knew it was enough. "What-what *happened* to me, that night in Geo's house?"

Victor grimaced. "Jack's devil got a hold of you for a minute. I nearly panicked when he did, but you were just so *angry* that after I wrestled him out of Jack, it was able to grab you without much of a fight. In fact, Jack had already been manipulating you even before you started working for him."

Lacey frowned deeply. "But I didn't even know him until—"

"Until he bought you dinner. But he arranged that, too. Even the Dark Ones have a bit of foresight. Not a lot, but they make excellent use of it. Jack—

the man—was looking for a woman like you to be on the 'good' side of his double life. He'd had his eye on you for a while, and I can't blame him. He even went so far, I learned, as to mess with your job search in order to keep you desperate. Then, when the time was ripe, he made you an offer he thought you couldn't refuse."

Lacey sat back in her chair and smacked her forehead at the realization. "So me making a fool of myself at B and B *wasn't* really my fault."

Victor smiled sheepishly. "Well, if you're honest with yourself, you *do* have a bit of a silly streak. You really must have noticed it, since you found *me* occasionally hilarious."

Lacey rolled her eyes.

"But seriously, he muddled your mind and led you into that natural, easy humor you do when you're unguarded, and... you actually gave a very clever answer."

"More like an embarrassingly *stupid* answer," she muttered.

"Hey, I laughed when I saw the replay."

Lacey cocked an eyebrow.

"Heaven… keeps records. We'll leave it there for now. The bottom line is, you were set up. A lot of guys like him like to lead double lives for a facade, some false sense of normalcy—who knows—but in the end, he only would have dragged you down to endless misery with him. I was sent to stop that, but nearly lost you anyway."

Lacey sent a mental hug again. "I'm just so happy you came back," she said softly. "Both times."

They went silent again and, after a minute, Lacey got up, took some red Jell-O out of the fridge, and then grabbed some instant-made mash potatoes off a counter. She set them both on the table, and with hands on hips, smiled with a sigh.

"Is dinner ready yet?" Nainai asked with childlike eagerness.

"Yes, it is, Nainai." Lacey wiped her hands on a paper towel, and went to wheel her grandmother into the kitchen, Victor still sitting at the table.

The wheels squeaked across the shag carpet to an opening at the table where no chair sat. "Smells delicious!" Nainai clapped.

Lacey was happy to at least provide a meal Nainai'd love. She gently tucked her against the table, and took her own seat. Nainai was made up so cute for the festivities, her white hair up in a bun, pink rouge across her cheeks, like she'd asked.

She was like a sweet doll. She deserved the best of things, Lacey thought. That pang in her heart entered once again over the thought of having no present to open. But suddenly, Nainai burst with joy, her dark eyes lighting up, "You got me a gift!"

Lacey's brow furrowed. She shared a confused glance with Victor.

"A beautiful angel…" Nainai nearly whispered in reverence.

Lacey picked up the little dollar-store statue in her hands, now remembering the story of how her grandfather always gave his wife an angel. With its porcelain wings and pretty golden hair, she guessed it didn't look half bad. Maybe it could have even passed for being worth five bucks. But when she went to hand it to Nainai, her eyes were clearly fixed straight ahead… at none other than Victor St. John himself.

The end.

A MODEL MURDER

PHOENIX PRIME

Author Claire Kane and this mystery series became a part of Phoenix Prime.

Phoenix Prime is a Ph.D. level workshop that spans approximately four months. It uses applied industrial psychology to address components of writing, marketing, branding, business and contract issues, productivity, etc. that combine Creative Writing and business perspectives.

The participants create a portfolio to showcase their work alongside students in doctoral programs in several major universities. The objective, in addition to expanding the professional growth of all the participants, is to study the impact of the independent author-publisher on the commercial fiction industry.

ABOUT THE AUTHORS

Claire Kane is an avid reader and writer, who enjoys going on zany adventures with her eccentric mother. She loves classic fashion statements, a good root beer float, and always eats with her mouth closed. And she of course has a weak spot for murder mysteries.

An engineer by day, a writer by night, Stan Crowe has lived more places than he ever imagined he would, and has more children than most imagine they ever will. Author of the collection, "A Comedy of Love," Stan wrote his first book at age five. Of late, Stan and his family have taken to waking up to Arizona sunrises.

Visit www.breezyreads.com for more info.